LIT
(6-2207)

Father of the Four Passages

By the same author

◆

Saturday Night at the Pahala Theatre

Wild Meat and the Bully Burgers

Blu's Hanging

Heads by Harry

Name Me Nobody

Father of the Four Passages

Lois-Ann Yamanaka

◆

Farrar, Straus and Giroux

New York

Farrar, Straus and Giroux
19 Union Square West, New York 10003

Library of Congress Cataloging-in-Publication Data
Yamanaka, Lois-Ann, 1961–
    Father of the four passages / Lois-Ann Yamanaka.— 1st ed.
    p. cm.
    ISBN 0-374-15387-6 (alk. paper)
      1. Single mothers—Fiction.   2. Fathers and daughters—Fiction.
    3. Mothers and sons—Fiction.   4. Las Vegas (Nev.)—Fiction.
    5. Hawaii—Fiction.   I. Title.

PS3575.A434 F38 2001
813'.54—dc21   00-042177

Designed by Abby Kagan

For Morgan Blair,

who appears when stars fall, and knows the truth of

this brutal life—my teacher, my friend, is the light that inhabits;

I walk because of you, breathe word and line because of you,

believe because you came.

Father of the Four Passages

The Keeper

SONNY BOY, son of Sonia, the only one I did not kill. Three, I killed. Number One in cartilaged pieces on a surgical tray. #2, like a dead feeder fish, flushed out and down. A third, buried in a jar behind my mother's house, fetal marsupial, naked pink.

Sonny Boy, son of Sonia, stop your crying on this bed, your purple wail without breath. Feel the squinting of my eyes, the gritting of my teeth, the closing of my fists. Here is my hand to cover your mouth. Here are my fists to crush your skull. Do you want to die?

They're smoking and drinking to your birth downstairs. And I'm the single artist mother, breast-feeding lounge singer mother, earth righteous minority mother. But I can't make you stop. Shh, they can hear you, godfuckingdammit.

Your body stiffens. Fists clench. You cry without sound. A blue boy. Let me bounce you, let me slap you, let me sing to you, let me choke you, let me throw you out the window.

I blow on your face. And in one long draw, you breathe me in.

I am the keeper of words. This is your word to keep: *God/the/son.*

♦

Dear Number One,

You are my first dead baby, a baby boy.

I am on the green bed in Granny Alma's Kalihi house. Alone, so Alone. My face is puffy and flushed. Scared, I'm scared. My belly is a round ellipsis. I don't know who to tell. About you.

Your aunt Celeste comes into the room and stares at me. My mouth opens, but no words come out. And then she knows.

You are in me.

And you need to come out.

She turns without a word from the doorway of the green room. You are four months old, she tells Granny Alma. Call Dr. Wee, who sits two pews in front of Granny at church every Sunday.

He will suck you out of me.

But you want to stay.

Salamander fingers, you cling to my wet walls until your body rips apart. You are the color of tendon in my sweet stew, little pod, with eyes, black beads, like a rat's. Your aunt Celeste's lovely eyes.

Love,

Your mother, Sonia Kurisu, age 17

♦

I hate my sister Celeste. Celeste who always reminds me that she raised me the best she could. Poor thing. Poor her. The kind of girl who's forced into substitute mommydom too early. Lots of sad stories about girls like her.

She found our mother wedged between her bed and the

wall, an empty vial of Seconal, bent spoon, lighter, and small syringe on the floor. Celeste was ten. I was nine.

Grace was fading out, eyes rolling slowly, a groan, a mutter. We walked her dragging feet to the living room couch. Celeste put herself between Grace's legs and held her body up against the picture window. Head floating on a neck made of rubber. "Call 911, you moron. Don't just stand there."

Grace took several short gasps for air.

Purple mommy.

So I blew in her face. A long breath that she held, her head falling.

"She's leaving," Celeste screamed. I dropped the phone, the cord spinning the receiver. And she was still.

I saw the couch indent beside Grace. I smelled the rotting carcass of goat, a maggot-filled belly, the explosion of flies wet with intestinal fluid and excrement. Her head slid in the direction of the Specter. Celeste covered her nose and mouth.

"Get up, Mommy, the Devil's come to get you. Stand up, Mommy. Grace!" I screamed at her.

I witnessed the summoning of the Seraphim as my mother willed her body to rise. She stumbled to the front door and leaned her body over the porch railing, her arms and head hanging. Breathing, breathing, until the ambulance rushed up our driveway and drove us all away.

Who the fuck knows why the police called our aunty Effie, who wasn't even a real aunt, to take us to her house. Our stay would be indefinite. I heard her calling the church's prayer tree late into the night.

"Grace. That's what I said. Grace Kurisu. The waitress at the 19th Hole. Painkillers and alcohol. She has that good-for-nothing husband. Oh, the big girl, Celeste's, all right. She's a strong Christian. Sonia, the little one, keeps talking about the

Devil. The poor thing's screwed up, I tell you. I'll call Frannie and all the deacons."

She told the story of my mother over and over again to anyone and everyone who wanted to know every goddamn detail of our lives and the Appearance of the Angel of Death, in Hilo of all places.

At eleven o'clock, the phone went still. I heard Aunty Effie brushing her dentures and a short time later, a muffled snore from behind her bedroom door. Celeste nudged me, motioning me to follow her. We left through the front door into the cool Hilo night and walked home.

It was Celeste who walked me to school every day, fed me canned goods and rice for breakfast, and told me what to say when the CPS social worker came looking for us. She got me on the sampan bus after school, down the icy corridors of the hospital, and into the room where Grace spent the next six nights. Every night, we were deposited at Aunty Effie's. And every night by twelve, Celeste made sure we slept in our own beds.

Sister/Mother, it all sounds so loving.

But she of the iron-fisted mommydom became the Sadist.

And I of the get-the-shit/mind/soul-beaten-out-of-me-or-else became the Masochist.

So your word, Celeste Kurisu-Infantino, twenty years later, I still fucking hate you, wife of Sicilian not Portagee, Michael Infantino; mother of Tiffany, fat and full of acne, and Heather who draws cat's claws in God's eyes, keep it for me, my: *Sister/sadist.*

♦

Dear Number One,

So who am I to blame a substitute mother for your death by suction? She raised me the best she could, right?

Love,

Your Mom, Sonia, age now

6

♦

Now:

I am on a black futon in a wet, warm room, red scarves over dusty lamps. Windows closed, curtains drawn, no sound but heartbeat and breath. Sonny Boy is asleep beside me.

When will I stop fucking up?

The pregnancy attention was what I wanted. I loved it. All of them giving me the best chair in the house. All of them putting pillows under my feet. All of them rubbing my belly for good luck. Feeding me, indulging me, venerating the earth mother. O, the possibility of bringing forth life from your body! they marveled.

When will I wash my hair?

Mark promised to buy a bottle of Prell, the fucking flake. My best, childhood forever friend, my little Markie, digging out on me every time I fuck somebody not to his liking. I miss him, I need him, I call him. But he's gone.

When will I stop fucking up?

I'm too selfish to do this mommy shit. Mark could do it. Mark who mothered me over the years. Mark who fathered me over the years. Mark who brothered me over the years. Come back and take care of this fucking screaming baby. Come back and take care of me.

When will the bleeding stop?

This afterbirth blood smells rancid and old.

When will I stop fucking up?

This isn't a dog I can tie up in the rain. Watch it shiver on a blanket soaked with urine and shit. Starve it, no money for dog food. Give it one kind pat a day. Beat the howling out of him. Watch him die. Bury him in the backyard. No more dog. Was tired of him anyway.

When will I rest?

My body aches from rocking, carrying, strolling, bouncing this boy who cries in steady, staccato bursts until he's blue:

Four to six in the evening, nonstop, he's fucking shrieking.

Ten to twelve, shut the fuck up, I put my hand over his mouth, dig my nails into his cheeks.

Four to six in the morning, nauseated, I weave my fingers into his hair and squeeze.

Ten to twelve, crying, I fall to the floor, watch him drop off the bed headfirst.

And in between, he sleeps. Maybe.

Overstim, they tell me. Darken the room. Talk in hushed tones.

Colic, they tell me. Turn him on his belly. Turn him on his back. Don't eat cabbage or refried beans.

These days and nights that blur in a myopic haze. And no one to talk to but this horrible pod my body made.

I hear somebody leaving next door. Lucky you.

They're all leaving Las Vegas. They write songs and movies about this phenomenon. Leaving Las Vegas with empty pockets, and the eternal struggle:

Should I use my last dollar to eat a hot dog or put it in this slot machine? Dumb fuck, you should've eaten.

I hear somebody moving in next door.

And the mailman's shoving envelopes under my door.

A letter from my father, a man who knows about leaving. Lucky him. Never looked back. Never wanted to look back.

Sweet Sonia,

A man stands in front of an old Chinese hotel in Kuala Lumpur, Malaysia. A concessionaire sells him watermelon juice. The man takes in the smell of peanut pancakes, coconut rice, and goat curries.

He's looking for a place to spend the night in the midst

of all the clatter and clang of the streets. The man wanders into a Chinatown. There's a Chinatown in every city of this world.

He finds a small Chinese hotel. Rooms, 25 ringgits, which is about four dollars. He sleeps early and long, full of rolls filled with chicken curry and cheeses. He drinks a delicious Chinese tea and falls into a steady slumber.

The next morning, he wakes full of huge red welts and an incredible pain that pulses through his muscles and into his bones. Are these mosquitoes? He searches the space of the room.

In the late afternoon, he passes a little mom-and-pop store full of cluttered shelves of strange bottles, dusty cans, and the odor of fermenting fish and mint leaves. The old woman sells him a can of insect repellent.

He returns to his tiny room overlooking a night market full of foreign sounds. The languages, sweet Sonia, the languages that he wishes to inhabit his body on lonely nights so he could speak to someone, these languages sound like music, like Italian opera or Hawaiian slack key. He knows the meaning of the melody from some place summoned inside his memory, and that he cannot understand the lyric does not matter.

This night, the man sprays his room before retiring to the voices outside of his terrace window over the streets that skein into alleys and crossings. But as he dozes, bedbugs begin to drag themselves from the crammed space of the bed.

These Malaysian bedbugs full of blood, his blood, are not lice with white, translucent bodies. These look like dog ticks, huge and gray, with two red lines on their backs that look like eyes. He presses into one of the dazed bugs and leaves the mark of his fingernail in its body. Hundreds of bedbugs pour out of the tears in the mattress.

The man sleeps well this night.

And the two red lines that look like eyes on the backs of the bedbugs? These are the marks on his body left by the bites—two tiny red lines etched all over him, front and back like shingles, the day he leaves Kuala Lumpur, languid and feverish.

May this letter find you in good health.

Your father,
Joseph Kurisu

I keep all of your letters, Father.

You who I search for. You whose words find me. The beauty therein. The emptiness without.

Now you keep this word: *Seek/and/you/shall/find.*

♦

Joseph left us for good in the time of blood. We all bled, Mama, Celeste, and I, the three house dogs, females in heat—stained panties, dog diapers, and sanitary napkin belts on the clothesline, bloody pads wrapped in newspaper in the trash. He had been planning to flee this all along, the bloodletting.

Grace could've slit her veins and he'd have run.

She came home from a long waitressing shift at the 19th Hole to find Joseph packing his duffel bag again. Hadn't he told her he would be leaving?

She said nothing to him. "Did you eat dinner?" she asked me. I shook my head.

"Dammit, Celeste, why didn't you cook for your sister?"

"Where's Joseph going?" I whispered to my mother.

"Did Jack's call him today? Did he drive the Japan tour to the volcano?" she asked Celeste.

"No, Mama," she replied.

I was eleven and bleeding for the first time. I hit myself

over and over until my vagina bruised and swelled. I stayed home from school for days.

Grace tore open a can of Spam and dropped the slabs of pink meat in sizzling oil. "Goddamn you, Celeste, can't you even cook some rice?" she said, slamming dishes into the sink.

"I'm out of here," he'd said to me earlier that day.

"Take me with you," I begged. I'd skipped school. Joseph didn't mind when he was the good father of some of my memory. Then, he loved the company. "Please, Daddy, don't leave me."

"No room in my duffel," he replied flatly.

"Then put me in a box," I told him. "I'll be a good girl. I promise."

"You are a good girl," he said, placing his warm hand on my face. "But Daddy's traveling light. No room for you. Sorry, pal."

I grasped on to his hand. "You love me, Daddy?" I asked.

"True love is freedom, kiddo," he answered after a long silence. "Freedom with a capital F."

"Joseph!" my mother yelled. And when he didn't answer, she picked up the empty Spam can and walked down the hallway. "Where the fuck are you going? How the hell am I going to pay the bills? Who's going to take care of me?"

"Get out of my face," he said to her in his fierce monotone.

I listened to the thud of her body against the wall. She slashed his face that night. He let her cut him open. Then he slung his duffel over his shoulder and turned once to look at me with vulnerable, fiery eyes, his hand stopping the bleeding. "See you, kiddo," he said with a mock two-finger salute.

Celeste clambered over the couch to stop Grace from hurting him more. I helped her pry the can from my mother's fingers.

"Run, Joseph, run!" I screamed. "Daddy!" I held out my arms to him. He paused for a moment, then turned toward the door.

"Run, Joseph!" my mother cried. "Wake up, Sonia, you stupid little girl." And then my mother turned her hatred on me. It would be days before I returned to school with black eyes and a bruised face. Celeste and I took the can from her fingers and laid her body down.

"I'm sorry, Sonia," she said. "Oh, look at your face. Celeste, baby, look at what I've done."

He was there, outside the picture window, looking back at the house he would not see for the next few years. I want to believe he placed it inside his memory for summoning on a lonely night. But he gave me that mock salute with a cocky smirk and a jerk of his eyebrows. I pulled the curtains shut.

♦

Dear #2,

You are my second dead baby, another boy. Here is a picture of me the day before you died.

I am in the small bedroom I grew up in at Granny Alma's house. I'm in my embroidered jeans and hippie gauze blouse. I'm wearing a crocheted bikini top, rose-colored, black-rimmed shades perched on my head.

There's a green bamboo bead curtain hanging from the doorway, hanging ferns in macramé plant baskets.

A long string of blinking Christmas lights encircling the windows. Fake snow sprayed on the jalousies.

I'm burning coconut incense in a small brass urn. Sitting cross-legged, leaning against my bed covered with a paisley gauze bedspread.

I'm reaching out one hand to you, see me, you must, and making a peace sign with the other.

One day, #2, the word will parallel the image.

Merry Christmas,

Your mother, Sonia Kurisu, age 18

♦

I never celebrate Christmas. Never.

I was twelve, Celeste thirteen. Joseph was gone.

Sweet Sonia, the name I had given to the girl who received his letters, knew he was in Thailand. This was the year Grace brought home a five-foot Christmas tree, a small but beautiful tree, which cost us all possibility of our own presents wrapped in red and green ribbons.

This was the tree she wanted to put in a rusty coffee can filled with rocks on the black lacquer table that Joseph had shipped back piece by piece from Chiang Mai. She wanted to give the illusion that it stood from floor to ceiling when we took the Christmas Eve photo, Celeste and I in red dresses, hiding the table with our bodies so he could see that fine tree, a Noble Fir.

That fuck you, Joseph, tree. We're doing just fine, you fucking selfish asshole.

When Grace placed the tree on the table, the tip bent on the ceiling, sending asbestos snow into its branches. And Bing crooning I'm dreaming of a white Christmas on the Muntz stereo.

"You don't need the table, Mama," Celeste suggested. "Why don't you just put the tree on the floor. Never mind if it's short."

She got her face slapped twice. I kept my mouth shut.

"Go get me the hacksaw from outside, Sonia," my mother said. "Get me a ruler from your schoolbag too."

My mother measured and marked. Her hair, flecked with rosewood, head down, wild hair jerking with the frantic tug of the hacksaw through wood. My mother cut off the legs of the lacquer table, one by one, wonderful smell of the fine rosewood and the snow of sawdust in our hair. In Celeste's wet eyelashes, on her sweaty nose, dust in my cough, I tasted roses in my astonished mouth.

We had no money whenever Joseph left us. He'd just leave.

Celeste wore a velvet yoked muumuu with butterfly sleeves. Me, a red pinafore with a lacy white blouse, both charged at the National Dollar Store. Where would she send the pictures?

"Stop, Mama. Please," I whispered. "We don't even know if Daddy—"

"Shut your mouth, you hear me, Sonia? Smile, dammit. C'mon, Celeste, big smile. Look at the camera. Sonia, you knock off that crying."

Later that Christmas morning, with the money Granny Alma sent for Grace to buy presents for us from her, she bought two airline tickets. Two one-way tickets to Honolulu.

At the airport, Grace was monotone. "Say goodbye to me," she said. I stared at Celeste, my mouth agape.

"Mama?" Celeste gasped.

"I'll send your things later," she said, turning.

"No, Mama. What's going on?" I asked. "Why are you sending us away?"

She refused to answer me.

"You take care of Sonia, Celeste. Tell Granny Alma she's allergic to shrimp." She gave her a push. "Go, there's your flight." Celeste took my hand in hers.

"I hate you," I said to my mother, who never turned back to look at me.

So I say it every day. Every day until the day she turns to look at me and hear me. Listen, Mama, keep this word:

Burn/in/Hell.

God/tHe/FAtHer

Dear Heavenly Father,

Forgive me for the constant sinning between my legs.

Forgive me for my low GPA last semester.

Forgive me my attraction to white trash and there's lots of it here in Las Vegas.

Forgive me my drunken whoredom full of promiscuous bravado and raunchy flirtation.

Forgive me for not filling out my student health insurance form at registration.

Forgive me my white feather and black whip wenching for money.

Forgive me for singing "Love ta Love Ya Baby" as the exotic Jade Kwan in my Lobby Lounge at the Fremont Hotel Thursday-night gig. It pays the phone bill.

Forgive me the full moon, the falling of a filthy egg into the moist pouch.

Forgive me unclean motel rooms, backseats of late-model gas hogs, and carnal trailers with stolen sheets.

Forgive me for missing finals due to a gynecological emergency.

Forgive me the seduction, the sodomy, and the missing videotapes.

Forgive me no paper trail of my third fuck-up.

Forgive me in this year of the dragon, this scraping of my innards again.

Love,

Sonia Kurisu, age 20

Dear Jar,

This is it, they say, the last I will ever kill. You, Jar, are my third dead baby. After you, they say, my body will never be able to bear a child. So I decide to go the route of feminine mythology.

I try the wire hanger first, of course. It makes me bleed.

I drink vinegar and vodka, and suck lemons. It makes me vomit.

I run for miles and jump from high places.

I pummel you and jolt you until I bruise and swell.

I force Mark, my childhood forever friend, to give me all of his antibiotics. I take the whole bottle. It makes me vomit, again.

I lift the couch, the dining room table, my bed, my desk, any and all heavy objects.

And finally, Mark comes over. "It's finals," he says. "How are you going to do it, Sonia, with all this unnecessary *stress*?"

So we close the curtains, lock the doors, turn off all the lights, and try the wire hanger, again.

You are born in the year of the dragon right on my living room floor. So much blood, all over us, all over everything, the violence and blood of your death.

Mark cries and cries. He finds you in the liquid sludge

on the linoleum. You're a boy, we think, whole and pink like a kangaroo without a pouch.

I put you in a jelly jar. Mark fills the jar with some formaldehyde from his zoology class. The TA likes him. My pet rat gave birth, he tells him.

I take you home over Christmas break and bury you near the night-blooming jasmine tree outside my bedroom window.

I say a prayer for you, I do. But I knew I would kill you. There are things I have always known.

Your mother, Sonia Kurisu

♦

The first time I bled, I was eleven years old. Grace told me it was a natural thing. All women have the monthly. One day, I will accept it and stop hitting myself. God gave me the blood so I could be a mother too.

One day.

But I knew Joseph left because of my blood.

I could not will the functions of my body to stop, though I prayed and prayed, and slipped away to Bible study at the house in Keaukaha that Pat Boone rented for the Youth with a Mission missionaries who'd wait for me in a beat-up Toyota at Kai Store every evening.

God woke me at six-twenty every morning, I was sure. If there is a God, He will wake me up at exactly that time. And that is what He did.

Joseph used to wake me up in the morning. A father who always said, "God? God who?" And laughed at me. "Effie's God. That's who."

But I knew there was a God who walked with Celeste and me to school. Who saved my mother from Seconal. Who gave me some sensibility amidst the clatter of this life.

There had to be. There was no one else.

Joseph was somewhere in Europe and my mother with a longhaired asshole orderly reading Stephen King novels at her bedside while some sitcom blared on above her.

There was God for me.

I felt dead. I couldn't be dead for Celeste's sake. How frightening to be Alone. She was walking me to the sampan bus. We were going to visit Grace.

A haole girl, college age, approached us. "You look like you need a friend," she said to me. Really, those were her first words.

"Yeah," I answered, "I think I do." Celeste turned to glare at me, probably for talking to a stranger.

"Have you heard the news about Our Lord Jesus Christ?" she asked. She was eating from a roll of sweet Marie crackers, silver paper spiraling. She offered me one.

"Yeah," I answered again, taking a couple of crackers from her. Celeste nudged me with an angry elbow. But I was so hungry.

"Do you have a personal relationship with Him?"

This time, I didn't answer. What was I to say? That He wakes me up at six-twenty every morning? That was as personal as it got. "No," I said to the girl.

"No, what?" Celeste yelled at me. She took me by the arm. "There's the sampan bus. C'mon, Sonia. Mama's waiting."

"I'll be on campus tomorrow," the haole girl called out to me. "My name's Kate. I'm with Youth with a Mission. Let's talk some more. Your name is?"

"Sonia," I answered. "Sonia Kurisu. Homeroom B-4."

Celeste rolled her eyes and shoved me onto the bus. "Why did you tell her your homeroom, you moron?" she said through clenched teeth. "Wait till I tell Aunty Effie. We're Baptist, idiot. You know God, stupid. You go to Sunday school."

As the sampan bus chugged off, I turned around to look at Kate. A light emanated from her torso, the light that pulled me back toward her even as we headed up Puainako Street. The road was paved in silver, a silver thread that led back to the girl at the bus stop. She was a Seraph sent from God to me on a wet road in Hilo town, Hilo of all places.

Me. Sonia Kurisu.

Every hair on my head counted, His eye was on this sparrow. There was no one for me, nothing but a road leading to the one God.

Then a letter from Joseph arrived. I took it as a Sign. I carried it with me to the hospital and had Grace read it to me.

Sweet Sonia,

A man enters the city of Rome. He notices the silver cobblestone roads, a sunny window reflecting the birds and dragonflies, when out of the blue sky, God makes a light rain. He knows it is for him.

There on a sidewalk in Rome, a gypsy approaches the man in the rain. She carries a soda box that she presses against his waist. She's trying to stop him, trying to tell him to give her something to eat. She is hungry.

Bells chime. The moon sways in a yellow-curtained window. The man tries to walk away from the woman who follows him down the road. And then he feels something underneath the box. A little girl is under the box trying to take the money from his waist pouch.

Meanwhile, sweet Sonia, bells chime. The man gets angry. He hits the box and it flies onto the cobblestone road, no longer silver, but a dull, mossy gray.

The woman curses and yells. The girl cries in howling vowels. The man becomes the culprit and they the victims.

All he wanted was to leave in peace. Is their hunger his responsibility? Or was the man simply being tricked by the woman and her daughter? Hunger was never the issue. He lost some sense of truth in all the noise.

There is peace for you amidst the din. True freedom, sweet Sonia, is not given, but seized. My love to Grace and Celeste, as always, they are in my mind's summoning place, and my mind is an ocean of love.

All joy,
Joseph

"Fuck him," Grace said, crying. "Peace and freedom?" she muttered as she turned her back to me. She crumpled his letter and let it fall to the floor. Celeste smoothed our mother's hair, giving me dirty looks and gritting her teeth. When Grace fell asleep, I crawled around the bed and found my father's letter. It was wet. I smoothed out the wrinkles, smearing his words, then shoved it in my pocket.

♦

Oh, Jar, find your peace.

The water surrounding you looked salty and gelatinous, a fetal comma, naked sea worm. You poured out of me, the smell of an old tidal pool at Onekahakaha Beach, low tide.

Mark told me to get rid of you, flush you down the toilet, put you down the disposal, throw you out with the trash and bloody towels. I said you deserved a decent burial. That we were both backsliding Baptists, but Baptists nonetheless, and if we prayed for forgiveness, we would be forgiven. Mark cried again. I couldn't make him stop.

I held the murky bottle you floated in up to the light. Mark gagged. I laid my hands on him to stop the misery. He laid his hands on me to stop the bleeding.

♦

Kate and the other missionaries greeted me at Kai Store with the warmest of smiles and embraces deep into my body. I wanted the monthly blood to stop as they laid their hands upon me in the house by the beach.

With the laying-on of hands and prayer, they freed me from 'io, who sat with yellow talons perched on the telephone lines as spiritual guardians of my home. The nesting pair of hawks left the lychee trees in our yard. I wasn't to be burdened by the pagan rituals of these islands.

With their hands on my body, they prayed for my mother, for my father, and for my sister to come to the light of Christ like I had. I repeated their every word for Grace, for Joseph, for Celeste, in Jesus' holy name.

So many tongues to speak in, I listened as my father must have listened to the music of voices outside his window at night, lulled to sleep by the lyric and melody of foreign sounds.

I prayed for my mother incessantly in my head, ashamed of the local dialect in my voice and entranced by the beautiful haole faces around me, the fluency of their prayers, immediate and poignant.

Kate of the curly hair, gauze blouses, and faded jeans played the guitar, and we sang hip hymns like "Pass It On." They raised their hands to the heavens, swayed, saying Amen and Praise You Lord. Brother Micah of the huge hands and gap between his front teeth sat cross-legged next to me. Peter, who looked like Rob Lowe, prayed in earnest for my salvation, and Emily, who kept her arm around me, smelled like carnations.

I needed to save Grace. I'd do it through God. It was at the Youth with a Mission islandwide celebration of Pat Boone's purchase of the old Travelodge hotel on Banyan Drive for a youth hostel that I learned prophecy.

Prophecy and Knowing I already possessed.

The prophet Robert Woods was there, bodies slain in the spirit, and tongues so extraordinary singing around me. This life seemed otherworldly and nothing else mattered—no mother trying to kill herself, no sister headed for early mommy-mommydom and squealing on me to the Baptists, no father gone into the world's spaces.

This was True Freedom. Freedom with a capital F.

I sat on a metal folding chair next to Emily, who held my hand in hers as Robert Woods worked the crowd by having a young Hawaiian man and a twentyish Puerto Rican woman stand as he prophesied over their lives.

How do you hide the blackness filling the spaciousness that hovers over your life? I am now certain that you can't.

The prophet pointed at me. Stunned, Emily prodded me to stand as the others had.

"Yours is a heart of stone," he said.

No.

"The Lord wants you to have a heart of flesh."

Amen.

"You need to be part of the family of God."

Praise You Jesus.

Emily cried. Peter who looked like Rob Lowe comforted her. None of them had received a prophecy.

That night at the house by the beach, Peter asked me to call my mother and tell her I would be staying with the family of God.

"No!" Grace screamed. "Celeste, get in the fucking—"

The phone line went dead.

"It's God's intervention on your behalf," Peter told me. "God's Will. He loves you, sister."

When Grace and Celeste found me that night under the

wavering fluorescent light of the liquor store by Onekahakaha Beach Park, I had been praying away a heart of stone.

"Fucking Holy Rollers," Grace said. "I'm calling the cops when we get home. And I'm telling Aunty Effie to ask the pastor and the deacons to deprogram you. They got you all fucking brainwashed."

Pray away a heart of stone, will away a heart of stone.

My father walked a path of stones in Italy that unhinged the silver light of the moon. Listened to the sound of peddlers pushing vegetable carts over alleyways in Kuala Lumpur. Walked a road in Kyushu paved with sea stones leading to a turtle's amber tears.

> *Dear God,*
> *Be with my father.*
> *Give the spaciousness of grace to my mother.*
> *God is good.*
> *Wake me at six-twenty tomorrow morning.*
> *Let me keep my heart of stone.*
> *Give one to Celeste.*
> *Protect us all.*
> *Amen.*

◆ 3 ◆

WAKE

I PUT MY TINY HANDS TOGETHER and prayed with a child's fervor and belief:

God, take me home.

And when I woke, I was a twelve-year-old girl sleeping in the tiny back room of Granny Alma's house in Kalihi, dirty curtains from Sears, and the slow crowing of a neighbor's rooster; pit bulls barking, yanking on rusty chains; the screeching of the city bus around a hairpin turn.

And when I woke, I was thirteen and drunk from too many Tom Collinses at the Stadium Bowl-O-Drome's Ten-Pin Lounge from Uncle Fu Manchu with his Lucky Strike embedded in the spit-white corner of his mouth; stolen sips of screwdrivers from Aunty Tokyo Rose in her teased Aqua Net do and tight turquoise capris; Granny Alma busy tending bar until one in the morning.

And when I woke, I was fourteen; it was midnight and I was stoned on shitty dope, staring at the waves, the full moon at Walls; a runaway hiding in the mock-orange hedges near the Waikīkī Shell, the cops chasing me into Kapiʻolani Park.

And when I woke, I was fifteen, Celeste dragging me from a crack house in Waimānalo; Doritos crumbs on the floor, Big Mac wrappers blowing across the table, dogs straying in and out of the open door, a sofa smelling like sweaty ass; my sister hitting me with a filthy mop she found dripping on a torn mattress.

And when I woke and woke and woke, I was Alone in a bar in Chinatown, cheap wine with a toothless man I called Gin Blossoms who always wore a wilted plumeria lei; a braless woman in a straw hat next to me singing Dionne Warwick songs over and over. Nobody knew the way to San Jose.

Take me home:

Because when I wake, I am in a two-bedroom walk-up in Las Vegas with Drake, warm beer in tilting bottles, a glass of merlot with lip-gloss rainbows on its surface, Percodan and Prozac strewn on the countertop, glass pipes, amber vials, burnt pieces of tinfoil, Drake passed out on the futon in the arms of a girl/boy drug friend, Sonny Boy mewling madly in the corner.

I wake with healing stones, fluorite and malachite, in my closed fist, the gray ash of incense on my skin, cigarette butts in a naked-lady ashtray near a black lighter, my sketches on the floor, a broken canvas with pieces of sky, bits of sculpture, torn music sheets, ripped photographs.

My breasts are engorged with thin, white-blue milk. Baby bottles on the floor, dirty Pampers full of diarrhea taped shut, receiving blankets covered with hair, an infant's sheepskin caked with vomit, a twisted tube of Desitin, and baby powder, a silky film on my skin. We cannot stop crying, Sonny Boy and I, towels strewn over the chairs.

I am screaming inside:

Shut the fuck up. Shut up, fucking rotten little shit. You better shut up right now or I will fucking kill you.

My teeth grit, my hands fold into fists, and I hit his face, squeeze his cheeks inside my closing palms. Distort his cry with my hands on his face and throat, until the sound makes me laugh. I have hair all over my wet hands, his and mine.

Okay, Sonia, breathe deeply, breathe. It's just another Sunday, I reassure myself. It'll pass. I'll make it. At least I'm not Alone. I cradle Sonny Boy's face in the protracted sunlight through the broad window.

Sorry. I'm so sorry, baby. Mommy loves her little boy.

Drake calls to me, the girl/boy giggling. "Leave the baby, Sonia, and come to Daddy. Let's make each other happy."

I get up off the floor. Sonny Boy, I cannot keep these words inside me. I try so hard every day. You must believe me. These words that hang outside of my lips like smoke I long to breathe in but simply cannot: *My/son.*

Sonny Boy, I had fertility to prove. Proven. Now I need you out of my life. Gone away in a tiny casket. Grieving mother all in black. All that mournful attention. Drake consoling me because *I* need *him.* And corn chowder in Crock-Pots at my door. How the living love to feed the grieving.

Sonny Boy, a painter cannot paint, sculptor sculpt, photographer photograph, musician compose, not without the experience; your birth was to enhance my art. Art enhanced. Now how do I get rid of you? All evidence of you. Everything. I should kill you. Artfully. I've done it before. What a requiem I would compose.

Sonny Boy, I had to birth you. I thought you were the blessing of a uterine lining, gone for what they all told me was forever. The possibility of my redemption, a miracle from God, who found me at last.

But You, God, had found me before, when they said that Kate and her Holy Roller friends had fucked my head with False Doctrine, Unbiblical Teachings, Unholy Lies, and Demonic Delusions.

You sat in the corner of the room when they thought they might deprogram me. Light You, Being You, All You, white inhabiting my every memory and moment.

You looked at me in the dusty church office full of Sunday school quarterlies, empty offering plates, wooden crosses over the doorways, the hum of the air conditioner, a red carpet, You, filling the room with seraphic light. So I put on my shades.

Aunty Effie sat sternly in holy disapproval with her hands clutching her Bible, there on the rattan sofa. She pursed her lips at me and wiped tears from the corner of her eye. Pastor Jimmy Hingman whose claim to fame was singing backup on Glen Campbell's gospel album *To God Be the Glory*, sat on the black executive's chair behind the big desk. He stared deeply at me, his hands in "Here is the steeple" formation. Deacon Apana sat, tongue clucking and head shaking at me, next to the desk in an old schoolroom wooden chair.

I watched the Holy Ghost outside the window hovering above the field of sleeping grass past the churchyard. The shifting of the wind tickled him, the free movement of rice sparrows through His gossamer shape. The Holy Ghost winked at You. I knew You'd seen him by the smile on Your beautiful face.

"*I love you,*" You said, loud as day, the light in the room ablaze.

"Deacon Apana," Pastor Hingman said, "would ya please turn on some lights? It's awfully dark in here. And open up the windas, would ya? Li'l darlin', would ya take off them sunglasses? It ain't even bright in here. We're gonna open with prayer."

And pray they did:

Purify.

Sanctify.

Rectify.

Disapprobation.

Calumniation.

Desecration.

Unrepentant.

Uncontrite.

Unatoned.

Beseech of Thee Your Mercy.

Grace.

And.

Love.

"*I love you, Sonia.*" Beside me, Christ the Son, His body gone from the cross on the wall, whispered softly in my ear, His voice a smooth sonata.

"Because the greatest of these is Love?" I asked.

"What?" Aunty Effie interjected, right in the middle of Pastor Hingman's fist-pounding, prayerful climax. She slapped my face. "Who the hell are you talking to, Sonia? You see what I mean?" she said. "They have her talking to the damn walls. Brainwashed, I tell you."

"Wake up, Sonia," Deacon Apana said in my face while snapping his fingers in front of my eyes. "I ask you, Dear Lord, to awaken this child," he said in spontaneous prayer as he held my face tightly in one hand and lifted his other hand to the ceiling.

"Li'l darlin'," Pastor Hingman said in his condescending holy voice, "do you hear voices talking to you?"

"Like they're talking now?" I asked.

Aunty Effie and Deacon Apana looked around the room and then at each other with great disdain. "They just showed the Joan of Arc film to her Sunday school class," Deacon Apana whispered. "She'll be speaking in false tongues in a little while."

"Are the voices speakin' to you now?" Pastor Hingman asked, his eyes roaming upward as I nodded. "The Devil plays some mighty evil tricks on weak minds, but it is the weakest link among us that is the strongest," he told me. "And that is why we are here to pray for you."

"Love is a trick?" I asked.

"Yes." Pastor Hingman paused. "Even love." No one spoke.

I looked around the room. Panicked, I looked to the field of sleeping grass, the sad reverie of smoke diffusing upward toward the sky. The Son who sat beside me rose slowly back to His place on the crucifixture over the doorway. And when I turned my eyes to the corner of that silent room, You had vanished.

♦

Grace vanished Celeste and me. "Say goodbye," she said, never turning back to watch us leave.

Mark vanished from my life every time I hooked up with another loser, another Drake, a poet without a pot to piss in, white trash without a place to stay, a wanna-be carpenter who promised to take care of me but had to enroll in vocational school first, an alcoholic artist full of angst, bartenders, drifters, drug addicts, a pit boss or two, stray underdogs but always good sex. They all eventually vanished too.

I even vanished myself, vomiting down to a size six, then four, then two, until Granny Alma force-fed me her power shakes full of some weight-gain powder from Longs and pureed bananas.

I vanished three babies. A hospital's toxic-waste bin, a dirty toilet at Magic Island, and a jelly jar buried outside my bedroom window.

I want to vanish Sonny Boy. Wake up one morning and find him gone. Put him in a jar on the shelf. A paperweight. A work of Art. His closed pink eyes. He's sleeping, that's all, I put him to sleep, that's all. What in heaven made me think I was mother material? Grace told me the monthly blood was for this, *one day*. This?

All my fuck-ups have to be learned behavior. We're not born fucking idiots, we become fucking idiots. And I mastered the art of fucking myself over into idiotdom very well. I drink too much, I smoke too much, I toke too much, I coke too much, Drake, me, and our new estrogen-addicted girl/boy best friend, who does nothing all day but eat our food, stare at my crotch, and wear smashing size-two DKNY knockoffs from T.J. Maxx.

Or was it not paying attention to Signs? The Miracle in each weary day. My Fate minus blessing. The open Door, the Road less traveled, the Riverboat leaving the dock. A Celestine Prophecy in each misplaced word.

The Voices vanished like breath.

Rigidity in my wrist. That's what it is. I know I can enter the realm of God through art. I should paint more. Glorify my impending disintegration. Try glass blowing. Do some deep breathing. Suffer more for the next note, the next measure. Maybe work with copper. Surrender to the bitter pill. Stare deeply into the spiraling pit. Drown the awakening.

I should lose this postpartum weight. Get shallow. Go shopping. Get back my Jade Kwan gig or reemerge as Tiger Lily Wong, now appearing Thursday nights at the Golden Nugget's 14-Karat Bar.

I want someone to blame.

Grace, easy.

Joseph, easier.

Blue-collar upbringing, yes.

Racism, yes.

Low self-esteem, good one.

Too many ethnic-female-with-dysfunction novels.

Which provide no solutions.

Because life provides no resolutions.

So we'll all be left hanging.

In our particular Victimhood.

God?

Granny Alma calls to remind me that "God loves you, Sonia, now make sure you take your One-A-Days."

Celeste Kurisu-Infantino calls to tell me, "Don't be such a crybaby. You made your proverbial bed, now lie in it. We'll be in Vegas for Reverend Cyrus Hill's Power of Love Crusade. We'll all be there to support you and the baby. Besides, God forgives single mothers like you, Sonia."

Aunty Effie comes to Las Vegas three times a year with her daughters Aunty Frieda and Aunty Frannie with a care package full of Top Ramen, Spam, guava jelly, and chocolate-covered macadamia nuts.

Aunties Effie, Frieda, and Frannie who remind me that "God loves you, Sonia. Now pray we hit the million-dollar jackpot." Pastor Hingman and Deacon Apana should have deprogrammed Aunty Effie from her lifelong gambling addiction.

"Wake up and be a good mother," Grace scolds. "It's just postpartum depression. It'll pass. If I could do it, you can do it. And really, you have no one to blame but yourself."

And Joseph. The vanishing father, the philosophical father,

the father who left me. Left Celeste. Left Grace. Left home. Joseph, whose words always found me over continents and years.

I've kept your letters as evidence.

The evidence of your bliss/ignorant beauty.

The evidence of your sick I/love/you.

Do I read too much, Daddy, those books with tawdry endings?

But how I love a happy ending.

Daddy, give me a happy one.

Sweet Sonia,

A man falls sick to severe dysentery. A woman enters his room with a small tray. Behind her, a little girl carries worn towels. The woman places her hand on the man's forehead, then turns on a small lamp.

On his bedstand, the man sees white fungus in a clear broth, a bottle of fermented tea, and a plate of grated coconut.

Outside, he listens to the distant rumble of approaching thunderstorms. The girl closes the window. When she notices the man's gaze, she covers her eyes with both hands but peers at him from between her fingers. The woman begins cleaning the man.

The man is delirious. He tells her about the west lake where he rode an old black bicycle, the lake so beautiful, the color of blue rock from the Buddhist temple in the hills of Han Zhou. How the rain spread over the water from the curvature of sky.

The woman wrings the dirty towel and begins wiping his neck. The girl holds a tiny wooden box, this girl who has the Buddha's ears. Pink light shines through them

when the girl looks up at the man. She looks like his sweet
Sonia.

The man begins to cry. He cannot stop his tears. The
girl climbs onto the bed. She crawls under the sheets and
moves the man's heavy arm around her. When she opens
the wooden box, she looks into the man's eyes. The music
is unrecognizable at first.

Beethoven's Moonlight Sonata. It is at this moment
that the man thinks of his sweet daughter. He knows he
must return home. This girl in the moonlight wraps
herself into the stink of his body, turns off the lamp, and
places the open box on the bedstand.

When he wakes in the morning, the tray of white
fungus broth, fermented tea, and grated coconut is gone.
The window is open, the sunlight comes, trembling in the
curtains. The girl is gone, the room silent, but for a tiny
wooden box still playing a Moonlight Sonata.

I will tell you, sweet Sonia, a prayer that I learned
years ago in a quiet synagogue in Amsterdam that this
little Chinese girl restored in me:

I believe in the sun even when it is not shining.

I believe in love even when feeling it not.

I believe in God even when He is silent.

Keep these words.

Tell Grace and Celeste that I will be home soon.

I love you,
Joseph Kurisu

Daddy, the sun has come, a fire in the morning. Just another Sunday, but flames rise from the ground of this desert
town, burn me from that Kalihi Valley suburb, blaze on from
Hilo, that sleepy bay town.

Sonny Boy falls asleep fitfully in my arms, his face and neck bruised. Asleep is the only way I love him. But this is Love, I am sure. Love, an ache he's sharpened in a girl given away, a girl never found, a girl never kept. Wake me when this is all over.

And the Voice of God, no pulse or flicker there, Daddy, His silent ire, years going on years now; God is a vanishing, invisible breath behind the distant clouds.

And it's every day I say, Daddy, no matter the geography of place or time:

Let this day end. Let it end with me dead.

Blue

SONNY BOY, you will love your great-granny as much as I did. You will love her because you will be forced to love her. She is all you will have on your day of no choice. You on her doorstep. You left in the tiny back room of her house in Kalihi. You, her daughter Grace's legacy of goodbye. Say goodbye to me. I am so sorry, Sonny Boy.

But this way, you will know your great-granny's love for everything lavender, her clean house, bleached whites, her Japanese sayings, one for every occasion, her sekihan rice and cucumber namasu, her itchy afghans and crocheted doilies, her Love of God. She will be here in Vegas with your Aunty Celeste for the Reverend Cyrus Hill's Power of Love Crusade.

Aunty Celeste who decided when we were girls to attend Kahala Baptist in an affluent Honolulu neighborhood while Granny and I went to First Kalihi in the ghettos. Aunty Celeste who became a fine Christian, who teaches Sunday school, chairs the Bread of Life foreign mission drive, sings Amy Grant songs for special services, and is the substitute pianist at her church. She holds some kind of national office for the Baptist convention. They're all really proud of their devout Celeste. I read it in the Baptist newsletter that Aunty Effie keeps sending me.

Hey, Sonny Boy, look at me when I talk to you. You want me to squeeze your face? You want me to snap your neck? Why won't you look at me? Frigid mother syndrome, somebody says to me in art history class. I shouldn't leave you with Black Bob, Drake's name for the man who moved in next door to us on the day you were born. Black Bob probably doesn't pay enough attention to you. Drake says I need to bond with you.

"Read Bruno Bettelheim, stupid idiot," Drake mutters. "He could wake up your sorry ass about failed mothers."

"You're not a failed mother," Black Bob reassures me. "I've consulted Jung and Piaget," he whispers. "I talked to the boys at length at a poetry reading in Kansas City."

Drake and the girl/boy refuse to baby-sit even if they do jack shit all day. Painting a series of teacup and Victorian home miniatures, writing his epic novel with a screenplay adaptation in mind, my ass. They *collaborate* in the apartment until late afternoon. The girl/boy gives him food stamps. I don't know what Drake gives it. They both need a bath.

Drake says, "I'll kick Black Bob's black ass myself if we even hear Sonny Boy whimper. Fucking nigger wants you, Sonia," he tells me all the time. "You need to wake up and smell the coffee."

Drake needs to wake up and stop living off the *fat of the land*, his clever metaphor for my body. "Nine months to make it," he says, glaring at Sonny Boy, "and nine months to shake it, baby," he says, clutching a handful of my belly. Clever motherfucker. "The kid isn't *my* life work," he always adds. "The kid isn't even mine. That kid for *my* art?" He laughs.

You are mine, Sonny Boy.

Mine Alone.

But Granny will be here soon, I promise. She will watch over you as she did me. She knows how. To love you.

♦

Granny Alma worked a day job as a part-time custodian at posh Punahou School cleaning toilets in the athletic department and a night job bartending and cleaning toilets at the Ten-Pin. Celeste and I could attend the private school on a work-study, partial-tuition waiver if we could pass the Entrance Examination. Celeste and I could bowl unlimited free games at the Stadium Bowl-O-Drome if we were serious about the Art of Bowling, which was not a mere Game.

Celeste passed. I didn't.

Celeste almost turned semipro. I hated the game.

"You try for Punahou again next year," Granny consoled. She sliced lime wedges and dumped them in a little bowl behind the bar. "I know you have brains," she said, giving me a couple of maraschino cherries, "because you're my daughter's child. Grace was a smart girl, you know." I watched Granny pour a shitty blanc for a woman with red lipstick smeared over the natural outline of her lips. "Don't worry, Sonia." She paused.

"What, Granny?" I asked, distracted by Uncle Fu Manchu's gesture for another Tom Collins. "Worry about what?"

"About school. I guess for now, you have to go to Dole Intermediate," she said sadly, like it was some death-row sentence.

It was.

Sanford B. Dole Intermediate was across the street from a public housing project in Kalihi called Kam IV and right up the street from the biggest housing project in the state of Hawai'i, KPT. The Honolulu Police Department's Kalihi substation was a parking lot away from my new school.

I was a little Jap surrounded by girls who looked twenty-one with high-maintenance hairdos, hickeys, cigarettes tucked behind each ear, lost virginities, and fucking tough-ass street attitudes; boys who looked twenty-one with homemade tattoos, gang colors, pagers beeping in every class, and knives, guns, and razor blades tucked away in deep pockets; teachers' cars were ripped off and torched during school hours.

Every day for me was an exercise in Simplicity. The Simplicity of my Survival.

Sweet Sonia,

There is a simplicity of a man's life here in Amsterdam. He buys beautiful rolls in the morning with various cheeses, rides a bicycle on bridges over canals, walks narrow brick-inlaid sidewalks where dandelions and tall yellow milkweeds grow from between the cracks.

He feeds his leftover rolls to the mallard ducks in the Herengracht, three females and two green-headed males unbothered by the "Wim Kam" or "The Lovers," empty canal boats moving about the brown waters.

The man hates chaos. He watches a woman and a man stop to argue on a bridge. Their dogs sniff in uncertain greeting. How much easier would it have been had the woman and the man exchanged a courteous but brief greeting? This simplifies the utter complexities underlying their meeting. The man wants it that way.

On this night, the man lies in a soft bed in a room that fills with orange streetlight. The room glows, the walls, gilded with bars of orange. He never closes the curtains. He is glad. He need not feel afraid of the dark and of his aloneness.

He hears an angry man yelling in the night. A heavy door slams. There is a woman with her face in her hands sitting on a dark stoop. The Dutchman does not need this woman. The woman does not need this man. A child in a flimsy nightgown comes out and sits beside the crying woman. They hold each other in this night of yellow lights in cathedral windows.

The man will return and return and return, his absence of spirit in the presence of his human form more apparent to the woman as the days roll on. They cling to momentary glimpses at happiness. But rather than binding themselves to joy, perceived or no, they must kiss it as it flies. Blake said that.

Do you remember, sweet Sonia, how I loved an evening cigarette out on the porch after dinner? Grace needed me inside to wipe your faces, put the leftovers in Tupperware, wipe the shoyu bottle, watch you finish your cup of warm milk, then read a story to you and Celeste.

I loved an evening cigarette out on the porch, reclining on the lawn chair, watching the sky turn orange and purple after dinner.

To Celeste and Granny Alma, my love. To Grace, my continued affection. Would I stop to chat with her had we met on the bridge? Yes, but the night is coming. I want to watch the passage of a flock of seabirds over the canal. It is time to water my flowers in the highest window box in the city.

All desire,
Joseph

Granny would read his letters to me, the calm rhythm of his words, a girl's bedtime story. She read them night after night until I memorized each line. The letter's edges frayed and melted.

"Would he stop to talk to me?" I asked Granny Alma every night.

"Who knows," she hissed, turning off the light.

"Would he?" I asked her silhouette in the doorway.

"What do you think, Sonia?" she said, closing the door.

Through the passage of time, the answer to my own question has never changed.

Granny Alma never chatted with the bums, the punks, the assorted Kalihi Valley working-class poor, and the mentally disturbed from Filipino care homes while we waited for the #7 bus to King Street. Granny had never learned how to drive.

I said goodbye to Celeste and Granny at the bus stop on King Street and headed deeper into that surreal urban ghetto, as Celeste headed toward a sparkling scholastic city. Up until the day she graduated from Punahou, Celeste would hop off the city bus one block before the manicured school grounds. She didn't want to be seen with Granny Alma, a lowly custodian, pretending instead that they weren't even related.

I was never ashamed of Granny. I helped her bus tables in the Ten-Pin. I washed glasses and wiped ashtrays. If she got slammed, Granny had me hustle around and restock the liquor. I carried buckets of ice to refill the ice bins. All of this busing and cleaning while Celeste doggedly did her Punahou homework in one of the dark orange booths. Pretending we weren't related, none of us, then reading thick-ass novels from a required reading list.

But I was slow-minded, Granny was sure of this, heading toward a bartending or janitorial job like her, or waitressing like my mother. And when the counselor at Dole Intermediate called to tell her I would have to drop an elective to take the mandatory Chapter One Reading class for students who fell somewhere below the thirtieth percentile, she nearly died of shame.

Chapter One Reading was a step above Special Ed. I hung

around the bathroom before the tardy bell and waited for the sidewalk to clear so that no one would see me as I slid into the classroom. Me and guys like Sam Cabales who didn't know his real name was Samuel so when the teacher asked him to spell it, he wrote *Sa-mule*. Ginny Asuncion who didn't know how to tell time unless it was a digital watch. Hector Edwards who looked like a mini Boo Radley and whose mother had a beard.

Granny called Grace, who blamed Joseph for my learning disability. It was a psychological scar I bore, so she said, because of his unpredictable absences. I didn't talk until I was four and a half, she said. And Joseph not until he was six. My father fucked me up emotionally and genetically.

Nothing said about her sending me away.

"But she reads all of her father's letters with me," Granny Alma said to Grace. "They're all tattered in a shoebox under her bed."

"She reads aloud to you?" Grace asked.

"I read them to her and then she reads them to me," Granny answered.

"After how many times?" Grace asked.

"I don't know. Maybe ten. Oh, sweet Lord Jesus," Granny gasped. "She's memorizing *his* words."

"Did she say she can read them?" Grace prodded.

"Yes. She said she just needed help with a few words," Granny said.

"Then Sonia's lying. The girl's a liar, Mom. You need to watch her. She's the spitting image of her father."

Granny enrolled me in a free after-school reading class at her church, First Kalihi Baptist. They prayed for God to raise our low SAT scores, help us overcome learning disabilities, motivate the unmotivated learners among us, and mainstream those in Chapter One Reading. We prayed before and after each session.

I prayed without ceasing:

God, take me out of Chapter One Reading. Make me a smart girl like Grace and Celeste. Find Joseph and make him bring me home.

Then one day, like an answered prayer, a package arrived for me from Joseph. In it was a copy of *The Diary of Anne Frank*. It arrived three weeks after my birthday, May 25. Celeste cried as she watched me open the present. Her birthday had come and gone months before. She cried even more as I read his letter aloud with my halting and limited reading ability, finally snatching the letter from me.

She had never been interested in his letters. But this one had come with a gift. An intellectual gift. A novel straight from her Punahou required reading list, and bragger's rights to her rich classmates, a novel straight from Amsterdam.

Sweet Sonia,

A man walks along a canal. He wonders if the reflection of a blue sky in the dark waters transforms its depths to azure like the waters off Pohoiki on a sunny day. You see, in the time the man spends in this city of Amsterdam, he never sees a blue sky.

But the man marvels at the houses over the canals built on cement posts. The blue-violet hydrangea and red and pink geraniums in plant boxes right over the canal, the man sees these plant boxes on ledges, on decks, and outside of windows.

It's five o'clock in the evening. There is a chill in the wind here and dull lights in windows. The man hurries past a black cat with green eyes in the window of a tea shop on the Herengracht.

He climbs the narrow stairs to his attic room

overlooking the brown waters of the canal. Dinghies covered with musty canvases shift in the tide. Canal boats leave a gassy trail of fumes and bubbles that never pop. The dinghies tilt. The man listens to the lapping water on the canal's edge.

Yellow porch lights outside of stoops go on and orange streetlights brighten the darkening roadways with a surreal luminosity.

Someone is whistling a tune not known to him, and for a moment, it makes him lonely. He strains to follow the melody as it trails down the narrow road.

Trees lose their leaves to the canal. A woman in a blue wool coat rides by on a red bicycle that looks like an old red Schwinn from the back of some child's garage. She pushes up her glasses, curly orange hair bobbing as she maneuvers around pedestrians. She has plants in her rusted metal basket. Maybe she is rushing home to put geraniums in an empty planter on a deck over the brown waters.

He will do that tomorrow. He will fill the planter in his window with magnificent flowers like the flowers he sees in the street vendors' stalls. Yellow tulips, delphiniums on long stems holding their tall blue-violet blossoms, gerbera the red daisies, euphorbia of the small yellow blossoms hanging, and pink or red geraniums. The man will spend the next day amidst the flowers in this city of gray skies—the gray skies and wind that makes a riptide of yellow leaves in the canal, the residue of some hurricane system named for a woman.

Sweet Sonia, when I looked up from the street vendor's stall, I saw a patch of blue and realized that my love for the blue is a condition of inhabiting days and days of rain.

My love to Celeste and Grace as always and a hope for all of you to turn your faces toward some blue on an occasion for flowers.

I love you all,
Joseph

I saw it all, the Amsterdam of Joseph's beautiful words. Celeste curled her lip at me, then beat me with Granny's back scratcher.

I asked Granny to reread the letter to me until the creases ripped. I taped the words together, my father's words.

Words that paralleled his image.

♦

Black Bob tells me he reads to Sonny Boy every day. He's still unemployed but wants to work in a casino downtown as a blackjack dealer. As soon as I take Sonny Boy from Black Bob's arms, he begins to cry, reaching his arms back toward him. Every day the same old fucking crybaby shit. Black Bob puts his pink palm on Sonny Boy's face. "I'll see you tomorrow morning, my little champ," he coos. When I walk into the apartment, Drake says Sonny Boy never cries as far as he can hear. Not a peep all day. He must be saving it all for you.

Drake is drunk, a mean drunk. The girl/boy's passed out. A crack pipe smolders in a tipped ashtray, cigarette butts all over the table. "So you think he's doing a good job taking care of your son?" Drake sneers. I don't answer. The girl/boy stirs. "Well? Hello? Am I talking to the walls?"

"How's the sweeping epic, Michener? And where's the paintings, the little miniatures?" I ask, putting Sonny Boy on the floor. He can sit up now. He heads straight for an empty bottle of Southern Comfort. "Pick up your shit," I tell Drake. The girl/boy turns over and pulls the blanket over its head.

"The problem with you, Sonia, is a lack of trust."

"What? Just shut up, Drake. You're drunk."

"You think I couldn't take care of the kid?" he yells. I turn away from him. "Well, you never asked, bitch." He pours a shot glass of cheap rum. "The epic?" he slurs. "Painting?" he laughs. "I got no muse. Just a fucking fat-ass old lady with a kid who only screams when he's with her. Now what kind of muse is that?"

I pick up Sonny Boy. "Where you going?" he asks, grabbing my arm.

"Out," I tell him.

"You just came from out, stupid."

"So?"

I pull the heavy door open. "You know why the kid never cries when he's with that nigger?" I stare at Drake, daring him to say something mean. "He's sucking his little pink dick all day. Would make me stop crying."

The girl/boy moans. "Drake? Baby? I'm hungry."

Drake laughs hard. "Hungry? I like that. Sonia's going to get dinner, baby." He pushes me out the door. Sonny Boy starts crying, again.

♦

Celeste threw Joseph's letter and the back scratcher at my face.

When we arrived at the Ten-Pin that evening, she headed straight for Granny Alma, who was blending a Midori daiquiri for Aunty Tokyo Rose. "Sonia stayed home and cut out from Dole." I hated the way she said "Dole," like it was some kind of whorehouse, hellhole penitentiary.

"But I finished the book Joseph sent to me," I chimed in, "the whole book."

I waited for Granny's slap. Instead, she put her hand on my

head and patted an empty space on the bar. "Well, how's that?" she said, bragging to an approving Aunty Tokyo Rose. "The *whole* book? All by yourself? How come?"

"Anne Frank, Granny," I started, Celeste pushing me out of her way, "a girl all alone in that attic, just like——"

"Oh, shut your face, Sonia. You're not alone. You have Granny and me. And you don't live in an attic, okay. Anne Frank was a hero. You are nothing. And don't forget, stupid, that you cut out of school," she enunciated in my face.

"Sit," Granny said to me. "Tomorrow, you go to school. And you know what I'll do for you?"

"What, Granny?" I asked. It was all Celeste could take. She stormed off to her dark booth and pouted.

"I'll ask that nice librarian, the pianist at First Kalihi, Mr. Jordan, to drive the bookmobile after school to the church parking lot for you kids in the reading class." I raised my eyebrows in astonishment.

I became well aquainted with Mr. Jordan, who'd haul the bookmobile into the church grounds and honk the deep horn for me to special-deliver books on Auschwitz-Birkenau and Dachau, thick historical documentaries on concentration camps. I borrowed biographies about the Nazis and Adolf Hitler, fascists and Benito Mussolini.

I read about the mountains of human hair made into rugs and cloth, human-skin lampshades, fingernail scratches in the concrete walls of the gas chambers, the extraction of gold teeth, and the smell of human flesh hovering above the camps.

I read about children put in rooms full of ticks to "scientifically" measure the duration of human life with parasitic infection. The children given away. The children left behind. The children afraid. The children abandoned. The children all Alone.

I read about the fate of the Franks—Otto and Edith, sister

Margot, and Anne. I pondered the whereabouts of Margot's lost journal. I studied the details of the small rooms and dark passageways in the Secret Annexe. I mapped my way up the Prinsengracht, and when I closed my eyes, I heard the bells telling time from the Westerkerk tower as Anne might have heard their chime. Through black gauze pulled taut and stapled over the windows of the Secret Annexe, I studied the chestnut trees. I saw Anne longing for blue.

I understood the image and the word:

Two sisters holding hands and walking away from Mommy.

Two sisters crying in the dark cold.

No Otto. No Edith.

Two sisters Alone.

Two sisters Dead.

Granny read every book with me so that I'd have someone to talk to about Anne Frank and inhumanity and demons disguised as men. These books and conversations occupied our slow hours in the Ten-Pin, and Celeste, not wanting to be left out, began reading *The Diary of Anne Frank* in her dark orange booth.

By the end of this school year, I was mainstreamed from Chapter One Reading. I chose Piano I as my elective even if I'd be in a class of students younger than me. The first song I would learn to play was the first page of Beethoven's Moonlight Sonata. I played it over and over for Granny Alma and Mr. Jordan on First Kalihi Baptist's baby grand piano on a Saturday church clean-up day.

"Your father would be proud," she said.

Sweet Sonia,

Come with me to the tall building on the Prinsengracht, through the front of the old brick building, past the crowd of foreigners, yourself included.

Have you finished reading the book I sent you a few weeks ago? I hope it arrived in time for your thirteenth birthday. Please share it with Celeste.

Now, come with me, sweet Sonia. Crawl through the bookcase's hidden doorway. Touch the porcelain sink, the walls of Anne's room, the face of Greta Garbo glued to the wall, the doorways, fading papers, cold metal stove, and marks on the wall made by a father to commemorate the growth of his daughters.

See another rooftop, another window, cathedral windows across the way. Tiled roofs are mossy gray. See a face in Peter Van Daan's window and brittle black trees full of lichen and moss. The windows, shaded with black gauze, are framed in white.

Come, sweet Sonia, and look out of these windows. See the gray sky and rocks amidst leaves on a rooftop below. The leaves are from a chestnut tree that has known in its rings of memory a day of blue sky in Amsterdam, where a girl sat on a lounge chair sunning herself before she forgot the true color of blue, distorted by black gauze; before she forgot the feel of sun on her bare shoulders.

When no one is looking, I rip a tiny space in the black gauze covering the window in Anne's room. In this act, I think of you, sweet Sonia and Celeste, my daughters, who must always remember the quality of blue and the passage we all take down dark corridors, up steep staircases, into empty rooms with faded pictures on the wall, to a window through which you can know the expanse of sky.

Sending my best wishes to Granny Alma and Celeste. To Grace, the sun on her pretty face in my mind's window.

My love to you,
Your father Joseph Kurisu

♦

My father would be proud.

♦

Drake yells at me from the doorway of our apartment, "Bring home a bucket of Popeye's chicken for Pat and me. And do the fucking laundry." He throws the basket of dirty clothes at me. "None of that Chinese or Korean shit, you hear me, Sonia? I got fucking rice coming out of my ears, dammit."

Black Bob steps out of his apartment with a load of his dirty laundry. He picks up my basket. "Need company?" he asks. I nod, holding back tears. We trudge down to the laundry room and start a couple of loads.

Sonny Boy falls asleep on a pile of Black Bob's unfolded laundry. We don't say very much in a kind of silent comfort, the kind old friends share. This realization all of a sudden makes me uncomfortable.

I listen to the spin and click of a zipper in the dryer, turn, turn, buttons clicking against the metal drum.

"Who is my father?"

It is a Voice that comes from nowhere.

"Who is he?"

"Sonia?" Bob nudges me.

I realize: it's not his voice. "Huh? What did you say, Bob?"

"My father, who?"

"Sonia? I didn't say anything." He gives me two quarters to start the load of baby clothes. "C'mon, girl. I don't want to be here all night. Not that I don't like the company. But your old man, um, um, um," he says in his disapproving singsong.

Through the window, I watch the sky deepen into indigo.

I see water, blue, my eyes do blink.

I am so hungry. I must be hungry, but I'm not hungry.

I hear a loud spouting, spray of water.

Is the sky raining?

Bob? Where are you?

Eyes do hunger.

No, blue sky, deepening water.

Then through the window slips a boy, seven, maybe eight, eyes black glass, and the clicking and chirping of a funny child's song.

"It's me," he says.

I look around. Bob snores soundly. His glasses slip down his oily nose. Today's paper spreads over his chest. Sonny Boy breathes evenly, sleeping on our warm folded clothes in the laundry basket.

The Voice is clear.

"Who are you?" I ask.

"#2."

Arms unfold into dorsals.

Feet, tail fin.

Tiny head.

Shiny amber shell.

I am losing my fucking mind. I work too much. I'm carrying too many credits. I need some sleep. I fucking hate this baby. I fucking hate Drake. The girl/boy leaves me no food. Celeste is coming. Oh, here comes judgment day. You will love your great-granny as much as I did. She will take care of you. She will take care of you. Bob can have you. No, I can bond. I am a Jungian. I am a backsliding Christian. Where is Mark with my shampoo? I am not a frigid mother.

A whistling spins from his mouth,

a chirp thrown into the sky, the laundry room, waterblue,

deepening indigo, a whistling sky,

the chirping room is a mouth,
a boy, waterblue, is it you,
my #2?

"Goodbye, Drake," he says, waving the waves back to the sky. *"Bob loves the Little Prophet."*

"What profit? I don't even pay him."

"Sonia?" Bob stirs.

Then out slips a boy, backward/falling, singing through the open window.

It's night but never night in this town. Fluorescent lights, garish brilliance. Bob gets up and lifts the laundry basket where Sonny Boy sleeps. He starts back upstairs. I follow him down the dark corridor, rustygold numbers on doors with peeling brown paint. I enter the dirty apartment, and look through the window. My hands tremble.

The sky is a remarkable shade of midnight blue.

5

Open Door

#2, IS IT YOU? It cannot be. I killed you, flushed you down a
filthy toilet at Magic Island. I tiptoe around the living room
with red scarves over lamps.

Promise me blue, my gone #2, the return of the sky.

Drake stumbles into a chair. He knocks books off of the
table. The baby stirs. I put my finger over my lips, *shh*. So he
shouts in my face, "Fuck you." The girl/boy lights the pipe.
Last hit, rock bottom. The baby shifts. Drake snatches the pipe.

A wind whistles through the window, gasps at first, then
howls in round vowels. Red scarves whirl around the room like
gossamer over sleeping grass, over a sleeping baby. The room
fills with an exposing light, the brilliance of yellow.

The girl/boy wants a second hit from the pipe and tries to
light it. The flame goes out, goes out, goes out.

Papers fly. Three pages of his epic and random notes
wheeze out the open door. Antique teacups, saucers, and photographs fall to the floor. But Drake says to the girl/boy,
"Fucking bitch—you been smoking my shit all day?"

The girl/boy looks at me, all in this moment of papers and
words spinning, scarves whirling, a fine Wednesday ash in an
exhaling breath around us.

I start laughing at them. The wind won't stop. So Words fly.

The apartment door swings opens. Bob enters the room and takes the baby in his arms. He points his finger in Drake's face, Big Black Bob, a warning, a threat in one finger.

I take Drake's clothes paints keys pipes computer discs brushes watch shoes wallet papers bills books CDs coins sunglasses cigarettes keyboard coffee mug and throw them all over the balcony.

"Goodbye, Drake," #2's little voice sings from behind me. I turn to the Voice, loud as the lights in the room, but it's gone.

I turn toward the door.

I see the back of two shadows, shades leaving the room, sucked out and inhaled as if in one long drag.

I see a man enter the room, a baby in a basket, a small miracle him still sleeping with all the wind in the skies. "Sleep, Sonia. I'll watch the door. Be sitting right here when you wake up," Bob says to me. "Lots of crime in this town."

♦

When I was fourteen, I wanted to be a criminal. Jingle Estrella and I were arrested for shoplifting cheap makeup and nail polish for Afi Sagatu and Lauta Tautele at the Waikīkī Woolworth's, at Kam Longs, at JC Penney. Freshmen at Farrington High School, all four of us were arrested for truancy near the store in Kalihi Valley that sold fresh goat. Arrested for buying crack near the back door of a Korean strip club on Kapi'olani Boulevard. Assault and battery at Peter Buck Mini Park below the H-1 freeway. Terroristic threats with an unregistered firearm at the Kalihi-Pālama Library. Minors in possession of alcohol behind the Stadium Bowl-O-Drome. I had mixed a batch of Tom Collinses for the four of us in a washed-out Harder's syrup jug. It was for me . . . innocent ghetto fun. It was for Granny Alma . . . the last of many straws.

As for Celeste, it must've been all those free games at the bowling alley that finally won her a full bowling scholarship from Punahou. Celeste who'd leave her orange booth when the crowd of low-class league bowlers cleared out near closing. She'd bowl intense midnight rounds with Uncle Fu Manchu, an almost semipro bowler and Granny Alma's boyfriend. He molded my sister into an interscholastic league bowling phenomenon. She'd appear on a cable access channel, rapt and focused, winning some major bowling tournament while Jingle, Afi, Lauta, and I got shitfaced drunk and stoned on stolen dope from Jingle's brother's stash. We caught the munchies, and teased Celeste's makeup, her dramatic ballerina follow-through, her smug and holy prayer, a silencer, one before each frame. And all the while, Celeste maintained a 4.0 at Punahou while chairing carnival and spring cotillion.

I was fourteen when Granny Alma sent me back to Hilo for the summer. She would return me to Grace every summer thereafter, every holiday, every long weekend, every chance she had to get me out of her hair.

"No ifs, ands, or buts, Gracie," she said to my mother. "Send Sonia back if and when she shapes up. And *if* is a small word that casts a large shadow."

I was belligerent. "She listens to no one, Gracie. Maybe Pastor Hingman can set her straight."

Out of control. "A damn Hurricane Sonia, that's what she is. I can't stop her."

A juvenile delinquent. "There's no other Japanese kids down at the cell block, you know, Gracie, just Sonia."

Out of control. "I'm blue in the face from yelling at her."

Insane. "Pray for her."

Out of control. "Pray for me."

And poor Celeste?

"Pray for Celeste, Grace. Sonia's an embarrassment to her.

They have the *same* last name, for chrissakes. Imagine if Sonia got into Punahou? Heaven forbid."

So Granny sent me Back. And Grace sent me Forth.

"Why can't she be like Celeste? She sets such a good example for her sister. I don't get it."

Whatever.

"And too bad for Sonia. Now she'll miss Baptist Summer Camp at Pūpūkea as further punishment."

Double whatever.

"And send her to Sunday school and morning service at Hilo Baptist. Have Effie pick her up and escort her there, if you have to rope and tie her."

Oh, shit. Not Aunty Effie. Fucking ballbuster.

"And make her join the choir. She can play the damn piano. I'll call her probation officer and ask if she can complete her community service in Hilo. Maybe at the church. Dammit, Gracie, the kid's a mess. Do something."

I got off the plane. The smell of Hilo rain and mildew in the jetway.

I laughed at Granny Alma, Celeste, Joseph, and Grace. I laughed at God, because in spite of them all:

I had made it home.

♦

I don't know how Mark gets word about Drake leaving me. But Mark comes back to me at last. He's knocking on the door. He hands me a bottle of shampoo. "About fucking time," I tell him.

"Fuck you, Sonia. It's not my fault you keep fucking up our friendship by hooking up with loser lovers," he says, pushing his way in. He picks Sonny Boy off the ground mid-crawl and wipes a smudge from the baby's face with the bottom of his T-shirt. He kisses his forehead, his cheeks, his lips. It's the first time Mark's seen him. No wind, still day, this early morning.

Bob leans his thick arms over the railing. Stares at the desert sky. He gives Mark an up and down who/the/fuck/are/you glare. Mark offers him a cigarette. Bob looks hard at Mark. He hasn't had a cigarette in a day, no money. His fingers linger on the open pack for a moment. He pulls one out slowly. The two of them smoke in silence. Meanwhile, the return of the sun from behind pink clouds.

We enter the ransacked apartment. Drake and the girl/boy have taken or broken everything. Bob and Mark look at each other. We step around overturned chairs, empty bottles, strewn trash. Mark puts Sonny Boy in his portable crib.

Mark gets the broom and starts sweeping up the broken glass. I get old rags and a bucket. Bob leaves and then returns with a cadre of cleaning products. "Went to the new-products fair at the convention center as a Kirby rep," he says.

"You big black phony," I tell him.

He shrugs his shoulders and laughs. "I'm going down to the 7-Eleven. Who wants some coffee?"

Mark and I raise our hands and continue cleaning. Sonny Boy hoists himself up and gums the edge of the crib, his knees buckling and bouncing. I look at him. Why can't he be a good boy all of the time? Cute boy. Good boy. Mommy's little boy. I cannot let Mark know how much I fucking hate this baby.

Mark steps over shards of glass. He puts his hand on my face. Then he opens all of the windows.

♦

The first time Granny Alma sent me Back to Hilo to be rehabilitated, Grace and Joseph picked me up at the airport. "Don't open the passenger-side window. It's broken," she snapped. They were her only words to me.

Mama, burn/in/hell.

"Kiddo, you better stop screwing up and find your damn self," Joseph sighed. "Get your fucking life together, dammit." He had been home for a couple of months.

Daddy, seek/and/you/shall/find.

It was late evening. We pulled into the gravel parking lot next to the taxi stand across from Joseph's favorite Japanese restaurant, Tomi Zushi. He and Grace walked down the narrow alley between the Mamo Theatre and Juanito's Barber Shop. I looked up the tall side of the theater, mossy lines of black mildew dribbling constant water off of tentacles of peat.

I watched my father's back, memorizing his shape like I did as a little girl. A tiny gold bell brought the o-san from the back kitchen with his "Hey there Mr. Joe, Missy Glacie. Rrong time no see."

"Play some songs for me," Joseph said, reaching into his pocket and putting foreign coins in my hand with a sly wink. My father always had change in his pocket for the two little girls he took to the same restaurant on Mamo Street years ago.

Change in our hands, Celeste and I would spend it all at the Hilo Comic Center and Kawate Seed Shop while he and Grace ordered miso soup, eggplant tempura, and chawan mushi. It was all so normal. Then he'd give us more money to play the jukebox.

This was no ordinary jukebox. Above it was a bandstand full of carved wooden musicians playing assorted instruments. When the songs began, heavy maroon curtains pulled open and the wooden musicians in their green tuxedos and red bow ties swayed in time to the tunes.

"Play some songs for me," he said on my first day back in Hilo. I listened to the change drop into the jukebox. A-5. A Moonlight Sonata, the Boston Philharmonic. The curtains pulled open and the lights on the bandstand flickered onto the faces of Ken-doll musicians.

"Time for chan-gee with the times," the o-san said to me as he placed a hot bowl of miso soup on the table. "All new doll-ru, fi-fu-ty per-centu off-u."

I was fourteen years old. I had lived with my grandmother for two years now. My sister was still with her in Honolulu. I watched the curtains pull open. And I wept. They were gone, the handsome wooden musicians, each with his own special face and expression.

"Not enough-fu bel-beto tuxedo on sale," he said to me as I stared at the bandstand. "So," he said, "I lea-bee some in the mod clothes. Ni-cu, lock and loll, no?"

There was no apparent order to the Kens who took the places of the wooden musicians. And when the band of Kens began to sway, they had real hair instead of wooden heads, their hair swinging madly out of time with the beautiful sonata. They all looked insane and out of control.

"Change is always good," Joseph said to the o-san, who left for the kitchen behind the indigo blue curtains on bamboo rods. "And there's a difference between change and chaos, you hear me, Sonia? It's all in the way you see things." He said these words to me, but looked at Grace.

"If she can see the difference. Or see, *period*," Grace said, glaring at me. "But *if* is a small word that casts a large shadow."

The o-san returned a short while later with a soda box full of the old wooden musicians lying like dead men with frozen hands and lips without instruments. I studied the holes in their hands and faces.

"For you," he said, shoving the soda box at me. "No goo-du big-u girl-san like you cu-rai, cu-rai, cu-rai." He kept shoving the box at me.

I was home.

So what?

Big deal.

I placed all of the mutilated musicians on a bandstand on my bureau in my old room except for three:

The tiny piano player with the face like a turtle.

The clarinet player who looked like Joseph.

The bass player with the pierced, bloody hands of Jesus.

I put them in my suitcase. I knew I wouldn't be staying.

Those musicians traveled with me back and forth across islands and oceans, hands and lips playing imaginary instruments, change in a jukebox, a child, a woman, playing A-5 over and over, studying the curves of their faces, waiting for the day of their footsteps through an open backstage door.

◆

Mark comes Back. He fills bucket after bucket with Pine-Sol, and, on his hands and knees, wipes months of filth off of the linoleum floors. Bob cleans the jalousies with old newspaper and sample-size Windex. I make eight bottles of Isomil for Sonny Boy and some tuna sandwiches.

Mark comes Back. He buys fresh bananas and apples to puree for Sonny Boy. No more Gerber bottled food. Rice cereal. "Mmm," Bob murmurs as he places Sonny Boy on his lap to feed him. I put a bib around the baby's neck and hand Bob a cloth diaper to wipe up what dribbles from the side of the baby's mouth. Mark starts cooking a spinach and tofu lasagna in the kitchen.

Mark comes Back. "Sonia, go take a bath. Wash your hair." Mark hands Sonny Boy to Bob. He lifts three heavy trash bags and heads for the dumpster out back. And for the first time, I bathe without worry or rush.

Mark comes Back. The table is set. Bob brings over a bottle of cabernet. I sit on the couch with a towel wrapped around my hair. Someone put the baby to sleep for me. I stare at Mark for a long time. The steam from fresh garlic bread rises in front of his face.

"Don't make it too nice for me, motherfucker," I tell Mark.

"What?" he asks.

" 'Cause I'll just fuck up again, Mark. Another Drake, another Benjamin, another shithead you hate so much that you end up hating me for choosing love——"

"Love? I love you so much, Sonia. I cannot bear to see you hurt yourself," he says. "And now, you have a baby to think about. It's not just you anymore."

"I miss you when you leave me alone. Mark, it's pain——"

"Fuck you, Sonia," he says. "You think I don't hurt? You choose losers over me. Our friendship is always the first to go."

"Forgive," Bob says, looking at me. He pours deep glasses of wine and passes the basket of garlic bread to me. He lights a candle Mark picked up at the market. "And forget," he says, looking at Mark.

"But it feels too much like family," I whisper.

♦

The first time Granny Alma sent me home to Hilo, Grace wanted to be a happy family. Joseph home. Me home. It lasted a week.

I watched from her bedroom door as she put on her makeup for work. She moved to the bed and sat cross-legged with a pillow wedged in her lap space. She patted the pillow for me to lay my head down.

Grace pulled my earlobe and scraped clean the pieces of dried wax from my ear like she did when Celeste and I were little girls. She laid each piece of parchment on a blue Kleenex. Sometimes she went too deep into the hollow of my ear and I tingled with sharp pain. Grace placed her hand on the side of my head to calm me, then continued the cleaning so close to my hearing. She smoothed my hair back with the palm of her open hand and I closed my eyes to take in the slow stroking.

"Granny Alma never cleaned our ears," I told her that day. "Do you think one day Celeste could come home so she can get her ears cleaned too?"

"Maybe." She paused. "I don't know. I don't know anything. I try to feel—but I feel nothing," she murmured. "Get going," she said, giving me a small push. "You're too damn big for this."

"You miss us, Mama?" The words clawed at my throat.

She didn't answer me. "When your father comes home from who-the-fuck-knows-where-he-went," she said, "why don't you ask him about missing you." She jerked her head and her thumb toward the door. "Go away from me."

My mother sat in front of her vanity, stared at her reflection from all angles for a long time, then put her face in both hands, her body shaking within her breaths. Grace painstakingly smeared layers of makeup on her wet face and when she left through the back door, ready to serve another round of drinks at the 19th Hole, no one could tell that she had been crying in the amnesia of the morning's sunlight.

♦

Another morning in Las Vegas. I need to write another paper. But there's too much need. Need shit wiped off his ass, need another bottle, need to watch the electrical outlets, get away from the TV, the curtain cord, bits of broken plastic on the floor, don't put the remote in your mouth. Need. Need. Need.

I need to paint. Been up all night with Sonny Boy's fever, 104 degrees and climbing. Put him in cold water? Lukewarm? He won't sit, he stiffens and screams. Get in the tub with him. Pour water on him. Tempra? No Tempra. Run to the 7-Eleven with Sonny Boy screaming in his car seat. Six dollars for this small bottle? I miss class for two days. Bob says to leave him, they'll be okay. But we're at the student health center, waiting, waiting, waiting our turn for amoxicillin. It tastes like bubble gum, dammit, swallow the shit, swallow it, you fucking stupid kid. Another fucking ear infection.

I can't do this. He's screaming, awake at three in the morning. I want my Life back. Nap when I want. Study when I want. Paint when I want. Shop when I want. Read when I want. Piss and shit when I want. Bathe when I want.

I can give Sonny Boy to Granny. No, then I'll be Grace, Part II. They're all expecting the sequel. I should give him to Grace. Poetic justice.

I'll kill him. No, I'll kill me. No, I'll kill both of us and put us out of our misery. Start all over in another Life. At four in the morning, my eyes cannot focus but on his open mouth, which has cried itself to a heaving silent wail.

I hate you. I hate me.

What kind of mother even thinks these thoughts?

Mark tells me to pray for strength. Pray like I have never prayed before. Know that this is God's Will for me. This pre-ordained Life I brought into the world. God has a reason for all things. Pray with the faith we had when we were kids. Innocent belief, bliss-ignorant children who loved God, who had nothing to lose. And forgive ourselves. We were just two college freshmen, kids really, who killed an unborn embryo, my third dead baby, right here on the floor of this apartment.

♦

When I was little, I prayed my mother wouldn't go crazy. I prayed for a normal life, a normal mother. By fourteen, I knew she was a fucking crazy, bat-out-of-hell lunatic. I remember the first time Joseph left. It was the beginning of her madness. I was four.

Grace worked at the 19th Hole bar at the Hilo Municipal Golf Course, while Celeste and I waited for her at Aunty Effie's. Everybody knew Gracie. Pretty Gracie, easy with the men golfers, buying them rounds, and married to that good-for-shit Joseph Kurisu.

And the women golfers, they gossiped about my mother, who garnered the attention of the men golfers:

"Her husband's a former science teacher, you know."

"Yeah, biology degree from MIT. How's that? Joseph's a classmate of my brother-in-law, Freddie Shimabukuro."

"What does he do when he comes home?"

"Wise off like Mr. Big Shot but he only works for Jack's Tours."

"Really?"

"What a waste of a degree."

"And how come Grace doesn't divorce him?"

"She's weak."

"And likes to flirt with all the sugar daddies, but she always has a way out. She's *married*, get it? 'Don't fuss around like that!' And then she slaps the hand touching her ass. 'See, I have a ring. I'm a married woman!' "

"My ass."

"Mine too."

"Another round, ladies?"

Her feet hurt after work. And we were hungry and little. She'd put Celeste and me in the bathtub and fill a large wooden salad bowl with rice, meat, and a canned vegetable.

Scoop, shove. Scoop, shove. Then take a bite for herself. Until the bowl emptied, she sat there on a small wooden stool, feeding us and crying.

I never toilet-trained until I was four, and I never wiped my own ass until I was seven. Aunty Effie kept telling Grace about the importance of consistency at the sitter's and in the child's home environment.

After we were fed, we were bathed. Grace attached a hose she ordered from the Lillian Vernon catalog to the pipe in the tub. She dribbled Prell on our heads. "Scrub," she said. And we did. Then she hosed down our heads. "Bathe and wash your own chingching good. Turn and scrub each other's backs."

And then she turned the hose on us.

She even washed the bowl and spoon with the hose and bathwater.

And every evening, we'd get on our hands and knees on one end of the living room and Grace yelled, "Go!" We crawled across the floor picking up strands of our hair, hardened grains of rice, dirt balls, tiny papers, and roach shit, then lay our individual booty across a bright green throw pillow. We did this four times across the floor each night.

"Celeste's the winner," she'd say. And the winner slept with Grace for the night.

It was pure obsession, from one to the next. They kept Grace running, finding control where there was none.

By fourteen, I convinced myself that she was out to drive me fucking nuts. I wrote to Mark in Honolulu every day of my stay that summer in Hilo:

Dear Mark,

I hate Hilo. I have no friends here which I guess was Granny's whole idea to get me away from Kalihi.

Grace said I cannot go to Baptist Camp Pupukea on Oahu. Not because it was Granny's punishment. But because we have no money. Joseph isn't working.

Your Aunty Frannie and Grandma Effie are sending your cousin Jacob to represent the Hilo Baptist youth group even if I have been the slave of the church because of my community service hours. Damn Jacob lied and said when he grows up he wants to go to seminary school.

Celeste squealed to Grace that you were my boyfriend. I said he is my *boy*, as in male, as in guy. And *friend*, as in boy, who is a friend. And if you must know, Mark is my best friend who I met in First Kalihi Baptist, by the way. But Grace doesn't think that a boy (you) and a girl (me) can do everything together, even if you do go to Punahou and me to Farrington, including chew each other's gum and do Geometry homework at the hellhole of a hot-ass after-school church tutoring class and still be only friends.

Your cousin Jacob is almost six feet tall and thinks he is the stud of Hilo High. I think he had sex with the assistant pastor's daughter but the other girls in the youth group aren't talking.

So the news is that maybe our Sunday School Board will vote for one Youth (who is not saved) to go to Camp Pupukea. Nancy Nakamura got saved. Plus her father owns an anthurium farm (rich). Claire and Shari Shimizu (not saved) don't want to go to camp. Plus their mother is an elem. teacher and they're related to Cafe 100. And Gregg and Bradley Tong Jr. are already going because Jacob is going and they want to score the Honolulu chicks even if they're all Baptist and look like us girls in this youth group (dorks). I know because I used to live in Honolulu. But think they listen to me?

I pray every night that it is me, Mark. I am not saved and we have no money, so who else could it be? Because I miss you and okay I miss Granny Alma. At least her house was normal and I had friends. Nobody yelling all the time and broken glass on the floor. (Long story about the glass, will tell you later.)

When you see Granny Alma at church, do you think you can ask if she has ten dollars somewhere from tips or gambling at the bowling alley? (Gambling is a sin, you know. I heard it on the 700 Club.) Tell her I changed my ways and no longer am a bitch.

You see, Mark, I know I will go because I pray. Prayer does work miracles, you know. Plus, your Aunty Frannie is on the Sunday School Board and Aunty Effie is church secretary and they're thinking of selling Mountain View rock cookies as a fundraiser.

I guess the part that is hippocrite is that I don't really want to go to camp to be saved, but want to see you, Granny Alma, and okay Celeste who's been my main mother all along anyway. Plus I have to see Jingle, Afi, and Lauta.

In other news, I have been praying for you to grow taller as you asked in your last letter to me. So you pray that the Sunday School Board picks me and I pray that God makes you tall, dark, and handsome like your cousin Jacob, but keep your own personality and not be a punk like him.

Pray for me. I'll see you soon at camp.

Your friend,
Sonia Kurisu

I lifted my thighs, sticky with summer sweat, off of the hot vinyl seats of the shrunken yellow school bus. I stepped into a swirling red dust cloud of other buses and beat-up church vans outside of the mess hall of Camp Pūpūkea.

Group leaders shuffled off in all directions carrying boxes and knapsacks. "The Big Island kids are here," someone with a safari hat and clipboard yelled.

Cliques of long-legged blond haole girls with Daisy Duke

cutoffs and bikini tops headed toward the beach; haole summer missionaries kicked off their leather sandals and dark
socks; and townie Japanese girls with heavy eyeliner sat outside
one of the cabins with townie Japanese stud-types in expensive
Quiksilver surf shorts.

I followed Jacob, who had taken a slight shine to me. I was
the closest thing to a townie "Honolulu" girl that he could
score that summer even if he was seventeen and I was fourteen. We edged our way along the confusion of guitar cases and
overnight bags, boxes of hymnals, and Love's hot dog buns. I
looked for Mark and Celeste over the dust and din.

Then I saw her. Celeste standing on the stairs of the chapel
in front of the beautifully carved doors. She was somehow
transformed in the sunlight of this morning. Straight golden-
auburn hair and pink frosted lipstick matched her fingers and
toes. She looked directly at me. I wanted to die right there in
front of that chapel in full view of all of Celeste's Punahou
Christian cheerleader long-limbed friends.

Jacob, Brad, and Gregg stepped up toward the landing.
"Who's the townie chick?" Gregg asked. "The one with the
lips. Over there. Pink lips."

Jacob looked at me. "She's——" he started, smiling at me.
"Isn't she your big sister, Sonia?" he asked, nudging my arm a
little too hard and chumlike. "Remember the picture you
showed me?"

"Yeah," I responded softly.

Jacob eyed me up and down and then Celeste. In his white
tank top, his skin looked bronze, his arms and shoulders chis-
eled. Jacob put his hand on my shoulder for a brief moment.

"Yeah, right. Sisters?" Brad said. "How come Sonia's so——"

"Ugly," Gregg finished.

"Hey, man, don't talk to her like——" Jacob started.

"Fuck you, Gregg, you Ching Chong Chinaman sitting on a

fence," I piped up loudly, not knowing why I said it the moment I said it.

"Shut up," Brad snarled at me. "Everybody's looking at us."

"You shut up," I yelled back, shoving him hard in the chest.

People began gathering around the chapel. Jacob pulled my arm.

"Well?" Gregg said in my face, Jacob getting between us. "Go say something to your sister, right now. Jacob wants to meet her, right, Jacob?" he said, giving him the eye and the eyebrows. I looked at Jacob and he at me. "Well? Jake?" Gregg challenged.

I was an ugly summer secret. Maybe I made it all up. Maybe he never took a shine to me. "Yeah," he said, giving me a slight push in the back. "We want to meet your sister."

I wouldn't. But not because of Jacob's sudden disinterest in me. Celeste was playing one of her passive-aggressive mind games. In that moment that our eyes met, I saw her face melt, then harden, within the frame of a second's time.

Brad stood with Jacob. They kept pushing me from behind. "C'mon," Brad whispered in my ear, "be useful or we sold all those damn rock cookies for nothing to pay your airfare to this stupid camp."

I stepped forward. Celeste stood under the rain gutter under the rooftop under the cross in some symmetrical beam of sunlight, the mouth of God's house open and dark behind her.

"Sonia?"

I turned around.

"Mark?"

My bag fell to my feet. He put his arms around me. I closed my eyes to the spin of that moment. "You prayed," were my first words to him.

"Of course. You asked, right, pal of mine? And you prayed too?"

"Yeah," I told him, burying my face in his shoulder. "I prayed hard."

"Then how come I'm still short?" He laughed as he wiped the tears from my face.

Toward the passion of this moment, Celeste descended the stairs.

"Oh, sis. Oh, Sonia," she cried as the cheerleaders gathered around us. Celeste eyed Jacob, then placed her cheek in the curve of my neck, sobbing, but without tears. I pushed her off me and turned to Jacob.

"Jacob Gomes," I said, "Celeste Kurisu. My *sister*," I yelled for everyone to know.

Mark picked up my backpack. I followed him. I turned to see Celeste, her sandals flung over her shoulder, barefooted, as she led Gregg and Brad toward some distant singing on the beach. Jacob lingered behind.

"Go," I told him. "Don't worry, I know all about leaving. There are things I've always known."

"Oh, knock off the deep shit, Sonia," he said, turning to follow Celeste.

But I didn't know:

Grace had asked the Baptists to purchase a one-way ticket for me. I would not be going home to Hilo. I would leave Camp Pūpūkea for First Kalihi Baptist, Granny Alma waiting for me with Uncle Fu Manchu in the parking lot.

Celeste and Jacob embraced in a dramatic summer camper's goodbye. Mark stood in the open door to the shrunken yellow school bus, holding out his hand to me.

At First Kalihi Baptist, Granny Alma lifted my bag without a word. I followed her to the old Cutlass, Uncle Fu Manchu waiting for us, engine idling in the heat of this summer's end.

6

Run

SONNY BOY SLEEPS ON THE BIG BED, Mark beside him, a long night preparing for grad school midterms. I am alone this morning but for Regis and Kathie Lee, a Baldwin brother, and a cup of coffee. Thinking about, "Maybe I don't need chaos after all. I can handle this life. God has answered my prayers for help. This boy I kept was for a reason." And now, I should go next door and ask Bob to join me, brew a carafe full of Yuban.

"Who is my father?" The voice of #2 asks. He sounds like the sea, the sea that sounds like waves and wind; but I understand him. His voice is a turtle's rise to the surface of ocean blue. A voice that shines with each intonation. I see his form in the reflection on the jalousies.

"Who is my father?" A voice behind him asks, muffled at first. It murmurs from what seems faraway but near. I stand, my knees shaking. I see light emanating from a box, unopened but aura throbbing from the inside out.

They stand there, outside my door, pulsing, moving, looking in, #2 and then out of the box, a man.

I will not lose my fucking mind.

I will enjoy the calm of these days.

No chaos.

No Drake, no girl/boy.

No maelstrom.

I will turn away from the edge.

But I ask instead, ready to leap, "Where the fuck is mine?"

The turtle boy, #2, spins the air of sea, dolphin whistling. The man laughs, a guttural bowel laugh from inside a closed space.

And then, I scream, pick up my bag, and prepare to run. Mark bounds down the hallway. Bob pounds his fist on my door. I pull it open, his arms outspread, stopping me. "Bob, you hear them?"

"Yes, I heard them," he starts. "I mean, no. I heard you screaming."

"Sonia," Mark calls, "what's going on?"

"Run," I tell them.

Bob sighs, puts his arms around me. Mark moves his hand through his tangled sleep hair. I sit down.

Because, just then, the Voices leave.

Sweet Sonia,

    The streets are narrow here where a man walks, and the lakeside gulf sounds like Hilo Bay. He watches the silent pull of a paddle through a taut stretch of water. It is so still this morning. The severance of water and sky seems an astonishing absence.

    This seashore town is full of old windows and dark doors, dusty little shops along alleyways paved in the ocean's stones. Today, the man finds himself in southern Japan, Kyushu.

    He bypasses several doors to take in the smell. A smell like tiny swarms of kiawe leaves on the surface of a muddy bay of a fishing town.

    He walks the line of shops that front the gulf. He sees shop after shop full of bracelets, earrings, necklaces, combs, and yellow glass eyes looking back at him, varnished amber tears that dead turtles cry. Shops full of turtle shells, and no one, but shells hanging from the ceilings. They're all for sale.

He remembers a Hawaiian man from Punaluʻu who caught a green sea turtle in the rough waters off of South Point. This fisherman gave the man some of the turtle's meat to taste. The fisherman went to a federal prison for that and paid a big fine.

So many turtles here.

The fisherman from Punaluʻu just wanted a taste.

And what about the man who saw shop after shop of turtle shells, all dead and gone but for carcasses filling dusty shop windows along a lakeside gulf? He's walking away. He's walking faster and faster down the narrow streets of a town, Kyushu, southern Japan. And he doesn't look back.

Sweet child, I will come to see your baby soon, then stop in Honolulu to see Celeste's children. Send my love to Grace and Granny Alma.

I love you,
Joseph

His letter is a Sign.

Who did I kill?

Turtle Boy, #2, why have you returned to this shore?

Didn't they tell you on the other side?

Little boy turtles who hatch from their shells never come back.

Only the girls.

"You know why he's telling you about the turtles, right, Sonia?" Celeste asks. "My God, you're really dense."

"Who? Joseph?"

"Who else? Hello? Wake up. You just read his letter to me. You still taking drugs with that god-awful boyfriend of yours?" Celeste asks, always an accusing mommy. "What are you on?"

"No. Nothing. The sea turtles. What were you saying?" I ask her.

"Oh, jeez. Listen, before Mama sent you and me to live with Granny, Joseph was home, right? He took us to Punaluʻu to see that Hawaiian guy he was talking about in his letter, Uncle Punaluʻu Melvin."

I don't want to hear her. Things don't Connect. Not since Drake left. He who I need/don't need/need/don't need. Pretending all the time for Mark and Bob, Sonny Boy and me: I don't need, but I want that motherfucker.

Things don't Connect. The Voices are back. Don't tell Celeste. I might be in for more deprogramming. Or some antipsychotic drug regimen. Or her latest cure-all. Therapy. Heavy-duty Psychoanalysis.

"I'm kind of running late, Celeste. For my Tiger Lily gig," I tell her as I powder on some dark blush. A sip of scotch with a back of two Canadian Tylenols.

Her voice becomes insistent. "Stop it, Sonia. The turtles. Uncle Melvin knew the hatch date. That's the turtle we ate, the mother of those babies that hatched in the sand. He caught her right after she deposited all those eggs in the sand."

I stop. Put my makeup on the table. Finish my drink in one long burn down my throat. "And that day Joseph took us to South Point, one by one, the turtle babies moved their tiny heads out of the shifting black sand——"

"And Joseph told us about survival and instinct. 'Pick one up,' he says to me, 'do it now and point it toward the mountain. He'll turn himself around and run to the sea. It's instinct, baby,' he says to me——"

" 'You just listen to your good old dad,' " I finish. " 'You got to know where you got to go. And you got to run there. Otherwise, you die.' "

"Joseph's survival, Sonia. He left us a couple of weeks later. All those little babies coming out of the sand."

"No mother in sight." I feel numb, good Canadian codeine, smooth scotch. "And a father's instinct telling him to run to the water."

Seek, Joseph, and/you/shall.

"He's still searching," I tell her.

"He's found nothing. The bastard's still running." Celeste begins to cry. She needs to knock off that shit.

"Call your therapist," I tell her. She hangs up the phone.

Dear #2,

Your father, you ask? It's not your turn to know. We shall proceed in a dignified manner. I will not run. And I will no longer lose my mind when I hear your voice. The passage begins with Number One.

Your mother,
Sonia Kurisu

♦

I was sixteen. Back in Hilo for another summer. And before that, Thanksgiving in Hilo, no money for turkey. Christmas, no time, no money to get a tree. Easter, whatever, too big for coloring eggs. Memorial Day, remember me, Grace? I was getting used to all the shuffling.

The Back and Forth.

Back to Granny Alma's: good girl for a month. Here comes Jingle's joint. My mouth couldn't resist. Hello, Afi? Mayor Wright's Housing? The dealer takes food stamps for ice? Lauta? Okay, black Russians. My granny's always working late. Come over.

Forth to Grace's: she's nice for a week. Mr. Tabata calls. He's married. Be nice to the sugar daddy. We'll be playing poker at Aunty Frannie's. I thought she was Baptist? Stop fucking judging me, you hear me? Want to go back to Granny's? She doesn't even want you anymore. Or maybe you want to live with your *father*? Find him first.

Back: Mark and I make plans. When he graduates from Punahou and me from Farrington, we want to go to a mainland college, together. We'll get summer jobs to pay our tuition. We'll Make It. We'll Show Them.

"But I'll be stuck in Hilo for the summer," I remind him.

"Then I'll stay with my aunty Frannie in Jacob's old bedroom," he says, "or at my grandma's."

"You would consider staying with your grandma Effie to be with *me* in Hilo?"

"Nah," he says, "I'll probably stay with Aunty Frannie."

Forth: Grace is nice. Joseph's home. She still plays poker on Friday and Saturday nights. Mr. Tabata never calls the house if Joseph's home. Good. No need to be nice to horny old Mr. Tabata. Even if he hangs out all day at the 19th Hole. Having her cake. Eating his. Why the fuck not?

Back to Granny Alma's: Jingle gets pregnant and keeps the baby. Mother, Father, and Baby Junkies. Afi's sent back to Samoa. Her grandfather's a very high-ranking chief. They cut off all of her hair. Lauta's boyfriend is thirty-one. Drives a Blazer. Works at the shipyard. Little wifey.

Forth again: We'll get summer jobs to pay for the tuition. We can Make It. We'll Show Them. Let's give it a Run for the Money.

Mark and I worked in Hilo as part-time dishwashers at Uncle Billy's Hukilau Hotel on a lunch-and-dinner shift. Then we worked at Fat's Union 76 at night, the two of us smashed into the small glass booth in the middle of the pumps.

Fat had been robbed a couple of times in the last few months and thought it wise to put both of us on the midnight-to-six shift. Like shrimpy Mark was some kung fu expert. And I could do a citizen's arrest with my finger gun.

At Fat's, I met Benjamin Hart. He was eighteen. His Korean mother punished him as a child by burning cigarette holes into his arms. One for every bad word. One for every bad thought.

I licked his holes clean. Even the ones on his dick. And every time we fought, he burned another hole into himself.

Benjamin was lean and angular, the two of us lying under his jacked-up Celica changing the clutch, me passing tools and wiping sweat from his brow with a red bandanna.

I deposited his paychecks from Fat's Union 76, made him a half-dozen egg-salad sandwiches wrapped in waxed paper every day, and drove him to and from work in the Celica.

"Damn kid playing maman-goto," Grace grumbled. "Don't be a wife until you have to," Grace said, glaring at Joseph. He had been home a few days after spending months in Bangkok.

"I thought Frieda's son Mark was your boyfriend?" Joseph asked. "Isn't that why he followed you to Hilo?" I didn't answer him. "Well?" I kept silent. "This is all so depressing," he said, walking toward the kitchen with his cup of coffee.

"Then why in the hell do you keep coming home?" Grace asked. She was in one of her Mr. Tabata withdrawals, irritated and curt. "I don't need you. And you don't need us."

"Us?" Joseph laughed. "And when was this ever a question of need?" Joseph rinsed his mug. "Need. Want—"

"I refuse to participate in your roundabout, full-of-shit rationalizations, fucking intellectual garbage."

"Shut up, stupid," he said to Grace. "Idiots," he said looking at me. "Next time, answer my fucking question, kid."

He shut Grace up. Me too. Joseph knew how to do that.

I felt sick. And I knew why.

Number One, you were three and a half months old, bubbling inside of me every Wednesday Bible Study, churning in Saturday choir, boiling on Sunday in the hot church, curdling as I washed dishes at Uncle Billy's, festering as I sat until morning in a glass booth.

I told no one. Not even Mark.

I could keep you. Benjamin had a good job. Fat was going to promote him to weekend shift leader.

I could keep you. I would make a good mommy. Benjamin would make a good daddy. We would be a happy family. We would be a normal family. And I would never be Alone.

Pastor Hingman said something in a Sunday sermon about the sin of sex before marriage. Abstinence. Celibacy. Unequal yokes. Abortion is Murder. Children of God. Ten Commandments. Thou shalt not kill. He was on my side, sort of, because I thought I would keep you.

I felt sick. And Grace instinctively knew why. She kept her composure. It was almost as though she had been expecting one of her daughters to come home with *the present.*

"Boys are lucky," she would always say. "They don't get stuck with the package." Once in a while, she called you, my Number One, the box, the bag, or simply *it.* "Boys are lucky. They've got legs to run."

She waited for Benjamin and me to come through the back door. And when we did, she sat us down at the dining room table.

"Abort it, keep it, or adopt it away," she said. "Get out of here. Go for a ride. Come back when you make up your mind."

I stared out the window.

Benjamin stared at a fresh burn hole in his hand.

Joseph stood at the kitchen sink. He tapped his boiled eggs one against the other. He peeled the shells off the shine of white egg and pushed it all down the In-Sink-Erator. He turned on the loud snarl of the disposal. I watched as he sliced each egg lengthwise and poured singular drops of shoyu on the severed yolks, the brown spreading out veinlike into fingers of murky ecru albumen.

"Get out of here," Grace yelled. "Make up your fucking stupid minds. I'll be waiting."

I turned my horrified eyes to Joseph.

Help me.

At first, he wouldn't look at me.

And when he did:

Whore. Stupid. Idiot. Baby. Bitch. Trap.

He stirred a spoonful of Pream into his coffee, the swirl trailing down the cup in an ever-lightening whirlpool.

"It's what blood will do," I told him as he turned to face me.

"Shut your smart-ass mouth, Sonia," he muttered. "This is so classic, don't you think, Grace? One of them with you in their blood."

"Then run away from this like you always do," Grace replied. "Your true freedom is all that matters. Fuck the rest of us, right? She's *just like you*, Joseph, your spitting image. Look at her, asshole."

My father gazed at me for an expressionless second. "I can't stand the sight of you," he said to me.

And then the words escaped. "I know," I said.

Benjamin and I would decide to keep you.

We could Make It.

We would Show Them.

Wrong.

Joseph would leave for Japan in a few days.

And Grace would send me Back.

Celeste would find me on my bed in a fetal curl.

"Granny Alma! Call Dr. Wee!"

I'll tell you, Number One, the secret of their Christianity: Silence.

And you and I the biggest secret of all. Because within days, like the briefest of whispers, you were gone, surgically sucked from my womb in a cold hospital. I watched you running, a child then a man, running naked toward the aurora of pink light coming from a corner in that hospital room; me, Alone, strapped like an anesthetized animal, staring at your cartilaged pieces on a cold surgical tray.

7

The Summoning

THEY ALL CONVERGE in the City of the Plain for the Reverend Cyrus Hill's Las Vegas Power of Love Crusade, flashing, steady red dots on my answering machine.

It's Celeste:
"I'm at the Hilton Grand. Call me right away. I mean it, Sonia. I want to take you and Mark to a fantastic seafood buffet here in the hotel. I hear the clam chowder's to die for. And I bought something for the baby. How is he?"

Celeste thinks her gift of an infant's hygienic sheepskin sent FedEx is the secret to Sonny Boy's *fabulous* sleep pattern. Help me, Celeste, the sheepskin's not enough. I'm dying. I'm scared. This baby. I've choked him too many times to count. Maybe I killed some developing brain cells. I slap his face all the time. I think he's a drug baby. Can't remember. Fetal alcohol syndrome. Can't remember. He fades in/out. Is it all in my mind? Only a mother would know: something's wrong with him.

It's Granny:
"Hello? Sonia? I'm at the Fremont Hotel. Can you call me? I hate talking into these machines. Hello? Sonia?"

Sonny Boy, you will love your great-granny as much as I did. She will take care of you as she did me. She will let me rest. She will watch you. I'm always Alone. Bob's found a job. Mark's at school all the time. The baby's not talking. Silent boy, maybe she will take you home with her.

It's Granny, again:

"Hello? Sonia? Do I have the right number? Is this the number for Sonia Kurisu? How come there's a man on your machine? This is Granny. I'm at the Fremont Hotel. Oh, for heaven's sake, I hate talking into these machines."

She will take care of you as she did me. Granny, I can't do it. Mark and me alternating class schedules and work schedules. His turn. My turn. Why did I have this baby? He's interfering with my fucking life. I hate him. You hear me? Giving a shit about somebody else all the time. Help me paint a sky, Granny.

"Sonia, this is Aunty Effie. You and Mark meet us at the California. Aunty Frieda, Aunty Frannie, and I have a care package for you. And bring the baby. He must be getting big. I hope the two of you found a church. We'll talk."

More Top Ramen and chocolate-covered macadamia nuts. I'll take the package and pass on the sermon about single motherhood and sin. It's guilt, that's what it is. Nothing's wrong with Sonny Boy. I hate him, that's all. Everything's wrong with me. I hate me, that's all. He's just fine. I'm not. Blue boy. Vacant stare. Just fine.

"Sonia, this is Aunty Frieda. Is Mark there? Tell him that after Reverend Hill's morning service, we'll be at the California Hotel. Meet us for lunch. And tell him not to be late."

They tithe 10 percent of their wins, Aunties Frieda, Fran-

nie, and Effie. Still sin. Love the sinner. Hate. Loathe. And Despise sin. And Whores. I can hear it in their voices, the mighty
Greek chorus that they are: Why does little Markie continue to
be there for *her*? A child needs a mother and father but she's
not the one for him. He's a martyr. She's a murderess.

Three fucking times, Aunties.

It's Grace:

"Sonia? Call me at the Fremont."

Grace, you cursed me. I want to blame you for every pre-
dicament gone bad in my stupid life. But then I would be a
Celeste-analysis cliché. Maybe you should take him. My son
doesn't need a mother or a father. Look at me. Made it through
this shitty life without the both of you.

"Hey, Markie. It's me, Jacob. Got here courtesy of my
mother. She thinks I'm going to the Cyrus Hill-billy crusade.
Right. Call me at the Golden Nugget."

His voice. It makes me think of Drake. I miss Drake. But I
can't tell Mark. Or Bob. Weak, weak girl. That's what they'll
think. Sick, sick girl. Missing that sicko psycho sociopath.
Needy, needy girl. Whine, whine, whine.

Jacob. I've missed you too, all these years.

Shit, somebody save me from this convergence. This celestial malfunctioning of our lives. The motion of stars and plan-
ets. A comet's path across the sky, foreboding. Mercury in
retrograde. The arrival of a full moon. Cosmic high tide over
this filthy desert town can only mean:

"Sonia, this is your father. I'm on my way home through
the States. I need a place to stay. Don't worry. I'll find my way
to your apartment."

This is your Father.

Where have you been, Daddy?

Father/God.

Where art thou?

Father.

Pass over us.

Father.

Who is my Father?

Where is mine?

All summoned at last to the City of the Plain.

♦

There are things I have always known. The power of summoning. Calling with the mind. Wanting, an ache, that pulled all my desires toward me by thought, obsessive thought.

When I was six, I summoned a fairy to my room to get the tooth I willed loose in a bowl of soup. It was the first I wiggled with the tip of my tongue until I felt the warm ooze of blood from the crater of gum.

Joseph was home. He would help me. He had not been home for any of Celeste's teeth. And the tooth fairy left her a quarter each time in Baggies tied with green twist-ums under her pillow.

Joseph always made dinner on Fridays, Swanson TV dinners. For himself and Grace, he baked Hungry-Man Turkey. For Celeste and me, Salisbury steak, fried chicken, or enchiladas.

I remember running out of the bathroom naked, my hair wet and dripping, to find the seat with the fried chicken. Joseph put a towel on my head then helped me put on my panties and nightgown. He led me to the seat with a hot bowl of Campbell's Chunky Clam Chowder.

"How come Sonia gets clam chowder?" Celeste whined.

"Stop complaining and sit down," he told her. "You got the damn fried chicken." My father started combing out the tangles in my hair, not the way Grace did, pulling and yanking until my scalp felt tender for the rest of the night, but working out each snag.

"Sonia has soup," he said, "because her tooth hurts. She's in pain."

"Yeah, right." Celeste glared at her oily fried chicken, the only section of the tin tray not covered with foil. "Not true," she said. "I ate carrot sticks. That's how my tooth came out, right, Mama? Tell him. Why's he the boss of us?"

"Because I'm the goddamn father, get it, you sassy little bitch," Joseph replied, "and what I say goes."

"Oh, knock it off, please," Grace said, exasperated. She removed the foil from her dinner, a rush of steam lifting out. "You're all hungry, right?" she said. "Then eat. Now."

"You want a bite, Celeste?" I asked.

"No. How come I didn't have soup when my teeth came out?" Celeste asked my mother again, this time with tears.

"Because that's life," my mother said at last. "And life is a game of want."

I moved the spoon full of dripping chowder to her waiting mouth. Celeste hit the spoon from my hand, sending the thick white gruel across the table.

"Sonia will make the soup for you, Celeste," Grace said. "Right, Joseph? Sonia's going to do it for you, right?"

He said nothing at first.

"Why me?" I pushed on the tooth.

"Fuck off. All of you," he said at last. "It's just a damn bowl of soup."

I wanted pain. I pushed on my tooth. I didn't want to hear any more.

"Well, Joseph? Answer your daughter. Why her?"

He poked at the melted bits of stuffing on his aluminum tray. "I already answered her."

"That's what I thought," she said. "It's you, Sonia. You take care of your father's shit. Eat it," she said. "All of you."

My bloody tooth plopped into the white space of chowder.

I put my tooth under my pillow that night. I turned my body to the wall and cried softly.

"Why are *you* crying?" Celeste whispered. Joseph and Grace screamed on in the living room.

"I'm scared," I told her.

"Of what?" she asked.

And not wanting to appear vulnerable to the weaknesses in my mother and father, I was strong, so strong, I could take my father's place in his absence, I told my sister a lie.

"I'm afraid of the tooth fairy."

Celeste called Grace, but Joseph appeared in the doorway.

"Here, sweet Sonia," he said, handing me a flashlight. "Sleep with Daddy's light and shine it on the fairy if you get scared. She might drop her bag of teeth, but who knows, she might drop her bag of money too."

In the morning, I found a dollar in a Love's bread bag under my pillow. Joseph was in the kitchen frying Portuguese sausage for breakfast, slices of white bread strewn on the countertop. Grace slept fitfully on the couch, a stretch of morning sun consuming her body inch by inch.

"How much money did the tooth fairy leave you?" he asked.

"One dollar," I said.

"You still scared?" he asked.

"No."

"No?" He turned the sausages with chopsticks. "Good. Can't have my surrogate scared of her own fucking shadow."

"Huh, Daddy?"

"Nothing," he said. "How come you're not scared any-more?"

"I felt her wings on my face, Daddy, when she was trying to take the tooth out from under my pillow. She touched my face with her soft wings."

"And then?"

"By the time I opened my eyes, shined the light, and looked all around, all around I looked and looked, Daddy, she was gone."

♦

"Sonia, wake up," Mark says, coming into the living room. He had spent the night in the library. "Your father's at the door."

"But he's gone," I mumble. "I'm scared of the tooth fairy, Daddy. Where?"

"Scared of what tooth fairy? Get up and answer the door. I'll make some coffee." Mark carries Sonny Boy into the kitchen. He sits him on the cold floor. Spinning pot covers. Spinning and flapping his arms.

I open the door. "Hey, there," my father says, "long time no see."

"Long time, Daddy."

Celeste has no time while in Las Vegas for the Power of Love Crusade, really, no time to see me or the baby. What with all the prayer meetings, revival workshops, devotionals, and music ministry discussion groups, it's lucky if Celeste can meet us for dinner. But she admits the clam chowder's to die for. So she squeezes us in for:

Appetizers.

Celeste blames him till today. I know she does. And she hates him with a passion, a fine Christian passion, the anger of

Jehovah of the Old Testament—the sin of this father, Grace's weakness, and the sister she would see dead for holding on to a pseudo/noble memory of Joseph.

Soup, and waiter, more bread, please.

Feed the baby solids. Mark, thank you for taking care of Sonia and Solomon. Stop calling him Sonny Boy, how gauche, how typically *local.* Where would Sonia be without your support?

Salad.

Don't you have anything better to wear? This is a four-star restaurant, you know. Mike gave me a Neiman Marcus credit card for my birthday. I'll get you some Anna Sui.

Entrée.

Joseph's where? No, I don't want to see him. In fact, I never want to read or hear another word Joseph says. And even though God makes no mistakes, the reason for all of them being here, especially Joseph, has nothing to do with me. I'm holy sure. And he can take that engraved tiger's tooth from Burma to hell and back for all I care.

Sister/sadist, inflict it with words.

Dessert.

Jacob's here? Really? I haven't seen him in years. Tell him I said hello. Mark, let's take him out to lunch. You too, Sonia. Leave the baby with Grace. Or better yet, leave him with Joseph.

Coffee or dessert wine?

No, please.

No.

No.

"Is the boy deaf, Sonia?" Joseph asks me in the apartment.

"What makes you think that, for chrissakes?"

"He doesn't respond to his name."

"Maybe because he doesn't know you, Daddy."

"Has Grace seen him?"

"No."

"Granny?"

"No."

"Something's wrong with him, Sonia."

"And who made you the expert on babies?"

"Nobody. But your boy—he isn't normal."

"So what do you suggest I do? What would you do, Daddy?"

"I don't know what I'd do."

"I know what you'd do."

A red light flashing.

"Sonia, it's Mom. Call me. I'm at the Fremont with Granny. Aunty Effie's driving me crazy. And Granny keeps muttering her prayers every time I drop a dollar in the slots, dammit. I want to see the baby."

A red light flashing.

"Markie, it's Mommy. When in God's name are you planning to call us? We're at the California, I repeat, California for the damn fourth time. Your grandmother and Aunty Frannie are beginning to take this personally. Sonia, honey, are you giving my messages to Markie?"

Mark's breaking his balls. A month away from graduation. An almost-finished thesis and then an M.Ed. in Counseling from UNLV. I am in my seventh year with no Bachelor's of Fine Arts in sight. Mark drinks too much coffee.

"Jacob wants to take us out for drinks," Mark tells me over dinner. "To celebrate my graduation."

"Me and you?"

"Yeah. He wants to see the exotic Tiger Lily Wong."

"Oh, jeez. And what about her sister, the sadistic Dragon Breath Kurisu-Infantino?"

"I didn't tell him she was here," Mark says.

"He knows," I tell him.

"He didn't say anything. But he saw that god-awful poster of you in the Golden Nugget's 14-Karat Bar. Said he likes your slutty look. Been in Alaska much too long. Five-to-one ratio, men to women."

"Prick."

"He said he'd really like to see you. And he has the care package from my mother. And Aunty Frannie. And my grandma." Mark sighs at the thought of the three F's: Frieda, Frannie, and Effie, the mad Greek chorus, mad at us for not returning their calls.

Jacob.

"Aunties too busy gambling and praying," I mutter.

"No. Sick and tired of talking to our machine."

My Painting III class fucking sucks. Every so-called artist in there slitting every other so-called artist's throat with vile remarks. One rotten morning class fucking ruins my whole day. And then I take it all out on Sonny Boy. I'm anxious, always anxious. One hand sketching, the other sticking a bottle in his mouth. Half my brain praying that he sleeps, so I can paint impressionistically about half my brain praying that he falls asleep. And when he doesn't sleep, I want to scream, "Take a nap, you little fucker, I've got art to create."

I knock on Bob's door. "Say 'Hi, Mommy,' " he says to Sonny Boy. He looks past me, silent. "Mommy's back from class. Say, 'Hi, Mommy.' He said it before," Bob reassures me. "We've been practicing, right, champ?" I take Sonny Boy from Bob. He cries for his surrogate father.

"Seen my father?" I ask, peering into my apartment.

"Not since coffee this morning. He came over with two big mugs from the 7-Eleven."

"Really?"

"Said something about the boy being deaf and how he's got strong teeth just like his mother. Went on and on about you being the most fearless girl he knows." Bob pauses, smiling and nodding. "Just like him. He said he had a couple of colored friends in college." Bob laughs and strokes Sonny Boy's face with the back of his hand.

"Thanks, Bob."

"God, I've got to get to sleep. This night shift's killing me," he says, arching his back. "Good tips, though."

Sonny Boy's body stiffens when I turn the key to the apartment door.

"Hey, Sonia . . ." Bob pauses. "These two ladies came looking for you. One looked like a Japanese Elizabeth Taylor."

"My mother."

"And the other one was old."

"Granny Alma. Oh, shit, I better call her right now."

"What's a kuro-chan?"

"They whispered it, right?"

"The old one did."

"It means black-boy-san. Sorry, Bob. Her old plantation mentality. Every time I tell my granny about you, she still refers to you as that negro. Kuro-chan? Haven't heard that one in a long time."

"Float like a butterfly, Sonia, just float like a butterfly."

Red light, Celeste:

"Aunty Frannie said you're meeting Jacob for drinks. Didn't I tell you I wanted to come? We'll talk old times. You'd better give me a call. I mean it, Sonia."

Sister/sadist. Talk? Evil words.

———

Red light, Grace:

"Where are you, Sonia? Granny and I took a cab to your place. Are you mad at us? We want to see the baby."

Burn, Grace, leave me Alone.

Red light.

"Sonia, this is your father. I'm at the airport. Sorry I didn't get to tell you goodbye in person. You take care of yourself and your boy. I hope you find out what's wrong with him soon."

Seek/seek/seek/and/you/shall/find.

You are the only one who knows, Daddy: something's wrong with him.

It's all my fault. I ignored him. I hurt him. I fed him bottled food. I didn't breast-feed long enough. I shouldn't have vaccinated him. I let his fevers get too high. Food allergy. Milk allergy. Brain dead. Unbonded boy. Frigid mother.

"Granny? This is Sonia."

"Sonia, I've been trying so hard to reach you."

"I'm coming to pick you up."

"Sonia, you all right?"

"No."

"Always no, you, Sonia. Why do I bother asking?"

"Where's Grace?"

"In the casino. Where else?"

"Good, leave her there."

"Don't talk like that about your mother."

"Help me, Granny."

"I pray for you every day."

It's night, but never night in this town. It's cool out here on the balcony, the lights, brilliant fluorescent all around me. Last cigarette, two Canadian Tylenols, and a tall glass of scotch for Tiger Lily Wong. Lots of *dignitaries* in the audience tonight. Celeste went and invited them all. As a favor to me.

There is a window across the alleyway. It is the first time I see this window. A bare bulb hangs. From ceiling to floor, I see bloodstained white feathers tied to long lengths of string. Gold origami cranes suspended with fishing line. A thousand and one pairs of wings floating on some night current. A thousand and one cranes for good luck.

An old man with liver spots on his bald head leans on the window ledge. Over and over he rubs his bumpy skull. Skinny man, thin white T-shirt. Yellow light. Bony arms, gnarled, bloody fingers. And then he looks up. At me. Camera/red/eyes like a photograph taken with a cheap camera that burns through my body.

He stands, still staring at me. Stabbing pain in my bones, my skull, my teeth. He touches the broken and bent golden paper wings on his back. He vomits into the alley. The smell of formaldehyde. Crows pick at the bits on the ground.

"Who is my Father?"

I turn to the voice. It's a new Voice. I see no one. I look toward the window, the old man leaning on his arms and rubbing his bumpy skull.

Behind him stands the turtle boy, #2, trying to straighten his broken wings. He's crying and crying, the flutter of gold flecks of paper in a room full of yellow light, the cling of gold paper to his wet face. Broken bottles all over the table and floor, glass breaking in the alley below, and then the smell of an old tidal pool at low tide.

Jar, my third dead baby.

You were not summoned. Why are you here? The old man tilts his head. Sad eyes, red. Have you always been here? Your room looks lived in, years. But you can't be here. I buried you in Hilo.

There's no mistaking you.

My Jar, living in the City of the Plain in a small one-room tenement full of golden cranes, bloody white feathers, and broken glass.

Born here in the Year of the Dragon on the floor of this apartment across the alleyway.

My mistake. I thought you water. I brought you home. I buried you deep in the ground on a volcanic island. You wanted sky. Just like me.

"*My father?*" the old man asks. "*Make me ash.*"

"What?"

Okay, snap out of it, Sonia. Another codeine and hard liquor fuck-up. Good job. Let your granny, Jacob, Celeste, and the F-Aunties see Tiger Lily sing all fucked up. And Grace.

Drake, call Drake. Get a joint, hash, some ice, or crack. Good excuse to talk to him. I heard Voices so I called you, Drake, baby. Come home to Mommy. I snapped. You know me. Yes, I'm begging for your forgiveness. Yes, I miss you. Yes, I love you.

I panic.

"*Listen,*" he rasps.

"*Listen,*" #2 repeats, "*the Little Priest is come.*"

Fucked up, Sonia, you are fucked up.

I bolt into the apartment and slam the door behind me. Lean against it.

Breathe.

Breathe.

I've got a gig in an hour. Me, Tiger Lily Wong. Breathe.

Two more codeine. Hands shaking, the bottle spills on the floor.

Sonny Boy stirs in the portable crib. No, you have to stay asleep, so Bob can sleep while he watches you. Papers rustle in a light wind. I close all of the windows. But when I turn, he sleeps, my baby, in a temple of golden paper cranes, white feathers brushing his cheek like fairy wings, this baby unafraid, this baby fearless. This baby my body made. This baby I let live.

8

Beautiful

Dear #2,

Why are you bringing the dead back to this shore? If I tell you what you want to know, will you make the Voices stop? Will you leave me the fuck Alone? Take them with you and go away. Don't make me hate you. It comes too easy for me. Just ask your dead brothers.

Love,
Mommy

Tiger Lily Wong wears Hong Kong sequins, the glam and slit of a red cheongsam, and red satin stilettos. She sings throaty and torchy, maudlin hits like Bette Midler's "The Rose." And means every word and every tear. But the Management of the 14-Karat Bar says that Tiger Lily can't drink in the bar and get her employee's discount unless she changes back into Sonia Kurisu in her faded Route 66's and white T-shirt from Savers.

Not that I want to meet Mark and Jacob looking like a fucking whore, but what the hell, *Jacob*. He always liked whores. And I hadn't seen him in a while.

And Celeste. She hates whores. The whore in me. The

whore in herself. Celeste who I hate more and more every time I see her. She makes it all so easy.

Stupid Mark calls her at the last minute. He says, "I promised her I'd call. Besides, she'd never even consider missing some Miracle of the Holy Spirit workshop to meet us at the Golden Nugget. It's downtown, it's a dive, and it's not even a one-star hotel."

But there she is, dressed to the nines in some churchy yet obviously Chanel suit. Coiffed and stuccoed, matted and high-maintenanced as can be, a trendy Kate Spade on her lap. Cute little Fendis on her tiny feet.

I had performed for them all two nights before, thanks to Celeste the sadist, who enjoyed every minute of my stumbling and mumbling over stupid, sappy songs, which according to Mark, I dedicated to each of them in turn. And then I sang "I Am Woman" and dedicated it to my best bud, Sonia Kurisu. Fuck. Too much codeine and scotch. Made a complete fucking idiot of myself, then ran backstage and took the bus home while they all waited for me in the bar. But Jacob never showed. Thank God.

Celeste's wearing some Yves Saint Laurent jasmine pure perfume. It kind of smells like night-blooming jasmine. But hers hangs thick like a toxic cloud. She's chirpy and light-hearted, drinking Perrier with a squeeze of lime with no pulp, if you please. She keeps one eye on the entrance. Small-talking about the fabulous workshops, seminars, and prayer sessions, her high-risk, high-yield investments, new BMW 740, and a yard in Makiki Heights full of night-blooming jasmine which she insists her Filipino garden boys keep in bloom *year round* with prayer and a proper fertilization regimen. Celeste, Mark, and me waiting for Jacob, now an hour late.

♦

The summer before Mark and I left for UNLV, Joseph planted the night-blooming jasmine outside of my bedroom window. And he planted ylang-ylang and honeysuckle that crept up the side of the house.

In my father's solitary yearning for beauty, I found him leaving pathways for me to follow, for me to find a way to inhabit worlds other than those of my own making. Worlds full of tiny, white jasmine, sweet ylang-ylang, and yellow honeysuckle that helped me to leave a small room, sometimes mine, in the Back and Forth of those days. Night after lonely night, their fragrances entered my worlds on a cool northerly wind. Worlds that returned every year when the flowers bloomed in season.

I could never explain this to Grace or Granny or Celeste, especially when I was a child. The way I would wake to Joseph watering the plants outside my window. The way I watched him hanging the honohono orchids he planted in coconut husks from the eaves above my room. Puakenikeni in a glass bowl on my bureau. These seasons of simple beauty. These seasons he shared with only me.

I could never truly hate him. I could never truly love him.

♦

Beautiful Jacob. He enters the 14-Karat Bar fucking flying high and drunk with some coke whore/white trash/skanky thin/permed hair/dark roots/blonde on his arm. Huge rose tattoo.

"Fuck the Ph.D.," he says, slumping down beside me, his hand on my leg and a kiss on the cheek, the blonde giggling and whispering in his ear. "Celeste, you look expensive," he says, reaching over the table to peck her face. "Hey, Markie," he says, giving his cousin a strong two-handed shake.

"What Ph.D.?" I ask him. He orders a Coors Light for himself and a wine spritzer with a twist of lemon for the blonde.

"Hey you, waitress, the peel only," she says loudly.

My waitress friend, Suzie, looks at me and raises her eyebrows. "Sorry," I tell her.

"Aunty Frannie said you had a few classes left and then your thesis at the University of Alaska," Mark says. "C'mon, man, you know you can finish. You're so close."

"And fuck her too," Jacob says. "Fucking bitch mother of mine ragging my ass all week long like I ever even considered going to seminary. She needs to wake up and smell the . . . punani," he says, nudging the blonde's neck with his nose.

Celeste is silent.

"I'm Jacob's cousin Mark," he says, holding out his hand to the blonde. "And you are?"

"Rose," she says, laughing at him and pointing to the tattoo on her arm. "Rose from Dubose. That's in I-o-wa," she says like we Japs don't speak-ee English. She has a chipped eyetooth.

"Whatever, *Rose* from *Dubose*," I tell her.

"Got a fucking problem, little girl?" Rose hisses.

"Plenty," I answer slowly, staring her in the eye. "And that's no lie, Rosie." The blonde gets up, and I push Mark to get him out of my way. Mark starts laughing uncomfortably. Celeste sighs deeply. Jacob puts his arm out in front of Rose from Dubose, so she sits down. He turns his drunken eyes on me.

"Still the mouth, huh, Sonia? Still the mouth."

♦

I was eighteen years old the summer Joseph planted the night-blooming jasmine. It was another summer Granny Alma returned me to Hilo. Uncle Billy hired Mark and me again at the Hukilau Hotel, this time as full-time dishwashers, scalding our hands raw for minimum wage and meager tips from the nicer waitresses.

This was my summer of dope. Jacob, who smoked a lot of hashish, slept with the new pastor's daughter, wrote a couple of fantastically romantic letters to Celeste after their summer-camp liaison, currently bonked some much older grad assistant in astronomy at Hilo College who sometimes came as his date to church functions.

"She called him 'Salty Peanuts,' " I said to Mark over the hiss of steam and water.

"Who?" he asked, laughing as he flicked water in my face.

"Pastor Wynne's daughter. She told me after the holy communion service. In the name of the Father," I said as I dumped a cup full of water on his rubber boots.

"Eh, stop horsing around," Tilly Maldonado yelled at us. She was the restaurant manager's ex-sister-in-law, a fat Portagee with a hatred-of-Japs complex. "Nani said you two idiots working the night shift for Mona Moniz and Carla Ruiz."

I looked at Mark. "We might as well work. We could use the extra money."

"What you said, you little Japanee? Got problems with your extra hours, take it up with the manager."

"No problem, Aunty Tilly," I said sarcastically. "We *want* to work, shit."

"Fuck you, Sonia, you townie Jap bitch. And stop laughing, you townie Jap midget. You go around acting big 'cause you from Honolulu, like you all this and all that. You didn't even have a choice, stupids. Now get your stupid asses in gear." She laughed too loud and too long.

After the dinner rush, Uncle Billy's Luau turned into U.B.'s, a hot spot for the Hilo College club crowd. Jacob was a regular.

The only reason I knew was Fat-Ass Tilly who made me, not Mark, empty the trash for the bartender twice a night.

Mark would look both ways, up and down the dark club, to see if anybody was looking. "Ready, set, go!" he'd say, and I would rush behind the bar for the trash. It was humiliating. All the beautiful college girls and me in my Uncle Billy's Luau apron.

Jacob leaned over the bar each time I ran out with his stony, drunken, "Hey, Sonia."

"Hey yourself," I managed to say in embarrassed half breaths.

"So how's your week been?" he asked.

"I just saw you in church, you nitwit. You and that airhead broad of yours." I gathered up some empty glasses, wet napkins, and dirty ashtrays off of the crowded bar.

"Do me a favor," he asked.

"I got no time for small talk, Jacob. What do you want?"

"Give this to Markie," he said as he slid me a couple of joints. Jacob let his hand linger on mine.

"Whatever you say, Jake, you the man, right?" I said, slipping the joints in my bra before I started my sprint back to the kitchen.

"Jake?" He laughed as he slid his arm away from the girl sitting next to him. "Tell Markie to wait for me out back after your shift," he said, holding on to my arm, sliding his warm hand down to my wrist. "I want to show *you*, I mean *both* of you, my favorite moon. The sliver of moon in case you ever eulogize me."

"Like *I*, I mean *we*," I said, "give a flying fuck."

"You got a mouth on you, Sonia, you know that? Dreary life, that's your problem," he said, tightening his grip around my wrist. "Meet me in the parking lot after work, then we'll have our own fun. No small talk, I promise. And wash your mouth out with some dish soap." When he winked at me, I nearly dropped all of the trash.

As I hurried back to the kitchen, I heard the grad assistant's laugh, heady and high, the clink of glasses and bottles in the smoky club, the steam of the washer finally drowning out the noise.

♦

Rose from Dubose keeps blowing smoke in Celeste's face. She rolls her eyes and fans the air in front of her face like a prissy socialite. Typical Celeste. It only makes the blonde do it more. "So, Jacob, your Ph.D. would be in?" Celeste asks, not completing her sentence.

"Astronomy."

I laugh.

"What's so funny?" he asks.

"I never knew her name," I tell him.

"Who?" he asks, his eyes narrowing on me.

"The grad assistant you were fucking in Hilo that summer. She was studying astronomy, right?"

"Yeah. Pearl? Berle? Some 'earl'-sounding name. I forget," he says. "She wasn't that good, you know what I mean, Sonia?"

"Maybe," I tell him. "You've always had such *high* standards." I fake-smile at the blonde. Jacob leans back in his chair.

"You think maybe I should transfer to UH-Mānoa?" Jacob asks Mark. "I've got to get home, Markie."

"Why? You got that big grant to finish your doctorate, right?"

"Man, I can't even fucking . . . I mean . . . I'm all . . . all . . . shit. Fuck all this shit, right, baby?"

The blonde leans her head on his shoulder. "It's okay, baby. Everything's gonna be all right." She looks like she's about to cry.

"Fuck what shit, Jacob?" Mark asks. "What are you talking about?"

"Nothing. Fuck it. Never mind. Hey, waitress," Jacob calls to Suzie. "A round of beautifuls, Coke back." The blonde laughs, a smoker's raspy, phlegmy laugh.

"What's a beautiful?" Celeste asks. "I don't drink. None for me if it's an alcoholic beverage."

"Grand Marnier and cognac," Jacob says, looking at me, "in a big, ass-round snifter. We'll drink to Markie's graduation."

Jacob keeps ordering rounds of beautifuls. I'm feeling it, but will not let him drink me under. After the fourth round, the blonde droops in her chair, and then her head falls forward onto the table. Her face pales. Jacob signals Mark to help him take her outside before she pukes.

A short time later, Mark returns to the table, alone. "He just stuck her in a cab," Mark whispers to me. "He opened the door and shoved her in."

"What? What happened?" Celeste interjects. "Where's Jacob?"

"And he told the driver to dump her outside the Fitzgerald," he continues, shaking his head in disbelief. "That's where he found her. He's washing his hands. Probably smoking some—"

"What an asshole," I tell him.

Jacob walks back into the bar. "Another round," he tells Suzie.

"Not for me," Mark says, signaling me to leave. "I've still got some studying to do. And I work early tomorrow morning. Bob's probably snoring Sonny Boy awake. Sonia, we'd better—"

"Markie, Markie, Markie," Jacob says condescendingly. Mark always hated that. "Always Mr. Do-Right."

"Well, Jacob, it's been nice . . ." Mark begins. "C'mon, Sonia," he says, pulling my arm.

"I'm staying," I tell Mark. His eyes widen, jaw tightens, and he shakes his head. "I'll see you at home."

"I need a drink," Celeste says at last, loosening the first gold button under her chin. "What a night. What a week."

Jacob holds up three fingers to Suzie. "That's my girl," he says, rubbing Celeste's shoulders. "We don't have to work tomorrow, now do we? And we've got lots of old times to catch up on."

♦

Jacob would meet Mark and me after work at U.B.'s, have me sell and deliver dope and coke to the valet guys, waiters, bouncers, bartender, and assorted coke whores. I felt like a cool drug-dealing bitch hanging out in a filthy back parking lot with Jacob Gomes, thank you very much, leaning against his souped-up Honda.

He allowed us to hang out with him, which was a big thing in Hilo. Mark really didn't care. He said he started having Benjamin Hart flashbacks from the summer before and did not care to relive that horror even if Jacob was his cousin. He was still a dickhead. As far as Mark was concerned, I was Jacob's mule. He had too much pride and common sense to do this shit for him. On and on, very responsible and sensible, Mark preached on and on.

"C'mon, Sonia. Let's go to Ken's Pancake House, eat, and just go home. Or maybe Mun Cheong Lau," Mark begged me night after night. "Fuck Jacob. I mean if you get caught, you screw up college."

"I get a slap on the wrist because I'm a juvenile. That's what Jacob said. If he gets caught, then he fucks up college because they charge him as an adult. That's why I do all the deliveries. And he pays me. We'll need the money when we leave for school."

"Fucking stupid. I don't need that kind of dirty blood money. Count me out," Mark said every night.

It was our one night off. Jacob wanted to meet Mark and me at the Hilo County Fair to pass a fifty-dollar bag to one of the carnival workers. It had rained all weekend, the slouch of the big-top tents wilting under the weight of the water. And when the wind gusted, the tents ballooned, sending the rain pouring down the sides.

We waited an hour and a half for him by the pay phones in front of the Civic Auditorium when out of nowhere, I felt his hands on my shoulders. "Ricky flaked. Sorry, girls, no dope to deliver tonight."

"We waited a fucking hour and a half in this damn fucking cold," Mark complained. "You prick. C'mon, Sonia."

"Blame Ricky," Jacob said.

"We don't even know who the fuck Ricky is," Mark whined. "And you don't even give a flying fuck about us waiting for your sorry ass on our one night off."

"Markie, Markie, Markie, why all the drama?" Jacob laughed. "Come," he said, jerking his head for us to follow him. Mark pulled me in the other direction. "C'mon, Markie-poo, forgive and forget," Jacob joked. We trudged behind him through the muddy field to his car.

"I forgive," Mark muttered, "but I never forget."

"Whatever, cuz," Jacob answered. He reached into the backseat and pulled out a red balloon. He handed it to me. "For you, sweetheart. Don't be so vicious with your mouth." To Mark, he gave a pot of night-blooming jasmine. "Plant it somewhere beautiful for Sonia," he said. "I won it, nah, stole it from the Plant Garden." He laughed.

"What's so fucking funny?" I asked, trying to be cool and ungrateful for Mark's sake.

"I got another present for my favorite two dishwashers. You've been such a boon for Uncle Jake's business this summer," he said as he ruffled Mark's hair.

"Eh, knock it off, okay, Jacob. Prick."

Jacob took the balloon from my hand. Tied to the end was a huge glass vial.

"The good stuff," he said after his first line, tipping his head back. "Froggy didn't cut it with all that baby laxative shit." We did three fat lines each in Jacob's car, Jacob whose body leaned into mine, who cupped his warm hands around mine every time I lit his cigarette with my lighter.

Before Mark and I left to walk into the slur of carnival music and spinning lights, Jacob tied the shiny red balloon to my ring finger. "I now pronounce you woman and balloon. Let me hang out with you guys," he said, following after us with a bottle of Southern Comfort.

"Us? Since when you want to hang with us?" Mark said as he walked off. "Let alone be seen with us."

"I like your company," he said, looking straight at me. "Always did from way back when." He put his hand on the small of my back.

Buzzing high, endless coke and Southern Comfort, Jacob draped his heavy arm around me. Mark, drunk and stoned, lightened up at last. Jacob took off his jacket and put it around me, the rain coming in sheets. There was a shitload of cash in its pockets. He held my hand and looked at no one but me.

◆

By the sixth round of beautifuls in the 14-Karat Bar, Celeste is shitfaced. "Joseph fucked us all up. And why he continues to write those philosophical, self-searching letters to you is what gets me." She's slurring but still incredibly polysyllabic.

"You're drunk. Shut up," I tell her. I take a deep drink from the warm snifter.

"Good shit, huh, Sonia?" Jacob says, leaning into me. "Like old times. A round of Southern Comfort," he says to Suzie.

"And I blame Grace," Celeste goes on. "When she put me on the plane with you, I had no one. No mother, no father, and going to live with a grandmother I had never met but once before at some dead uncle's funeral. The family of God is the only family I know," she slurs. "I want another beautiful, Suzie," she calls to the waitress.

"Why not blame God while you're at it?" I ask Celeste. I finish the last of my drink.

"Because my heavenly Father took their place." She puts her head in her hands. And then she looks up at me. "But poor you, Sonia," she says sarcastically, "you had nobody. Pinning all of your hopes on a ghost-father. I feel so sorry for you. You still have nobody."

I look at Jacob. He looks at me. I want to cry. He takes my hand in his, stroking my wrist with his fingers. "She's drunk," he whispers in my ear. "Let her go."

Celeste starts sobbing. "And for heaven's sake, I look at Tiffany and Heather and think how could anything but a cold-hearted, psychotic lunatic of a mother send her babies away forever? You answer me that, Sonia."

"Relax, Celeste," I tell her, "before you say something you might regret."

"What? Like you? You've been engaging in a lot of the regrettable," she slurs. "And I'm not talking verbally."

"Shut up, Celeste."

"I know you want to give Solomon to Grace, or Granny, or me." Celeste's drink arrives. She swallows it down, slams the glass on the table, and orders another. "So, fuck you, okay, So-nia. Don't you sit here and tell me that it never crossed your mind."

I am silent.

"She's doing pretty good with those big-ass words," Jacob says, patting her hard on the back. "You got a Ph.D. in vocabulary? No, you're drunk, right, Celeste? C'mon, let's not get ugly."

She stares hard at me.

"What, Celeste? Why're you looking at me like that?"

"Because if there's anyone I despise as much as Joseph, it's you, Sonia. Why in God's holy name do you feel the need to value what he says in those awful letters and what he brings home from those godforsaken alleys he wanders into to get a good deal on fake, pirated goods is what gets me." Celeste downs her next drink, no Coke back.

"Despise?" I push myself away from the table and get in her face. "Try hate. I *hate* you, Celeste. I really do. You have an evil, vile mouth. But I'm going to save the rest of the whys for when I'm sober and have both you and Grace in the same room."

"I can still kick your ass, Sonia," Celeste says, standing up on her wobbly Fendis. Her Kate Spade falls to the floor. "You're still nothing. C'mon, think you're so tough, huh? You little slut."

I shove her away from me.

"Sisterly love," Jacob laughs, "always turned me on." He takes Celeste's arm and leads her out of the bar. I flop back onto my chair. Suzie puts a hot cup of coffee in front of me.

"Sonia, honey, you've had enough. Want me to take you home? It's almost morning."

"No," I tell her. I put my face in both hands. I won't cry. I feel the tears burning behind my eyelids. When I look up, I see heat waves moving in undulating invisibility. I shut my eyes again, breathe deeply in and out so that the alcohol clouds in front of me. I try to shake it off. I look for Jacob. Nowhere.

I turn around. And then I See. Number One and #2 sit in the next booth. They're having piña coladas garnished with little pink umbrellas, pineapple wedges, maraschino cherries, and mint leaves.

"Who is Mine?" #2 mouths at me.

"No!" I scream.

"It *is* almost morning," Suzie repeats as she refills my cup. "I'm taking you home."

♦

When I woke after the night at the Hilo County Fair with Mark and Jacob, one eye opened to the sting of morning light in my bedroom. I watched the chalky red balloon bobbing in the corner. It made me sad. I should've let it go off into the sky.

At the top of the Ferris wheel Jacob told me, "Let the balloon go, Sonia. Watch it fly off."

"No," I said, "I'm taking it home."

Those beautiful, shiny carnival balloons. This carnival balloon that Jacob gave me, the balloon that pulled in the wind as we rode the Ferris wheel, followed above me as we cruised through the tents, by morning, dead in the corner of my room.

I listened to my father's shovel cut into the mossy soil outside my window. He planted the beautiful night-blooming jasmine that would grow long arms of thin white flowers to heights beyond the rooftop. I watched an aimless balloon.

I turned to the hard brown back sleeping beside me, softly moved my fingers over his spine, down toward the arc of naked ass; I watched his steady breathing until he turned and put his face in the curve of my neck. I stroked his hair. He reached for his jacket and placed it over my cold shoulder, then pulled the comforter over both of our naked bodies. He put his hand between my legs. I smelled his fingers. I knew what we had done. And then, we did it again.

◆

Jacob stumbles back into the 14-Karat Bar.

The turtle boy, #2, lifts his amber head.

I watch Jacob's last gulp of his beautiful. Amber burn, but sweet. He takes me by the hand.

I turn and hear tears falling, the clink of stones on a cheap linoleum tabletop.

"Turtle Boy, #2, stop your crying."

Number One, like light from an open box, stands. Such a handsome man, a prince. He puts his hand on Turtle Boy's shiny head.

"You want me to hate you? Both of you?"

Jacob puts his hand on the small of my back and leads me toward the door.

They won't stop crying, cups full of amber and murky salt water.

"Leave me Alone."

I take a last look at them.

"*Mine?*" #2 mouths.

"If I tell you, then leave me Alone."

Turtle Boy's eyes widen, satiable knowing.

"Meet your maker, #2," I tell him. "Jacob is yours."

9

QUIET CHAOS

LAS VEGAS HEAT makes my car a kiln. I look at Sonny Boy sweating in the car seat next to me. Where we are headed is of small consequence. All of a sudden, his eyes meet mine. Something inside grasps at my throat:

Sonny Boy's eyes hadn't *seen* me for months.

Joseph, you were right, the only one who could see. But you Leave me with just words, words that I am forced to keep:

I hope you find out what's wrong with him soon.

To everyone else my Sonny Boy's so cute.

Looks just like you, Sonia.

Has your nose.

Your eyes.

What a big boy.

Lots of hair.

Just like you when you were a baby.

And lucky for you, so quiet.

Wait till he learns the word *no.*

And who's the father?

You Leave me with words, Joseph, always leaving. When I was a little girl, so still, the day after you left. Someone missing from a favorite chair, different milk in the fridge, familiar sounds missing from around the house, slippers and shoes in a modified disarray, empty spaces on the clothesline.

And this time, not even a goodbye. No kiss on the forehead, a ruffling of a little boy's hair. Just words on an answering machine.

Talk to me, Daddy. You see, Sonny Boy has stopped talking. All of his words, gone. He has stopped looking at me. All eye contact, vacant and beyond me. I need his words. His utterance of *Mommy*, gone into distant silence. And again you Leave, when only you and I believe.

Sonny Boy's sitting on the floor. He's gnawing on the hygienic sheepskin. He doesn't answer to his name, softly spoken, loudly screamed; my pleading, begging, answer me, Sonny Boy. He gazes away, intense.

Mark sits on the couch. "Okay, Sonia," he says, "let's say for a moment that you're right. Something's wrong with him. What?"

"If you ask me," Bob says, "I say he's come whole. Nothing's wrong with the champ."

He's deaf?

I tap my fingernails on the tabletop.

Yes, he's deaf.

How do you test a toddler's hearing?

But he wasn't deaf before.

So I hide in the kitchen and bang on a pot. I whistle, I clap, snap my fingers. I blow on party-favor horns. I punch the wall. Sonny Boy turns to look for the sound.

Sonny Boy's sitting on the couch. He's gnawing on the hygienic sheepskin. He doesn't make any sound. Silence but for eggs boiling on the stove.

Mark sits at the dining table. He's graduated, an M.Ed. at last. Bob lies down on the floor in front of the TV. "He's fine, Sonia," Mark sighs. "He just has one of those type-one introverted personalities. I'll ask my early-childhood professor what he thinks. But let's just give Sonny Boy some time."

And the Greek chorus rises:

"It's because Sonia let that kuro-chan watch him since he was an infant," Granny Alma says.

"Her abandonment traumatized him," Aunty Frieda says.

"I'll call the prayer tree," Aunty Effie says.

"He doesn't respond to his name?" Celeste asks.

"She didn't let me see him when I was in Vegas," Grace says.

"You spent all those ungodly hours in the casino, Gracie," Granny Alma says. "That's your fault."

"She said he was talking," Aunty Frieda says.

"She was writing down all the words," Grace says.

"Maybe Sonia's lying," Aunty Frannie says.

"Again," Grace says, "she's just like her father."

"Is he a retard?" Celeste asks.

"Nobody's a retard on my side of the family," Grace says.

"Trust God," Aunty Effie says.

Sonny Boy's spinning and spinning and spinning. He's not joyful in the frenetic round and round of his movement. It's his eyes. They flicker back and forth in his head. Mark tries to make him stop. He won't. I try to pick him up but he arches his back and screams. So I put him down. And Sonny Boy spins.

I'm watching Sonny Boy in the car seat next to me. Where we are headed, this child and I, is of urgent consequence. He turns his eyes toward the window, and in its reflection I see the back-and-forth flitting of his pupils.

Little boy who cannot manage the overwhelming world of passing cars, buses, vans, and trucks;

mottled sky, brilliant sky, rainy sky;

varieties of trees, leaves shivering, rustling all at once, all directions;

night lights, fluorescence in pinks, blues, reds, yellows, Sally's staggered dance high above, lobbies full of lights;

hotels whizzing colors and heights, reflection off of glass, a sudden refraction of unbearable sunlight;

the radio on talk, talk, talk;

wind through the vents and windows, the smell of exhaust, bakery, car freshener;

the feel of an itchy blanket, scratchy new shirt, wet diaper;

and kaleidoscopic tastes.

Simultaneously overwhelming him.

His wide eyes pulse back and forth, the rocking of his head in some metronomed staccato this world plays for little boys who cannot manage its multifaceted sensorial enormity.

Sonny Boy's sitting in a cardboard box. He's gnawing on the hygienic sheepskin, a bald piece of gray chamois. Mark drags the box around the room.

"You're a train."

No, I am a boy in a box, his eyes say.

"You're a tugboat captain."

No, I am a boy in a box, his silence says.

"You're a race-car driver."

No. Everything moves too fast, this world spinning by me, his fingers in his ears say.

Stop all of the noise.

Make the world still.

Leave me Alone.

Celeste keeps calling me. Making up for pissing me off with her drunken bullshitting blame in the 14-Karat. "Mike's father's accountant's son didn't talk until he was four," she consoles. "He was one of those premies, but he works for Mike as a janitor in the warehouse now. He's slow-minded but perfectly functional.

"And Grace said that Joseph didn't speak until he was six. She said his brothers did all the thinking for him.

"And Aunty Frannie said that Jacob didn't talk until he was five, can you believe it? So anyway, his baby-sitter did some pagan ritual of feeding him the boiled uterus of an ox to make him speak. I think it involved a variety of poultry, too. Apparently, Jacob began speaking in sentences."

"But Sonny Boy has absolutely no speech now," I tell her, my words choking in my throat, "and he used to say words, Celeste."

"Have you ever heard of speech therapists?" Celeste remarks. "I mean, isn't Aunty Frieda's son an educator with a master's degree who networks with these ridiculously redundant agencies for the handicapped?"

"Handicapped?"

"I mean . . . kids with difficulties . . . you know . . . Dammit, Sonia, consult your pediatrician. Don't you think he might have some insight into the situation?"

"I guess. I don't know what to do. But Mark thinks. You're right, there's nobody to blame but me. And Bob says. You're all right. I fucked up. So I was thinking. And Grace thought. All I wanted was a normal child. And Granny Alma keeps saying. So I was wondering. Why can't life be normal for me? And Aunty

Frieda suggested. Life is pretty normal for everybody else, right? Then Aunty Effie told me. Should I? And Joseph——"

"Where is that bastard?"

"China," I tell her.

"Oh, for heaven's sake. You know, Sonia, the more I talk to you, the more I realize that you are probably overreacting to this whole thing as some misguided ploy to get us all worked up enough to hop a plane and——"

"Fuck you," I tell her.

"I beg your pardon?"

"You and your fucking chaos, Celeste. You're the one building this to fever pitch, so you can come to the rescue."

"Me? It's *your* chaos, Sonia. All yours."

I hang up the phone.

Sweet Sonia,

A man travels the countryside on a small road with few trees, the rickety old bus passing rice field after rice field in this brown landscape outside of Han Zhou, China.

The man is quiet and still. He does not remember his destination as he puts these words on paper. But he remembers that no one looks at him, the old woman with the basket full of snakes, the young girl in red, the man with few brown teeth, the boy with baby's blanket, no one.

The man sees a whirlpool of dust on the road up ahead, dust that momentarily blinds him, thrashes at his skin, swirls into his mouth, particles around him, and the smell of urine and dung. He regrets taking the day trip.

But when the man opens his eyes, he sees the boy with the blanket wiping his own eyes. For a moment, they gaze at each other on this tired bus where a woman steadies a basket of snakes, a young girl shields her face, and a man with few brown teeth pulls at a boy's gaze, that for a moment, restored a wandering man's disenchanted spirits. What quiet amidst the chaos.

May you find that in your boy, sweet Sonia. May he gaze at you with brief eyes. My regards to Grace, Celeste, and Solomon of the distant tiger's birth.

I love you,
Joseph Kurisu

I love you?

Say You, God? Say You What? What about Love?

"Say you receive the Little Priest," a turtle boy's voice says.

"Say this," God says. *"I love him."*

"Say you trust Him," Jesus Christ, gone from the crucifix on the wall of this apartment, says.

"All of this sayeth the Three in One," the Holy Ghost proclaims, steam and smoke rising outside the window.

"God makes no mistakes." A princely voice from a box.

"A Divine perfection." An old man's voice from across a filthy alleyway.

"The Little Priest chose you." A turtle boy's voice.

"We all did." Open box, illuminate.

"We all choose." Across an alleyway, golden cranes, gloriole.

Fucking Liars. All of you.

♦

Mine was the little girl's hand riding out the back window feeling the sting of rain on my palm.

"God made a rain for you," Joseph would always say.

We drove through a grove of mango trees in a cool March, the rain, a lifting steam on the silvery road.

"Smell the mango blossoms," my father said to me, the

116

shell gingers flowering on the roadside, the tinkling of wind chimes hanging from the branches of the trees, meanwhile, the sweet wind through the car window.

My perfect father, a child's flawed vision memorizing the shape of his head, his neck, his fingers pointing the Way.

My perfect mother, scarfed hair and sunglasses, a young Japanese beauty.

Big sister humming a child's lullaby beside me.

He stopped the car and spread a picnic goza in the filigreed shade of the mango trees and watched Celeste and me play a finger-string game.

Diamond.

Pinch two crosses.

Go under and pull open.

Pull open the halo of sun, the woman in the moon, the moaning seas of Keaukaha.

"God made a rain for you."

I fixed my gaze on my father's face.

"Does God love me?"

"Yes, sweet Sonia."

"Then why does He take you away?"

He glared at me and then at my mother. "Why do you always fucking ruin things, huh, smart mouth? It's you, Grace, you filling her head with lies."

Perfect father.

Perfect mother.

He walked to the car and shut the door behind him, turned on the radio, leaned his head back, and closed his eyes. He never looked at me until the day he left town, a heavy rain and furious winds the night before, the mango blossoms flustering in white dispersal. The quiet chaos of my childhood.

♦

Say You, God? Say You What?

I'm praying for Sonny Boy in the car seat next to me. Where we are headed is of Absolute consequence.

Mark parks the car, gets the baby bag, and walks beside me. Child my body made, little pod, you are two years old. I carry you, baby boy, toward steel elevators that pull open like doors to a morgue. A morgue door that opens to another heavy, institutional door, and another and another. The dead weight of these doors, and the absolute sound of their closing.

Nurses. Fill out this form. Intake, health insurance, and questions. Diagnostic Testing. Let's eventually do a psychiatric, psychosocial, psychobehavioral, complete physical and auditory examination. We'll need to set another appointment for this test. And that test.

A door yawns open. Doors beyond that door. Follow me. Down a fluorescent-lit hallway. The nurse lightly knuckle-knocks on the last. Behind it is a woman with red hair and green eyes.

There are trains and huge tops on the floor, blocks, a tent with pillows, and soft animals. We sit on the floor. She blows bubbles. And more bubbles. She rolls Play-Doh on a low table. She says nothing all the while.

I look at you, my Sonny Boy. This is it. I feel myself crumbling. Some Death in your eyes. Or was it my own? This I know. Somebody will die here. Somebody dies here Today. Mark puts his hands on my shoulders.

This woman with red hair and green eyes: Specialist. Doctor. How quiet your voice. How soft your touch. How beautiful your eyes.

"Your son, Solomon, is severely developmentally delayed."

Liar.

"I don't want you to be afraid."

Fuck you.

"Your son is autistic."

No. Please. This happens to other people. The Evil ones who deserve karmic payback. The Saints among us who welcome adversity.

Sonny Boy looks at me.

"He's listening to every word I say," the woman with red hair tells us. "Your reaction is very important. Take a deep breath."

Mark takes my hand in his.

Everyone's eyes on me, waiting. The world stops.

"Oh, God!" I scream.

Sonny Boy, startled, runs into Mark's open arms.

I hear the Angels singing his diagnosis; God rejoicing his developmental disorder; the Three in One exulting this genetic mutation my body made.

A Divine Perfection.

Did the boy gaze at you, sweet Sonia, with brief eyes?
Yes, Daddy.
Then all is well.

Her words beyond *autistic* make little sense to me. Talk, talk, talk. Her lips keep moving. She's so pretty. I see Mark nodding, concerned and benign. I hear breath and heartbeat, dull thumping in my ears.

No. Mommy, help me.

No. Daddy?

How the world collapses into this one moment. It's not the shattering of glass, the tailspin into the dark hole, the falling off of the edge. I know all of that. It is this: I did not kill this child. How I had hoped in his birth that God would forgive me everything I had done in this Life. God's grace, my own at last, abundant as air. I would not have to know more struggle. Why let the weak struggle most? I've tried to be Good.

Stop fucking me up the ass.

Oh, God.

Say You, God? Say You What?
The answer is a Voice that sounds like my own:
One Death.
Two Death.
Three Death.
Somebody dies here Today:
Four Death.
It is me.
Dead inside a churning darkness that feels like a whirlpool, sucking me deeper into myself; every cell tingling and heightened; the quick descent into a numbing catalepsy. Because I know, because they knew:
Number One,
#2,
Jar,
and Sonny Boy:
We chose this Life.
We knew what chaos this Life would bring.
And yet, we came.

10

Sing

I STARE AT SONNY BOY in the tiny living room. It is one o'clock in the morning. He has not been to sleep. He watches his hands, a rhythmic flutter-trance, marveling at his tiny fingers rippling and purling at his command.

Mark had promised to stay by my side, day and night, to see me through this. Because:

I am not to call Drake.

I am to get out of bed, brush my teeth, and comb my hair, daily.

I am not to do illegal or prescription drugs.

I am not to drink until I fall face-first into my own vomit.

I am to feel this Death, I am to grieve, to cry, to accept, to move on.

A bottle of splendid gin outside my apartment door. *Love, Drake.* A joint laced with sweet white dust. *Miss you. Love, Drake.* A secret lullaby on the answering machine. *I love you, Sonia.*

I sit in a rocking chair by the window, day and night. A dormancy of my choosing, my metabolism slows with each dark breath. It feels oddly vegetative. No water passes through my parched lips, no food. The world is two-dimensional, yet seconds, minutes, and hours, cubic. I don't want to bathe. The indifference of this detachment is all I can muster. My feet are dirty.

Mark promises he will see me through this. But he leaves this night for a graduation party. Some pretty Chinese girl he did an internship with at a shelter for battered women.

"I have to show face. It's a big party. I can network. Claire Yee's very well connected. I like her a lot. You need to get out of the house. You need to snap out of this. And everything will be okay, I promise. Why don't you want to come?"

Because.

One-fifteen in the morning. Sonny Boy starts lining up his toys. When I step on the cars in the dark and move them from the middle of the floor, he screams, picks them up, and throws them at me. He realigns his tiny Hot Wheels, red/yellow/green, red/yellow/green.

Bob was drunk with me post-diagnosis, three days and nights in a row. He's reading *A Personal Matter*. "I met Kenzaburo Oe on a stopover in Seoul," he says, "right after the war. He was on his way to Zurich."

I fall face-first into my own vomit.

One-thirty in the morning. Sonny Boy coos at his fingers moving in the orange streetlights. Plasticine turtles all in a row.

One-forty-five. I am not to disrupt his order.

Sweet Sonia,

In an alley in Pusan, a man eats a bowl of noodles prepared by a sidewalk vendor. The boiling swamp cabbage and mung-bean sprouts tangle in a thick broth.

He watches the flies in a frenzied dance over what looks like a fish head. Large ants tread a winding path near the curious mania of pale roaches.

The soup steams in a cast-iron kettle. The embers crackle as a little boy with dirty hands and a yellow shirt tends the fire with a small bamboo pipe.

A tabby cat with live maggots in one eye lifts the fish head with her tired mouth. The flies disperse, the roaches scatter. The man is distracted by the marching of militia in the street.

He turns back to find the little boy in the yellow shirt picking maggots out of the cat's delirious eye, popping the white worms with his fingernail. He sings a child's song.

I must come home. Sweet Sonia, will you and Solomon share a bowl of miso soup with me? Wakame, hokigai, and bean sprouts in a clear broth with symmetrical cubes of soft tofu that I will place in Solomon's mouth? Do you think he would sing me a child's song?

I love you,
Joseph Kurisu

Sing?
The angels didn't.

Celeste calls. "He's so damn clueless, Sonia," she says. "When did you tell him about Solomon?"

"A couple of weeks ago," I answer, monotone. "He called. I told him. Everything."

"What did he say?"

"He started telling me a story about sea turtles," I tell her.

"How appropriate. Typical Joseph waxing philosophical when everybody else is losing it. *He must come home.* Give me a break."

"Once the male sea turtle escapes from his shell, he scrambles toward the water—" I begin to tell Celeste.

"Why bother figuring out his cryptic metaphors?" Celeste

complains. "If I remember correctly, he told you this a long time ago, Sonia. Knock it off."

"And he swims away."

"So?"

"He never comes back to the beach. He's not supposed to come back."

"So? What are you saying? Because frankly, I couldn't care less what Joseph's saying. And you are beginning to annoy me big-time."

"Only the female comes back, again and again. If nothing kills her."

"And now, you sound *just like him*," Celeste says loudly.

" 'What does your instinct tell you, sweet Sonia?' he says to me. 'Tell me, Sonia.' "

"Do you hear me?" she screeches. "*Just like him.* Dammit, Sonia, that's supposed to hurt you."

"I don't know what my instinct tells me, Celeste." The phone line hums but for her breathing. "Tell me."

"You need to come home," she says after a while.

"And Joseph?"

"Need you even ask?" she says.

I am silent, because what I recall scares me:

Joseph in the kitchen stirring a teaspoon of Pream into his cup of coffee. Eating the half of a boiled egg and staring out of the window.

My horrified eyes: Help me. My hand reaching for his, and my father's refusal to meet my gaze.

"Sonia, you there?" Celeste asks.

"Yes."

"Fish rot from the head down," Celeste says.

"What?"

"Joseph's the reason for Solomon being the way he is," she says.

"God is the reason," I tell her. The phone line hums but for her hard breathing.

"You have to go back to church. What is God saying to you? Everything means something. Why can't you get it?" Celeste starts crying.

"We used to talk every day and every night, God and me. Nothing, heard nothing lately. Maybe the Three of them are whispering among themselves. I hear a lot of whispering."

"Don't tell me you're hearing voices again, Sonia?"

"I said I heard nothing. Why don't you fucking listen to me? I can't do it, Celeste. I thought God was through with punishing me. God loves me, right? What's going on?"

"Come home," Celeste pleads. "Just for a few days."

And then the line goes dead.

The night gives clarity.

This cannot be happening to me.

Stars?

Moon?

Rain over the City of the Plain?

Why?

Blame God.

The End.

Two in the morning. Sonny Boy, son of Sonia, gets angry. His body stiffens. He clenches his teeth, his fists, and throws himself down. His pupils blacken as he hurls his head onto the floor again and again.

No way to comfort: Come here, baby boy.

His arms flail.

No words: Let me hold you, baby boy.

His body stiffens.

Don't touch me. It hurts, your touch.

No words, just guttural screaming and crying.

I'm screaming inside:

God help me.

But in these moments, Sonny Boy draped in some unearthly rage, God never hears me, my prayers unanswered, as the boy's hands lunge for my eyes.

"Maybe we should go home," Mark says.

"What are you talking about?" I ask. I watch him clear the dining table of his loose grad-school papers.

"Here," he says, handing me a manila folder. "Bob and I did some research on autism. We want you to read this. We're going to see you through this."

"I'm not reading this shit," I say as I throw the folder at him. "You read it and tell me all about it. Oh, you wouldn't understand. And I can't talk to you about it."

"Why?" Mark asks.

"And I can't talk to Grace or Granny or Celeste, either. Somebody's tapped our phone line," I tell him, exasperated. "There. Are you happy?" I say, yelling into the phone. "Now you know that I know, so take the fucking tap off my line."

"Sonia?"

"I *know*, Mark. There are things I've always known. You know that I know, right?"

"You've been in touch with Drake? You've been doing shit with him? What kind of shit? When, Sonia? You're all fucking paranoid," he yells.

He's tired. So tired of me. He might as well Leave. And it might as well be about Drake. I can't, I won't be a mother, a best friend, a lover, a daughter. I want to lose myself in Junk before Mark loses me again. A Junkie's oblivion, a Junkie's disregard, a Junkie's oversight, a Junkie's reverie.

"I *know*," I tell him.

"You know nothing," he says.

I light a cigarette. "Think what you like."

Celeste calls, again. "Sonia? Mark called me last night," she says.

"So?"

"He said"—she pauses—"that you've been smoking that methamphetamine again. Is that why you're hearing voices? Tell me."

"He has a fucking big mouth. Nothing. Don't you get it? Nothing. Listen, bitch, what about the word *nothing* don't you understand?" I yell at Celeste.

"What? What did you say to me?"

"Stop fucking harassing me," I tell her. I light the pipe. Smooth smoke. Sweet descent, smoky fingers that slide down into me and grab onto the pit of my belly. "There, you happy?" I yell.

"Who, me?" Celeste asks. "What's going on?"

"You happy, you fucking alcoholic junkie? My own fucking sister. That's what you wanted?"

Drake slams the door behind him.

"I can't come home, Celeste. Not like this. This shit's nothing like the shit I did back home. Something told me, 'Don't do it, Sonia.' Not the white synthetic shit. I mean back in Kalihi, it was a shitload of white shit, but white shit from plant life, you know, coca. But Drake and me, we—I called him. Mark told me not to, and I tried not to, really I did, but I feel so fucked up. I mean, there's nobody on this planet like him. He's going to help me with Sonny Boy. Now that has to count for destiny, right? You read *The Celestine Prophecy*? He'll adopt him. He'll take care of us. And the shit's so cheap. I have to clean up this apartment right now. It's filthy."

"Where's Mark, Sonia? Listen to me, Sonia. Where is Mark? And where is Solomon? Answer me."

"I don't know."

"Oh, Sonia."

"Don't 'Oh, Sonia' me."

"You better bring yourself and Solomon home."

"My, my, now that's a proposition. I don't think I even know where home is. Maybe I should ask Joseph. Oh, he wouldn't know. But neither do you. I figure home is some place below my rib cage. Lodged in my belly. But I can't make me rise up through my chest and out of my mouth. Dark, Celeste, dark. I couldn't come home if my life depended on it."

"You know you can, Sonia," she tries to reassure me. "You've always known."

"I know nothing. We need lightbulbs. This house is dark. And I don't have any cash."

I knew.

I heard the Voices singing.

And I sang with the Voices because I loved God. And God loved me. He told me so.

They killed the knowing in me. They prayed the Voices away. They made sin of my ability to hear. I blame them every fucking day of my life.

But in the end, I know.

I killed God in me.

◆

The singing began in the afternoons I spent with Celeste under Aunty Effie's porch. She watched us while Grace worked at the 19th Hole. I knew the life stories of the people in Aunty Effie's house.

"They sit in her kitchen," I told her, her eyes wide as she took a swig of the warm soda I'd stolen for us from Aunty Effie's garage stash. "They drink o-cha and eat tsukemono. And they're humming o-bon songs."

"Aunty Effie lives alone," Celeste said with nonchalance, the hairs on the back of her neck standing.

"One's this old lady who looks just like an old, old Aunty Frannie. She thinks Aunty Effie talks too much. And she's mad 'cause Aunty Effie threw away the Buddha house where she used to live."

"Right."

"I keep telling the old lady that Aunty Effie didn't throw it away. It's in the back bedroom. The one full of mothballs. But she can't get off the kitchen table. I don't know why. You want to see the Buddha house?"

"Stop it. You're making me scared," Celeste told me. Still, she always wanted to know more. "Anyway, Aunty Effie's Baptist and Buddha is against her religion. You don't know nothing, Sonia."

I widened my scary eyes and stared at her, humming the o-bon song, slow.

"I'm telling Aunty Effie that you're telling me devil stories." She had been afraid to join me after I told her that someone was following her besides her own shadow, and she caught it playing by Aunty Effie's lychee tree. I took a warm, melting Tomoe Ame from a box crushed in my pants pocket. I passed one to Celeste, who washed it down with her soda.

"There's this one little boy who's always in the kitchen, right by the fridge. He can't get to sleep. And he looks just like Joseph. A little boy Joseph. He likes me because I eat those coconut crackers."

"Ask him if he wants one," she dared me.

"You ask," I said, staring at her. "He's looking right at you."

Celeste swiveled her head from side to side. "Where? Where is he?"

I looked at the boy. And then a tear ran down my cheek. "No, you're wrong. You don't have to stay here."

"He has to," Celeste warned.

"Listen, I can see the light," I whispered. "Over there," I pointed.

"What?" Celeste screamed. "No, don't listen to her, Joseph, stay."

"Shut up," I hissed. "You want Aunty Effie to hear us?"

"Aunty Effie!" she screamed.

"Go see God," I responded. "Go home. And one day, you can come back and be with me. Tell me everything you've seen. Yes, the angels sing. I heard them."

"No!" Celeste covered her ears. "Daddy!"

"He's singing to me. Listen." I pulled at her hands.

"Daddy, come back."

"Listen," I whispered, taking her hands in mine.

"I can't hear anything. Stop it."

And then I joined the boy. "Praise God from whom all blessings flow. Praise Him all creatures here below. Hurry." I sang louder. "Praise Him above ye heavenly host. Praise Father, Son, and Holy Ghost."

"Make him stay," Celeste said as her body crumbled.

Aunty Effie screamed from the door above us. "Sonia! I hear you defiling the doxology. Celeste, where the hell are the two of you?"

Aunty Effie yanked Celeste's arm as though the power of the Holy Spirit Himself possessed her, sending her hurling into a patch of peonies. I crawled farther under the porch, out of Aunty Effie's reach.

"You come out right now, Sonia," she said while slapping Celeste's face with her broad hand.

"He went into the light," I gasped, "and they sang, *Gloria . . . Gloria . . . Gloria.*"

Aunty Effie pulled me out from the dark space under her porch and beat the shit out of me with her house slipper. All the while saying, "Gloria, my ass, devil child."

♦

Two-thirty in the morning. Sonny Boy stands in the dark kitchen. He opens the refrigerator door. A gasp of cold vapor envelops him, the white light against his back. He flaps his arms and disperses the mist, the heavy door bumping, bumping his side. Meanwhile, the light flickers on and off behind him.

I am in the rocking chair by the window. I hear all of their voices in my head responding to my three basic complaints:

1. I have to sleep. *What did you think it was all about, earth hippie mother? I know—you thought that the single mother/artist phenomenon was so politically "in" these days. The child would be a cutie-pie genius like Kathie Lee's Cody. And you would've raised this child all Alone. What a fabulous accomplishment. What a beautiful child, inside and out. Sonia, you finally did something right.*

2. I have to finish this semester. *Seven years of school and no fine arts degree? You're a musician, no, you're a photographer, no, you're a painter, no, you're a sculptor, no, you blow glass, no. Maybe you should drop out. Maybe now you can drop dead and everybody would think you did Sonny Boy a favor. Why not choose a drug overdose? At least you'd get some sleep.*

3. I still have to work two jobs. *Sonia acts like she's the only one eking out a living in the face of adversity. Always full of the same poor me, pity me complaints. And always going from one maelstrom to the next. You never end, Sonia. Your life is a series of crises, uphill conditions, dramas, plights, predicaments, catastrophes, and emergencies. State-of-the-art victimhood.*

I look at Sonny Boy. Why won't he sleep? *You made your bed.*

Always making my own bed.

Sleep.

Fuck, I have to sleep.

Bob knocks at the door. He's home from work.

"Made good tips tonight," he says, lugging a heavy box with him. "Got this train set at Wal-Mart for the champ." He sets up the tracks, tired Bob. "Even remembered to get some batteries." I rest my head on his shoulder. Sonny Boy sits in the middle of the tracks. The train chugs on with the flip of a red switch, lights, smoke, loud train sounds.

Two-forty-five.

Three.

Three-fifteen.

"Where's Mark?" Bob asks.

"At some classmate's graduation party," I tell him.

"How come you didn't go?"

"They're drinking all night. I had Sonny Boy. I mean, what's the point . . ."

Three-thirty, the train pulls round and round. The noise, the whistling, the smoke. Sonny Boy flaps and jumps.

Three-forty-five.

Bob falls asleep.

Four.

A knock on the door. It's Drake, loaded and filthy. His hair's matted on one side like he'd been sleeping in a pool of saliva. He puts his finger over his lips. The train winds on and on. We step outside into the hot air.

Absolut in a brown paper package. I'm crying after four deep swigs. He pushes the bottle toward me. It's all mine.

I have no words for *this.* I want no one to know. I feel so ashamed. One in ten thousand births. Man, I've got fantastic odds with the devil's luck. I tell Drake, beg Drake, the bottle's almost gone, don't tell any of our friends. Hippie earth mother, single artist mother, breast-feeding lounge singer mother, righteous minority mother made a deformity, an aberration, a mutant pod, a silent freak of nature.

He promises to keep his mouth shut. Do I have twenty bucks, by the way? He feels sorry for me. Pity for me. But empathy, not sympathy. He'll be There for me. Make it part of his Novel. Share his advance and royalties with me. By the way, do I have twenty bucks?

"Here, to help you sleep."

"But I can't ever sleep again unless Sonny Boy sleeps. Who's going to watch him?"

"Here, to help you sleep. Halcion. Put it all in a Ziploc."

"But I can't sleep unless—" Drake never hears me when he's high.

"Here, to help you kill the pain. Percodan. Here, don't be depressed. Prozac. Put them all in a Ziploc and take it when you need it. Don't fret the small shit. Besides, I got lots more." Drake walks over to the stairwell to take a piss.

I stare at the pills in the palm of my hand. Beautiful yellows. Speckled blue-and-white time-release capsules. Shiny azure ovals like the waters off of Pohoiki. I hear angels singing. And then, I take them all.

I was right.

Angels do sing.

Golden cranes swirl about me, slapping my face with broad white wings, pecking at my eyes: *"Wake up, wake up. Come back."*

"Oh, Jar. Why is your chest bleeding?"

He doesn't answer me. A voice from gurgling water rises and moans. *"He is weaving a blue silk cloth for you,"* says #2,

Turtle Boy, *"a cloth light as feathers, in the apartment across the alleyway."*

I look beyond them. Angels do sing in yellow light from a cardboard box. Number One?

"You brought me lightbulbs. I needed those. They're always on sale at Wal-Mart."

"Wrong light, mother." A princely man emerges from the cardboard box, a man whose cartilaged pieces remained on a surgical tray, Number One.

"You ran naked for the light in the corner of a hospital room. But you tell me, 'Wrong light.' Go away. All of you."

"The Little Priest, the Little Priest," #2 cries, water blue, light falling around him, eyes do blink, head spin, round and round the train's slow drag behind the closed door.

"But the light," I tell them. *"Gloria . . . Gloria . . ."* My vision blurs, the Three of them in one. Their voices sound like insects buzzing. Then the chamber doors, my eyelids, shut.

"Come back," he begs, a turtle's amber tears that clink on concrete.

I was right.

Angels sing.

But not where they send you for taking all of Drake's little pills.

Angels sing on the way There.

Not very bright, the lights, There.

I see:

Noose lacerations in cold, pink flesh, still raw and wet: *beyond hope, there is the child's jump rope, the worn belt, the necktie, or the electrical cord.*

The slurp of slit wrists, razor blades slicing white muscle and blue vein: *horizontal or vertical, there is a sound to the skin's new seams, then tissue spreading open, and blood; the sound of warm water, the collapse of a body onto a cold floor.*

Shot-off faces: *odd, the man with half a head who learned sign language here, and two eye blinks for yes, one for no.*

The mouthless who gave blow jobs to .45s: *cry wolf and despair, ye brokenhearted.*

Jumpers from high places with knee bones protruding from chests broken open: *a freeway overpass into rush-hour traffic, two retarded girls holding hands.*

A gunshot in a bleeding heart: *walter, r.i.p.*

Druggies with cold sweat and shaking hands: *past pins and needles, sudden rush in dick veins, between the toes, heavy blood vessels under the tongue.*

Them who carry lungs black-filled with carbon monoxide: *did you sleep at last in the front seat of your buick, sweet jay?*

Them who carry lungs like pink-veined balloons filled with seawater: *blue-faced, ocean blue, windex blue, cadaver-white eyes.*

None with scars.

And me. Until I hear the angels sing.

"Sonia?"

I'm nearly dead in front of the apartment door.

Shallow breathing, comatose sleeping.

Bob pulls open the door. I fall face-first into my own vomit. Mark stumbles over me and calls 911.

I lift my eyes and see my Sonny Boy, asleep in a celestial sphere of light, his earthly body in the middle of the train tracks.

Never mind the train dragging round and round on dying batteries, headlight flickering.

My son sleeps in daylight.

It is seven-fourteen in the morning.

◆ 11 ◆

Birds

MARK GETS ON THE PHONE.

"What? I can't believe this," Celeste screams. "It's history repeating itself. Grace overdosed on Seconal when we were kids. Sonia found her. Like mother, like daughter. Oh, sweet Lord Jesus. I'll be there on the next flight out."

"She What?" Granny Alma gasps. "How many pills? Who found her? Where was Solomon? O Heavenly Father, protect our Sonia. Damn Hurricane Sonia, when's this all going to end? No promises, but maybe Uncle Fu can cover for me at the Ten-Pin."

"She Did What?" Grace punctuates each syllable. "Oh, God, what on earth—she's a mess. Did someone contact Joseph? No, I don't know where he is. I never know where he is. Only she knows."

I open my eyes, tubes in my arm and face. And then I see him: Daddy, you found me.
Seek/and/you/shall.

"We're moving home," Mark whispers to me in the hospital room. "I'm not giving you a choice in this, Sonia." Sonny Boy climbs onto the high bed. Bob shuts the heavy door.

I chose to die, you idiots.

"You're moving back to Hilo?" Joseph asks.

No.

"I'd have an easier time finding a job in Honolulu," Mark answers. "My mother's there. She said she'd help take care of Sonny Boy."

I hate Aunty Frieda, passive-aggresive bitch.

"You can finish your degree at UH–Mānoa," Joseph says condescendingly to me.

Fuck school. Fuck life.

"I'll miss you, champ," Bob says as Sonny Boy raises his arms to him. He carries him to the big picture window.

Come with us.

"No, got things to do here in Vegas," Bob says, averting his eyes from mine.

"What, Bob?" Mark asks. "What did you say?"

"Nothing," Bob tells him, "just talking to the champ." Sonny Boy stands on the chair next to the window and flaps his arms. "See all those ants below us? Here and there and everywhere to go, but never where they matter most."

Daddy.

"I hope I can get a refund if I cancel my trip to Nepal," Joseph says.

Places to be. Mountains to climb. Motherfucker.

"And your granny said we could live downstairs in her Kalihi house," Mark consoles.

No, please, no.

"And Celeste said she'll help us secure services for Sonny Boy," Mark reassures.

Redundant agencies for the handicapped.

"Sonia, are you listening to Mark?" Joseph asks. "Is any of this making sense to you?"

Chirp, autism, chirp, autism, chirp.

"What have you got here in Vegas?" Mark asks. "Only more trouble. We need to go home." I look at Bob.

I've got Bob. The eyes of home not watching me, saying, "Typical Sonia, blaming everybody else. Not taking her bitter pill." And Drake.

"Baby girl, Drake's dark," Bob says. "You got darkness here. Go home. Listen to Mark."

Come.

"No, I need to stay," he says.

"Huh? Who are you talking to, man?" Mark walks over to the window to quiet Sonny Boy's frantic hands. He looks quizzically at Bob, who shrugs his shoulders. "I've already made some phone calls to set up interviews, Sonia. Say something."

I open my eyes, cold hospital feet. And then I see her: Grace.

Like mother, like daughter.

You don't know it yet, like Granny Alma never knew until the moment Celeste called from the pay phone at Honolulu International:

Sonny Boy is yours, payback time, the reckoning. Burn, Grace.

"Sonia, we started packing up your things," Grace tells me, holding a pink plastic cup with bendable straw to my lips.

Fuck off. Too late to be a mother to me.

"With Sonny Boy's condition, maybe Mark's right," she continues, "you both need to stay in Honolulu."

That's what you think.

"How did this happen?" Joseph asks with a deep sigh.

Condition?

This?

Autism, fuckheads, say it:
Autism.

There's a knock at the door. Bob stands to answer it. He puts Sonny Boy on the bed. Celeste barges in all decked out in DKNY black. Granny Alma's behind her clutching a big Bible. Celeste grabs my face, then holds my limp body to hers. Sonny Boy screams.

Let go, bitch.

"She hasn't spoken a word to anyone," Grace whispers to Granny, who puts her arms around my mother. "She's been catatonic."

The Back and Forth of my life, together at last.

"Drugs will do it, Gracie. And alcohol. All the drugs and liquor finally did her brain in," Granny whispers back, "drugs, alcohol, and kuro-chan derelicts," she whispers even softer, looking side-eyes at Bob.

"Welcome to Sin City," Grace says.

Casting stones.

"Knock off the silent treatment, Sonia," Celeste says, continuing to tough-love me. "You tell us what's going on in that head of yours right now, or we will all assume that this is just another one of your misguided attention-seeking attempts at pity."

Sister/Mother.
Sister/sadist.

"We should all leave Sonia alone," Joseph says. "So she can do some soul-searching on her own."

Good idea, Daddy, leave Sonia Alone.

"You know, I saw Maya Angelou on the Oprah Winfrey show, and she told Oprah that she went mute to regain power over those who hurt her," Celeste says, walking over to the mirror above the sink to fix her lipstick. "You're playing stupid mind games, Sonia, but you're only hurting yourself. We have to decide what to do about—" She pauses, looking sadly at Sonny Boy. "Him." Celeste crosses her arms. Her mirrored reflection glares at me. Nobody speaks for a long time.

Silence, sweet.

"You know, I met Maya Angelou at an Amway convention in New Orleans," Bob says all of a sudden. Grace, Granny, and Celeste stare at him, mouths agape. "She avoided the French Quarter like the plague so I read her palm, lovely palm, dipping our toes near a little dinghy docked on the Mississippi . . ."

Granny rolls her eyes. Grace shakes her head. Celeste raises her hands in Bob's face. "Are you crazy?" she screams. "My sister tried to off herself and you stand here telling us some cockamamie story about a fantastically famous poet who you never have and never will meet."

Oh, Bob.

"She's a beautiful soul," Bob whispers in my ear. "Just like you, Sonia."

"Did she tell you?" I ask him, my voice raspy. Everyone stops yakking. The power of silence, the power of words. My throat burns from the harsh scraping of tubes shoved down for the stomach pump. "Why the caged bird sings?"

Of course she did, little girl. Bob puts his hand on my face and smiles at me with utter tenderness. *Keep humming.* He walks out the door, Joseph behind him.

It is morning, cold. Bob sits with Grace at the dining room table. Joseph sips a cup of 7-Eleven coffee. Mark takes Granny on a box-hunting expedition. Celeste goes with them. She says she needs a shitload of her personal favorite cleaning products, if we expect her to do a decent job at getting back my deposit on the place.

My hair is uncombed. They've put away my rocking chair.

I'm humming a soft and slow o-bon song as I wipe a spot on the kitchen counter over and over. Bob looks up and gives me a good grin. "Take the dining room table, the lamps, the bed, and the couch," I tell him. "What else?" I ask myself, surveying the mess of an apartment. "All the dishes and glasses. You need pots and pans, right?"

"You should sell all of it," Grace deadpans. "You could use the money. Stop acting like you're some philanthropic charity."

"Mind your own business, Gracie," Joseph says.

She glares at him. "And don't sponge off of Granny when you get to Honolulu. Get a job right away even if you have to flip burgers on the graveyard shift at McDonald's."

Bob walks over to the refrigerator and gets a bottle of milk for Sonny Boy, who stirs awake on the folding mattress. "It *is* cold, I promise," Bob says to no one.

"What?" I ask.

"Isn't that so, Sonia?" Bob asks. "You made it a couple of hours ago."

I nod slowly as Bob puts the bottle in Sonny Boy's sleep-groggy mouth.

"He shouldn't be on the bottle. He's almost three," Grace complains. "It'll ruin his teeth."

Bob says nothing, and I'm so tired of Grace's shit.

"Don't waste your energy wiping down the counter," she gripes at me. "You should be resting. Celeste's just going to do it all over again with some rich-people disinfectant product."

Bob strokes Sonny Boy's hair. "He says he likes it cold—" he starts, then catches himself. He looks at Joseph.

"He said what?" Joseph asks.

"The baby's blanket is filthy," Grace interrupts. "Wash all his things before you pack them, you hear me, Sonia?"

"Right when his eyes open in the morning," Bob says to Joseph, "just stick a cold one right in. After naps too."

"Why tell him?" she snaps at Bob. "He won't be around to do it. Maybe you should help Sonia settle in to Granny's," she says to Joseph. "The rest of us work. You don't have a job to go back to in Hilo."

"Listen, Grace," Joseph says, "what's with all the hostility? Give Sonia some peace and quiet. I'm sorry, Bob, for all the imposition and thank you for—"

"Hostility," she enunciates, sarcastic and low.

"And if you put it in his mouth right when his beautiful eyes open," Bob continues, "he won't be a grouchy little champ. Can you remember that for me, Joe?"

"Are you deaf? I told you you're wasting your breath on him. You got any helpful hints on child rearing, you tell them to me," Grace yells at Bob, her hard finger poking at her own chest.

"You?" Joseph yells back. "Some mother you've been."

And then, they start in on each other:

Historically.

Chronologically.

You did This.

You did That.

You said This.

You said That.

A putrid, green rage.

Sonny Boy's face begins to contort into a cry. Bob picks him up, the bottle dangling from Sonny Boy's quivering lips, and carries him outside. I drop my dirty rag on the counter and follow him out.

Bob shares his cigarette with me. We watch as Sonny Boy moves his hand along the metal railing, back and forth in front of us. It sounds almost musical.

"You can't give the champ to your mother," Bob says.

"What?" I tell him. "Who said anything about giving him to her?"

"You did," he says, taking a deep drag.

"No, I didn't. I never said it aloud—" My breath shortens.

"What, some kind of karmic payback?" he says, handing the cigarette to me. My hand shakes as I take it from him. I want to scream. I want to cry. Sonny Boy tugs at my pants and I pick him up. He peers over the high railing. "C'mon, Sonia," Bob says at last. "You leave that to God."

"Merciful God," I tell him, stubbing the cigarette out under my angry foot.

"So much love, little girl, so much love," Bob says, his arms outstretched and wide.

Why won't the words *Fuck you, Bob*, come out of my mouth? Mute, I stand next to him who makes my son laugh, who makes my son sleep, who rises with him; who comforts me, who drinks with me, who restores me; who watches our door.

"Come with us," I ask him, so soft, it is a whisper that leaves on a cool wind.

"I can't," Bob says.

"Yes, you can," I say to him, my teeth gritted and certain.

"I won't," he says.

"Why?" I ask him. "We need you." I feel my body collapsing inside.

"You got everything you need. He made sure of that, the keeper of dreams. Dead, but now alive, hey, fancy that. Lost, but now found."

"What are you talking about?"

"I have to stay." Bob turns toward the alleyway. I follow his gaze.

There's nothing there. No window illuminated by a bare

lightbulb. No old man with age spots on a bald head folding golden origami cranes for his bizarre crane mobiles hanging from the ceiling. And in some crazed panic, I run toward the stairwell. I want a closer look. This is not possible.

"There used to be a window," I point, "over there. An old man in a white T-shirt and khakis. He leans over the ledge. He rubs his bald head. There's origami cranes everywhere." The panic rises.

"He'll be back," Bob says, walking away from me now. "Some warm night." He lights another cigarette and leans his huge body over the railing. "Pulled out all his chest feathers making some blue silk cloth. It's too cold right now."

"What?" Sonny Boy stands beside me and takes my hand in his. I hold on tight.

Jar of the open window, born on the floor of this apartment in the year of the dragon, born by way of feminine mythology, the infamous wire hanger, you came whole and pink. I put you in a jelly jar and buried you under the night-blooming jasmine tree outside of my bedroom window in Hilo. I knew I would kill you.

My Sonny Boy, beloved of Bob, born in the City of the Plain, you came to me on the day a huge man moved in next door, everyone else leaving Las Vegas. They write songs and make movies about this phenomenon. My lover called him Black Bob, the man who arrived on the day of your birth. I know now, my Sonny Boy, my Solomon:

You came, he came for a Reason.

"When is Jar coming back?" I manage to ask Bob.

"He needs the mountains, Sonia, thin air, like the Sierra Nevadas. You got mountains where you're from?" Bob asks.

"Yes." My answer is small. "Mauna Kea. Mauna Loa." I start to cry. Sonny Boy holds my hand tighter. I hold him close to me. "But I buried him. I put him in formaldehyde in a jar."

"It's all about second chances. You and your mother, dead but now alive. Lost? Not a forever condition. He needs air, Sonia, some rarefied air."

Bob takes Sonny Boy from my arms. He holds on to Bob's neck and draws back to take in all of Bob. Sonny Boy places both of his tiny hands on the plane of Bob's broad face. They resume their embrace. "Tight, tight, always a tight hug, champ," Bob says to Sonny Boy, who hums a child's song in Bob's ear.

"Why does the caged bird sing?"

"Terrible life, isn't it, Sonia? Look what God's done to you, to Sonny Boy. Blame God, right, Sonia?"

"No."

"Repeat that for me, please."

"No," I tell him again.

"It's God inside us all that keeps us singing no matter how bad it gets, ain't that so, champ?"

I hear Mark arguing with Celeste about grout and mildew. They're down the hall by the elevators. Granny Alma's complaining about the dirty boxes they found in a dumpster downtown. The fighting from inside the apartment stops.

"Little girl," Bob says, holding on to both Sonny Boy and me, "this will be goodbye. You give Mark my best." He hands my son over to me. I watch him walk toward the urine-stained stairwell. I turn toward the clamor fast approaching the apartment door. I see my father looking out of the window at Sonny Boy and me.

"Bob!"

When I look back for him, I see a window, illuminated with

golden light. White down feathers drift on an immaculate current of inner air. And golden birds in flight, a thousand and one, in a perplexing concert of wing and sound.

Sonny Boy waves a slow goodbye.

Bob.

An old man stands, his white paper wings outstretched. Tiny golden birds light on his shoulders. Standing next to him in the gloriole of that light is our Bob, beautiful Bob blowing kisses at Sonny Boy and me, radiant Bob, waving goodbye to us from the apartment across the alleyway.

12

Fate

BOB DISAPPEARED off the proverbial face of the earth.

My phone calls are answered by the telephone company's loud screech in my ear, "I'm sorry, the number you have reached is not in service at this time."

My letters to him come back *Return to Sender* with the stamped red finger pointing at Granny Alma's address in the corner of the envelope. But I write him every day, address the envelopes:

Bob
Las Vegas, Nevada

Dear Bob,

Do you believe in Destiny? That everything that happens to us, every person we encounter is never an Accident?

I miss your voice and your kind face so very much.

I Love You,
Sonia Kurisu

I was destined to listen to their bullshit. Celeste, Granny Alma, Aunties Frieda and Frannie in constant cahoots with

Aunty Effie and Grace. All of them nagging me about going back to church. All of them tsk-tsking about God's punishment on me. And all of them crawling up my ass trying to infect me with their collective horror stories on autism.

"You know what the Japanese say about bachi," Aunty Effie says. "This boy is Sonia's bachi for all the evil she did in the past. Must be a helluva lot of evil. It came back three times worse."

"She gave me so much heartache when she was living with me," Granny Alma says. "I don't want to believe in bachi, but Sonia's abortion was a horrible, horrible sin. The girl never repented. Till this day, that baby's in my prayers, and I say, 'Lord, forgive my granddaughter, for murdering that child.' "

"It's bachi on all of us," Grace says.

"Not me," Celeste says. "Excuse me, ladies, but I go to church. I pray daily. And I never ridicule the infirm or handicapped."

"Not me," Aunty Effie says. "I've always been a strong Christian. There's absolutely no reason for God to judge me in this matter."

"Not us," Aunties Frieda and Frannie say. "We've been members of Hilo Baptist since we were born. And we've been praying for Sonia for years."

"Maybe it's your bachi, Grace," Granny Alma says, "yours and Sonia's."

"Mike's secretary's nephew's son is autistic," Celeste tells them. "He started self-mutilating so they had to put him in restraints all day. And his bedroom is completely bare because he started breaking everything, bare, I tell you. They boarded up the windows, no bed, no curtains, no nothing."

"Frannie's Friday-night poker friend told her that a child gets autism if the pregnant mother abused drugs, alcohol, caffeine, or nicotine," Aunty Frieda says. "Sounds like Sonia, right? All of the above and more."

"You know how uncaring and unaware Sonia can be,"

148

Aunty Frannie snipes. "What in heaven's name made her keep this child? Not that I advocate abortion, but adoption is a viable option for unwed mothers these days. The boy might've gone to a family equipped to deal with this kind of burden."

"One of my teacher friends told me that there's a high incidence of mental retardation with autism," Aunty Frieda says. "And Down's syndrome. And attention-deficit-hyperactivity disorder. And obsessive-compulsive disorders. And Tourette's. And schizophrenia."

"Did you see *Rain Man*?" Aunty Effie asks. "Do you think Solomon's going to grow up and know how to count cards on the blackjack table?"

"And you'd be the first in line to take him with you to Las Vegas to hit your deserved million?" Grace asks, irritated.

"You should talk," Granny Alma preaches, "spending whole days and nights in those sin-ridden casinos. Maybe *you* need to go back to church, too, Gracie."

"My Hawai'i Pro-Life Coalition's co-chairman's neighbor's cousin was autistic," Celeste says. "She said he head-banged and screeched all day with no eye contact whatsoever. His parents finally opted for a total-care institution somewhere in Delaware. Out of sight, out of mind. The rest of the family is *finally* back to normal."

"Maybe he'll be some kind of savant," Granny Alma says. "I saw this autistic man on *Sally Jessy* sculpting these beautiful horses. And then this other woman on *60 Minutes* who wrote symphonies but never took a day of piano lessons. And this Japanese autistic man on KIKU-TV who played the flute in a solo concert performance just like Pan himself."

"I saw on TV that Sylvester Stallone has one of them and Father Mulcahy from *M*A*S*H*," Aunty Effie says, "and Dan Marino and Doug Flutie and Boomer Esiason too, you know."

"And Frieda's favorite writer," Aunty Frannie says, "the

one who wrote *Valley of the Dolls*, Jacqueline Susann. She had one, right?"

"And I read in *Newsweek* or maybe *Time* that Albert Einstein and Bill Gates were autistic," Grace says.

"Oh, for heaven's sake, Solomon will be severely incapacitated," Aunty Frieda says, "and Sonia needs to prepare for the worst. He's going to get older and stronger. And not so cute anymore when he's able to beat the living daylights out of her in one of those autistic rages Celeste keeps talking about."

"It's an absolutely debilitating disorder, I tell you," Aunty Frannie adds. "Let's not get her hopes up. His future is stacking canned goods at Star Market. And that's the best-case scenario. The worst-case scenario is that the boy needs to be put away in some state facility or one of those Filipino care homes."

"It's medically untreatable, right?" Celeste asks. "It's a brain disorder, right? Maybe we need to look into rigorous drug-treatment plans. I mean, they treat schizophrenics and all those other brain-damaged retarded people, right?"

"Bachi," Aunty Effie repeats.

"Love."

"Who said Love?" Granny Alma asks.

"I did," Grace says.

"You should talk," Granny says. "You certainly *loved* your girls. Celeste straight into years of therapy. And Sonia to death, well, almost."

Sweet Sonia,

A man stands on a bridge overlooking a large river in Kathmandu. Pigs grunt their bodies through the shallows as they root in the mud along the bank. Storm drains and sewer pipes spill into the river. A child plays alone, his naked body glossy from the brown waters. Beside him, two boys skip stones into the debris moving downstream.

Shanties and vegetable gardens line the banks. An old woman sells her wares along the sidewalk of this bridge where a man stands trying to avoid bicycles, rickshaws, tukutuks, taxis, cars, motor scooters, and buses.

The man searches this old part of Kathmandu for the Lord Shiva who led his people from a disastrous flood in the mountains and built a large temple and platform near this river.

The man gazes at an old government building full of the dying. They bring a body from this building, a body wrapped in a white sheet. They anoint the dead with water. The man watches them place the body on the platform strewn with pieces of wood and straw. And as the body burns, sweet Sonia, the fragrant flesh crackles, orange sparks rising in black clouds of smoke. The man sees the knees of the dead rise up, the head, still, staring at the heavens.

The char of this human body amounts to a quart of ash. They wrap the ash and bits of bone in leaves, then offer it to the river. The man sees an old woman give food in a leaf bowl to the waters. She steps into the gray cloud of human remains and bathes herself.

People along the river splash themselves with this holy water as women continue washing their laundry downstream. The naked boy who plays alone moves into the chalky waters.

The man walks along the riverbank past many beggars, those with leprosy-bandaged hands. He drops barley, rice, and a couple of rupees into their cups. He is surrounded by them, this man whom they mistake as a savior; this man who seeks his freedom in journeys to sacred mountaintops.

Tomorrow I will hire a Sherpa to take me to the highest of elevations my body can tolerate, where the air, thin and vacuous, burns my lungs. There on the Himalayas, I will offer incense and candles, food wrapped in leaves, holy water from a brown river, and ash. I will say a Buddhist prayer, a Hindu prayer, a Shinto prayer, a Muslim prayer, and a Christian prayer for Solomon. Prayers, sweet Sonia, for freedom of his spirit trapped in silence, prayers for healing.

> I love you both,
> Your father, Joseph Kurisu

You taught me a simple prayer, Daddy. Say it for Sonny Boy on your sacred mountaintop:
I believe in the sun even when it is not shining.
I believe in love even when feeling it not.
I believe in God even when He is silent.

Should I speak aloud, Bob, would you hear me?
Hum, little girl.
Bob, is that you?
Hummmmm.
I try to talk to Sonny Boy with my mind. I think he hears everything I say. The Voice that talks back to me is soft like his face.
What say he to you?
My body is broken but my spirit is whole.
What say he to you?
Listen always for my Voice.
What say he to you?
Seek the angels who walk among us.
What say he to you?
Rise from the ash.
What say he to you?
Love me.
Then love.

I don't want to believe their horror stories. How they want to frighten me back to the doors of the church that I cannot pass through. How my turning to God makes me a hopeless, hypocritical cliché. How when the storms come, they laugh as I run to the church, pray with fervor, join the choir again, and attend their Wednesday Bible studies with a glad heart.

Faith is He can. Hope is He will. No church but He.

How they lack faith. How they kill hope. How they all feel so self-righteous in their silent belief that I deserve this. How I am a faithless girl who lost her God.

A mustard seed is all you need.

And nothing is impossible unto me. How do I remember God? His words etched on the cells of my body. Reach out my hand and touch the hem of His garment in a noisy crowd of followers, teachers, apostles, the rich, the educated, the faithful.

Who touched Me?

Me, Sonia Kurisu.

And what sayeth you, child?

Child?

You are a Child of God, little girl.

Me? Sonia Kurisu?

What sayeth you, child of mine?

Heal my son. Oh God, what am I saying? My faith is transient. My faith is convenient. And I touch Your garment in desperation. On good days, Sonny Boy is a gift from You to me, a blessing. On bad days, he is the enormity of my suicide, his needs slicing my throat, my wrists, open and bloody. There is no cure for autism. What is the reason for this? God makes No Mistakes, right? Then how does God expect me to heal my son?

The Little Priest came to heal you.

What?

All of you.

How?

Unconditionally.

Why?

The Three in One.

The Trinity?

The Three, Sonia, claim your Three. No more blame.

Oh, Jar.

Speak aloud, little girl.

Bob, listen. My father's always told me what to do.

Then Do.

Dear Jar,

You need rarefied air. The kingdom of mountains, the depletion of oxygen in altitudes above the cloud line. I will take you there, I promise. I will release you, ashen you, in your flight of finding. Breathe your father into yourself.

You never ask me like the others do, "Who is my father?" This is your sadness, I know. There were many lovers at the time of your conception. Had you asked, like the others do, I would not be able to tell you. You will never know. This is my sadness.

Broken paper wings, white bloodied crane, in Japanese mythology you are endurance and long life, a thousand and one of you mean good luck, golden paper folded and hanging from the ceiling. You are the tsuru of nobility and elegance trapped in a lonely apartment in the City of the Plain.

My father has written to me a Sign. This is how I know I will set you free. But you must promise me that in your flight of finding, you will tell me, Jar, boy without father:

You discover Truth. You understand that you are *my* son. You understand that you are forever a child of God.

Love,

Your mother, Sonia Kurisu

Mark's helping Granny cook a healthy stir-fry. Aunty Frieda's certain that Sonny Boy's diet needs to be all natural, nothing canned, dyed, or preserved. She begrudgingly shops for our "fresh veggies," which are "good for active seniors *and* children with autism," at the People's Open Market or in Chinatown, except on the days she has her high-impact aerobics class.

Sonny Boy's playing with my hair. He's ticklish around his neck and on the bottoms of his feet, giggling at my touch. There is a tiny knuckle-knock on our door. *"Open door,"* he says, loud as day, so loud I wonder how no one else hears him. He frantically takes me by the hand and places it on the doorknob.

I stand there for a moment. Sonny Boy pushes my arm. I pull the door open. A rush of mountain air hums around us. There on our porch sits a white box. I look around for the deliverer. No one in sight but Sonny Boy stepping past me and into a square of afternoon light. He cocks his head to one side and looks up toward the mountains above Kalihi Valley.

The box is addressed:

Sonia Kurisu

Granny Alma's house

I hold the box in my hands. Light peers from tiny pores perforating its surface. I lift the flaps slowly, and like wings, they catch a southerly trade wind. The box opens. Inside I find:

Four yards of exquisite blue silk wrapped in fine rice paper and a note:

My Mommy,
  Promise me ash for my flight of finding. Then I will be yours.

13

Rain

LOVE TRANSFORMS OVER DISTANCE.

Like rain on hot concrete. Like rain on river water. Like rain on sun. All transformations.

The sun intensifies through steel and glass in this autism specialist's office in downtown Honolulu. Sonny Boy, she will tell Mark and me what to do. What she says is Simple:

Every movement you make, we must make. Every sound you utter, we must utter. Until we know what you know.

"And what is that?" Mark asks.

"That's for you to discover with Solomon."

"What the hell does that mean?" Mark asks. "*Discover?* Oh, please, give us some concrete answers."

Seek the angels among us.

I hear you, Sonny Boy. I look at this specialist with sea-green eyes.

"How? How? How?" Mark stammers on. "Why? Why? Why?"

"Just do," she says. Such peaceful wisdom, sea-green eyes.

We leave her office. "Sonia, you better start asking questions. You better research. You better get on the ball. You better network. You better, you better, you better. And stop trusting what all these so-called specialists tell you to do, dammit, if it doesn't align with current research and data."

Sonny Boy, I want to move like you move, sound like you sound.

As soon as we get home, Mark wants lunch first. A cup of coffee. A little *Montel.* A short nap. We need to grocery shop. Toilet paper is on sale at Longs. Then maybe a trip to Hamilton Library for some data on this method.

I will not wait.

Mark, tired after an hour with you and me, tired of jumping on the couch, screeching wild vowels, running in circles, laughing at fluttering fingers, flapping rubbery arms, rolling on the floor, opening wide mouths in front of the mirror, bouncing heads on the bed, falls exhausted onto the floor.

I don't stop.

Seven hours, I move with you. Seven hours, I sound like you. Because it is Simple:

This is the language of your body.

All of a sudden, you look at me, Sonny Boy, your frenzied world grating to a halt for you and me. I am on my knees. You place my face in your hands. I place your face in mine. And we hold on tight like Bob says with our eyes locked in mother-and-son covenant:

I made you with my body. Your father is known to me. Until the Time of your knowing, understand this:

You are mine. I will never Leave you. I will love this distance away.

Understand the motion of diminishing distance, all of you:
Jar,
You will rise from the ash.
Number One,

You will inhabit light.

#2, Turtle Boy,

I will listen, then Do.

"Then listen, Mother," #2's voice from water rises, *"they are all coming toward the Little Priest."*

I start taking art classes at the university. I see Jacob near the geology department. He doesn't see me.

#2, Turtle Boy, see him.

Your father studies the stars, galaxies full of billions of the young and hot-white, the old and red-dying, dusty spirals and ellipses; he touches the curves of the moon's canyons, mountains, canals, and plains; your father whose broad shoulders hunch, feet shuffle as he walks ahead of me, eyes cast downward, clouded yellow.

#2, his eyes want the heavens, but he is worn.

I follow him into the Institute for Astronomy, a dark building with 1950s marbled tiles chipped in shoe-blackened corners. I follow him up two flights, past bulletin boards tacked with yellowed news clippings, old photographs of scientists, astral hemispheres, and torn posters of the Mauna Kea telescopes.

#2 of the ocean, swim beside him through celestial bodies.

He steps into a dusty office. He stares at his computer with a *Star Wars* screen saver, green pennies strewn on a faded desk blotter, Jacob hunched over in an old office chair. He turns on a lint-caked fan. He doesn't see me, but says, "What can I do for you, Sonia?"

#2, you know but he doesn't; what he made with his body.

I move into the doorway of this room, see a desk covered with Styrofoam cups filled with cigarette butts, a dirty pillow on a brown rattan love seat, plate lunch boxes stacked near an overflowing trash can, stacks of books, strewn manila folders full of loose papers.

"Give me a ride home," I tell him.

I will love this distance away, Sonny Boy, transform it like rain on hot concrete, like rain on river water, like rain on sun.

The sun pushes into the hot conference room. A child's desk, a child's orange chair, a therapist, and wooden blocks wait in the middle of the room. They want to train personnel on the use of this New Method. They want to model the Method on you. Surrounding you are pychologists, psychiatrists, special-education teachers, speech therapists, occupational therapists, physical therapists, educational assistants, social workers, health-care providers. And me.

"Do this," the therapist tells you. She places an orange square on a blue rectangle.

"Do it, Sonny Boy, just do it," I tell you with my mind. "Show them you can do it." You lift your fingers slowly and place an orange square on a blue rectangle.

They whisper, take notes. Somebody claps for you. The therapist hands you a Chee·to.

"Do this," the therapist tells you. This time, an orange square on a blue rectangle on a green cube.

Again, I tell you with my mind, "Do it, just do it." You place an orange square on a blue rectangle on a green cube. The therapist hands you a Chee·to.

They shuffle papers. Smile at your compliance. This Method will work! By George, I think we've got it! More of them clap for you.

"Do this," the therapist tells you. Now, an orange square on a blue rectangle on a green cube on a red triangle.

You look for me in the midst of this humiliation, this condescension.

"They're almost done with you, Sonny Boy. They have three other autistic children lined up to finish this training session. Just do it. I'm so sorry."

Monkey.

"No."

Doggie.

"No."

"Do this," the therapist repeats.

I see it in your eyes. Then in the clench of your jaw. With one mighty swoop you hurl the blocks off of the tiny desk, get out of your chair, climb over the table, and lunge at her eyes.

You are crying uncontrollably as I carry you away. They talk loudly. Debrief. Analyze. Discuss. Conclude.

My body is broken, Mommy, but my spirit is whole. Take me home.

Home is the basement of Granny Alma's Kalihi house.

Outside, baskets of hanging ferns line the rafters of her porch; in her yard, red and pink torch ginger, yellows and whites, a mango tree, a mountain apple tree, avocado, delicate palapalai, wild impatiens, healthy anthurium, and purple heather. She waters and weeds daily, Sonny Boy following her in his garden boots with a bucket full of his collection of tiny rocks.

Jacob steps out of the car. Sonny Boy wanders the herb garden, following the path of volcanic river rocks that Mark laid for Granny one Sunday afternoon. I call Sonny Boy's name. He approaches us with a handful of lemon mint. Jacob reaches his hand for Sonny Boy. I expect him to turn and run. Then Jacob puts his hand on Sonny Boy's face. No words. Sonny Boy tilts his head and rests himself in a stranger's palm. The lemon mint falls to the ground.

"I better go," Jacob says without a word of goodbye.

"We should've called Jacob's office or left a message with the astronomy department's secretary," Mark tells me. He points me toward some empty stools at the bar. "Why do all these sleazy bars have red interiors?"

"Your mother wanted him to get the word today," I remind him.

"And how come he doesn't have a phone in his apartment? I tell you, he's going over the edge. He looked terrible, Sonia, that day he dropped you off. And I mean, everybody has a goddamn telephone, for chrissakes."

A couple of women with green tassels on their tits and G-string panties circle the room. "Oh, I get it," I whisper to Mark. "Green tassels for Club Wizard of Oz. So clever, these Koreans."

"Shhh," Mark says to me. I sit next to him at the bar. I don't see Jacob. A tit-tasseled woman slides onto the bar stool next to Mark. He greets her with his patented fake smile.

"How bad is Aunty Frannie?" I ask him.

"Bad enough. She's moving in with my mother, for now, so she can shuttle her around for all those tests. Aunty Frannie refuses to stay with Jacob in that little shithole of a roach-infested apartment by the university."

"He looks like a fucking mess," I tell Mark.

"He's smoking big-time, you know," Mark says, like he knows some big secret that I don't.

"What? Just tell me what he's doing." I act as though I couldn't care less. Mark reads me and smirks.

"Ice," he says at last. "Every day. He doesn't even bother to hide the shit every time I go over. That's why he looks like the return of the living dead. And can't finish his Ph.D."

"I feel sorry for him."

"Stop it, Sonia, dammit, just stop it. Let him hit rock bottom. Alone. Short of that, we'd just be enabling his habit. Enough. I've had enough of you and your—" Mark stops and changes the subject. "So many of my boys, brothers, uncles, sisters, aunties, cousins, and parents smoke that shit. They can pretty much make it in their kitchen. So what? You plan on saving all of them, too?"

"Drinkee?" the waitress asks. "Buy me?"

"Man, I hate these places," Mark complains. "Two Coors Lights," he says, reaching into his pocket for money. "You saw that, Sonia? She had her hand on my thigh."

"Good for you," I tell him. "Why didn't you tell her, 'Drinkee only if you suckee my dickee.' "

"Very funny. That would be drinkee and another hundred. Past those marvelous bamboo curtains over there. No thanks."

I look around the dark room. A fat businessman sits at the edge of a small stage as a girl spreads her legs, unfolding wet labial lips in front of his sweaty face. The girl rolls over, then lifts her crotch as she masturbates for the grunt next to the large speakers. She lets a haole worm smell her hands then moves his face toward her large pink nipples. An unshaven local guy puts his arms around two girls in his booth.

Mark rolls his eyes and scowls. "Jacob got a master's in astronomy and he's bartending in this shitty Korean bar. What a loser. Where is he?" Mark swivels his head and scans the dark room. "Nowhere to be found. Let's go. We can leave a note on his apartment door." I don't move. "Let's go," Mark repeats. "Sonny Boy might wake up and pull a fit on Granny."

"Hey, Cindy," I call to the waitress who's been whispering

and laughing with another slut whenever I look at her, glaring at me up and down with a sneer.

"My name not Cindy."

"Whatever. Where's Jacob Gomes?"

"He no come in till eleben," she says, irritated and sassy.

"Eleven?" Mark says, grabbing my elbow. "How's them hours? C'mon—"

"Give me a beautiful, Coke back, Cindy," I tell her.

"I said my name not Cindy."

"Well, listen, Cindy, you want a good tip tonight from Uncle Markie here, then when I call you Cindy, you answer. Understand?" The girl snubs me and walks away.

"Why are you being such an asshole?" Mark asks.

"You wear green tassels on your tits and walk around in a G-string, you pretty much deserve no dignity even from a lowly state worker."

"Did you call Sonny Boy's social worker for the appointment with that new psychologist?" Mark asks. "I had a couple of messages in my box at school. And she came by my office today. You better get in touch with her right away."

"Stop being such a nag," I tell him, taking a deep drink from the snifter. "I'll call on Monday, no biggie. Sonny Boy and me, we've been—"

"No biggie? Sonia, you idiot, we have to get maximum services for Sonny Boy. These social workers have a hundred and twenty cases each. And the psychologist's booked for two months. I told you to set an appointment right away. And don't call me a nag. You think they worry about you?"

"Eh, fuck you, okay, Mark. Don't you ever call me an idiot."

"He's your son," he says matter-of-factly.

"And you truly believe that I don't know that, motherfucker?" I get up and head toward the rest-room door.

"You could've fooled me," Mark snipes.

163

"What? You know, this is fucking hard shit for me, Mark. You and that fucking Celeste. And Grace. And your goddamn mother. All full of lip."

"Lip? Me? You better wake up, Sonia, 'cause in the end, he's your son," he repeats. "Nobody's going to save him but you."

"Me? Fuck you." I want to cry. I'm trying so hard, but everything I do or say is never enough for Mark.

"And try not to ruin your makeup," he says as I walk away. "Jacob's due in at eleven."

"What's that supposed to mean?"

"You figure it out," he says. "You're no idiot, right? From the frying pan right into the fire," he mutters. "Nag, my ass."

Cindy slides onto my vacated bar stool. "I dance next song for you. You put dollar in here," she says, pulling open the elastic of her G-string. She slips her hand inside herself, turns, and looks right at me.

Mark pulls a dollar from his stack of folded bills and tucks one in. I stalk off toward the deck in back that overlooks the swampy canal. A fish turns in the darkness of the water's scum. A muddy smell drifts in the wet air.

I watch the cherry of a cigarette burn then fade in the darkness in front of me. "Always Mister Morality, good ol' boy-san, that's our Markie," a voice begins. "Don't fight it."

"Jacob?"

"Sonia," he says as he steps into the dim light. He looks old, but beautiful and tall. He kisses my forehead. I put my arms around him. He's wet. "I got caught in the rain," he starts, "yeah, the rain."

"Yeah *rain*, right." We stand there for a moment of unbearable silence. "Thanks for the ride, you know, the other day."

"Small talk? You? Sonia Kurisu? C'mon," he laughs. "You got no time, remember? Come here. Let me show you something." I step toward Jacob, who looks up past the banyan tree overhanging the canal, the sky black with white clouds. "Look," he says softly, the chirp of a gecko, the tinkle of leaves, rain, his eyes scanning the night sky.

"Sliver of moon," I tell him. Slowly, he takes my hand in his. He's dripping with sweat. "Must've been some real good shit, Jacob. Or real bad."

"A dreary life," he answers. He turns toward the kitchen. "Sliver of moon," he whispers as he disappears, his shadow lingering in the yellow light from the back door of Club Wizard of Oz.

I will. I will love this distance away, know the language of rain on hot concrete, rain on river water, rain on sun.

The sun's yellow light remains outside of rooms with doctors and nurses holding you down for three arduously slow vials of blood. I cannot even look into your eyes as the needle moves into your vein. I don't even know why they need the violence of this blood work.

He is your son.

The neurologist finds no Fragile-X gene, so no mental retardation. The allergist finds nothing. The auditory-test technician indicates nothing's wrong. The psychiatrist finds no depression.

He is your son.

The pediatrician weighs and measures monthly. I allow his vaccinations to flood your body with millions of tainted antigens. It takes three of us to hold you down.

He is your son.

Should we do an MRI?

Your son.

A CAT scan?

Your son.

More blood. More blood.

Mine.

Think fast, Sonia, more blood? More tests? They always conclude: There is nothing wrong with your son. Physically, at least.

Aunty Frannie needs a quadruple bypass. Aunty Frieda's in constant, hand-wringing, dramatic distress. Aunty Effie arrives from Hilo. Granny Alma cooks dinner for everybody on hospital watch. Celeste delivers dinner after her nonprofit or volunteer work, Heather's soccer, and Tiffany's ballet. Mark takes Sonny Boy to the hospital with him if I have class. Jacob sees me at the bus stop near the Buddhist Center on University Avenue. He pulls over. I get in.

"Hey," he says, flicking cigarette ash out the window.

"Hey yourself," I tell him. He pats my thigh.

"Where you headed?" he asks.

"To the hospital," I tell him.

"Good. That's good."

"You going?" I ask.

"Somebody stole it," he says, passing the cigarette to me, his hand shaking.

"What?" I ask as I take a couple of drags, then pass it back to him.

"My shit, man. All my shit right out of my fucking apartment."

"Good," I tell him. "That's good."

It's late when Jacob arrives at Aunty Frannie's room with a bouquet of red Mylar balloons and a potted plant. He kisses Aunty Frannie.

"Where were you?" she rasps.

"Fiftieth State Fair," he answers. Aunty Frieda clucks her tongue at him disapprovingly.

"Jacob," Aunty Frannie begins. She's so tired.

"This haole grad assistant's been nagging me to take her and—oh, forget it." He stops. "Sorry," he says sarcastically, holding out his arms to the entire room. He ties the bouquet of balloons to the nightstand, then looks at Sonny Boy sleeping on a rollaway bed. He takes one and ties it to his tired finger. "I brought this for you," he says, holding the potted plant to me.

"Night-blooming jasmine?"

"I won it—"

"Nah, stole it," we mutter together. He lifts one eyebrow at me and smiles. Mark sighs. Loudly.

Jacob walks around the room. "Take this orchid home, Celeste. Take this fern, Aunty Alma. And Aunty Frieda, all of these fucking violets."

"Jacob!" Aunty Frannie scolds.

"They're from all of our friends," Aunty Frieda finishes. "And Aunty Grace sent the orchids." She shoots a see-what-I-mean-about-your-good-for-nothing-cousin look at Mark, who nods his judgmental head in agreement.

"I don't want any potted plants in this room, you hear me, Grandma?" he says to Aunty Effie. "Anybody who sends my mother potted plants wants her to take root and stay here. And she's not staying here, you hear me?" He places his face in his hands and rests himself on his mother's belly. I put my hands on his back.

"Let's go, Sonia," Mark says, taking my elbow in his hand. He lifts Sonny Boy, who sleeps on his shoulder. The red balloon bobs on a draft of air-conditioning. Mark unties it from his finger and releases it. I watch the balloon drift along the ceiling. "Let's go," he says again, this time stern and hard. I turn and follow him out the door.

Distance transforms love. Diminishing distance. You are my son. You and I have shared a heartbeat within a body. You heard the sound of my voice through water, muscle, membrane, and skin. And I, the sound of your voice, a childlike lowing, inside my body then inside my head, the spoken words of your silence.

The Toddler class for Children with Disabilities plans an excursion to the beach. We'll go on a little picnic to enhance our social skills, community learning, bus etiquette, communication skills, et cetera, et cetera, et cetera, killing many therapeutic birds with one stone.

I tell the speech therapist, the occupational therapist, the physical therapist that you will want to swim. They won't be able to keep you away from the water, the feel of wet sand under your bare feet.

"Oh, he can play in the sand," a therapist says with a smile.

You will want the cool water on your skin, the taste of salt water in your mouth.

"Oh, he can't go in the water. Liability issues," a therapist says with a frown.

"Maybe I should keep him home," I tell her.

"But he needs social skills, community learning, bus etiquette, and communication skills," a therapist says with pursed lips. That and all of the et cetera, et cetera, et cetera.

"Then I'd better come along," I insist.

"Oh, he needs to be more independent," a therapist says, shaking her head at me.

"He won't understand why he can't go in the water," I tell her.

"Then this will foster communication skills," a therapist says impatiently.

I force them to let me go along. There is a grassy hill where they spread their blankets.

"We'll just keep him far away from the water," a therapist recommends.

You smell the ocean's mist, taste it in your mouth, feel the trades on your face, then you move toward the sound of waves. "Stop, Sonny Boy, stop." You run from me. "Stop, please, stop." None of the other children run from the therapists.

There is a stone wall. There is a long drop to waves swelling and smashing against its side. "You cannot go in the water," I say with my mind as I chase you. "You cannot go in the water. You cannot go in the water." I am frantic. I should've kept you home. I told them this would happen. You run faster. "Sonny Boy, listen," I say as I catch you by the arm, expecting a struggle of epic proportion, "you cannot go in the water."

You stop. You sit on the wall. You begin to cry. "You cannot go in, you cannot go in," I repeat in my mind, a mantra begging for your compliance. You listen to the waves, breathe deeply, watch the horizon, the movement of a seabird overhead. You calm yourself. Still, I expect you to jump. "You cannot go in, Sonny Boy."

"Get out of my head," you tell me, loud as day, the spoken words inside my head.

And I comply.

Boy from inside me, boy my body made, you amaze me. We sit on this wall together and watch the incoming swells, a gray sea drift, mighty whitecaps, the churn of a murky riptide, you and I in a reverent silence.

With rain on hot concrete comes a steamy humidity.

With rain on the Kalihi stream comes a raging brown torrent.

With rain on sun comes a momentary rainbow.

It's raining again. I need to get home. Granny Alma needs to get to work.

I walk up Granny Alma's long driveway lined with tropicals all in bloom, the smell of this house in the valley intense and sweet. Jacob's car sits in the garage. Granny opens the downstairs door for me.

"Come, quick," she says. "Look at this." I step into the room. "I can't believe it, Sonia," she says, putting her arm around me.

Sonny Boy sits cross-legged in front of a huge aquarium. His hands are folded on his lap. Jacob sits cross-legged next to him, his finger pointing.

"Turtle," Jacob says softly.

"Tur-to," Sonny Boy repeats.

No hands flapping madly, no screeching, no fingers in his ears to eliminate overstim, no tantrums, the jumping of a nervous system triggering rapid and illogical neurons.

Orange clown fish move in and out of filigreed black coral; a tiny balloon fish stops to examine the eyes outside of the glass; a butterfly fish reaches its probing snout into a sea stone's barnacled crevice. The water's fluent trickling is repetitive and soothing.

Jacob puts on the fluorescent light. Sonny Boy's eyes widen, reflected in glass. Granny Alma wipes tears from her eyes, reflected in glass. "He's talking. To *Jacob*. I have to go," she says as she kisses Jacob on the top of his head. "Take the stew in the Crock-Pot to the hospital, you hear me, Sonia? Celeste has a church-board meeting tonight." She kisses Sonny Boy's face.

"Fish," Jacob points, oblivious to Granny's kiss, her commanding voice, her tears, her leaving, the shut of the door.

"Pish," Sonny Boy repeats.

I sit beside Jacob. "Why?"

He looks at me soft, then hard. "Fucker stole my shit," he says at last. "All my cash, all my shit," he repeats. "So I did what I had to do. Yup, motherfucker's got nothing now and got his ass kicked, too. But this, I told him, I could use this." He stares into the aquarium.

I have nothing to say. I watch my son, awestruck by the movement of fin in water, the glide of colors, a tidal meandering in glass, the oceanic sound of bubbles, the briny smell of a reef. "Then, why here?" I ask.

"Don't get me wrong, okay? My place is too fucking small." He puts his hand on Sonny Boy's back and rubs him slowly.

"I can't upkeep a saltwater tank," I whisper. "The system's so delicate. The whole thing might crash. And then what?" I look at Sonny Boy and imagine a Richter-scale-ten tantrum over dead fish on the surface of murky water.

"Champ and me will take care of it," he says.

"What did you call him?"

"We'll get seawater from the Waikīkī Aquarium every weekend. Catch a manini or two while we're there. No crashing allowed, right, champ?"

#2, Turtle Boy, smiles, his reflection behind me. I turn quickly, but he is gone. Sonny Boy stares at the balloon fish's hummingbird fins fluttering.

"Jacob. The baby, the boy, I—"

"Shut up, Sonia. Now listen," he says, "I already bought the scuba man, you know, the one you connect to the air pump?" I nod. "And the sea chest opens."

"It's full of jewels," I tell him. He nods slowly.

"Jacob—"

Mark pulls open the door. "Hey," he says to Jacob. "We better get ready to go to the hospital," he says abruptly to me.

"I better go," Jacob says without a word of goodbye. Sonny Boy's eyes follow him across the room.

I stand at the open door and watch Jacob's car pull away. Brisk trade winds disperse dying yellow leaves from the treetops. And inside this valley, it has rained on sun.

◆ 14 ◆

Blood

AND ONE MORNING WHEN I WAKE, I take a hold of what is Mine. Sonny Boy sleeps beside me. It is not just another day. This Life. Every second, every minute, every hour since the utterance of his diagnosis, Time ticking against him, Time ticking against me. Time is Death. Death is Time.

This Life is all about one moment that changes us forever. Just one, each of us. The door opens. We choose. We never come round again.

This is my story. Sonia Kurisu. Bred to believe in the power of Implication:

Blame my mother. She abandoned me.

Blame my father. He abandoned me.

Blame Celeste. She mothered me to death.

Blame Granny Alma.

Blame Reaganomics.

Blame pop culture.

Blame Prozac.

Blame Smirnoff.

Blame all of this spiraling dysfunction.

Blame God.

Find comfort in the Victim.

I am *not* a Victim to this Life.

Steadfast defiance, this time of now comes from a place I cannot name. But I know that every event, every person, every circumstance in this Life has brought me to the words:

"Your son is autistic."

At first, the words unhinge me. I try to Exit, stage left. But God escorts me back.

And I come back knowing.

I am the Hero of this Life.

And fuck anybody and everybody who thinks otherwise.

Because one morning when I wake, I look at my son asleep beside me. Face of the cherubim, Thorn of my side, Reason for being here, Reason for choosing me, all of my moments colliding into this one of sun through dirty curtains from Sears, the slow crowing of a neighbor's rooster, pit bulls barking and yanking on rusty chains, the screeching of the city bus around a hairpin turn. Perfect Imperfection. Complete Incompleteness:

You and I are Home. Not in a house full of beds and chairs, dishes and toothbrushes, but in undeniable covenant. Home is the possibility of return.

The door opens. Celeste's six-year-old arrives on my doorstep. She comes in with a McDonald's breakfast and a pink Barbie backpack.

"Watch Heather for me, Sonia," Celeste says, all out of breath, as she pushes Heather's back into the house. "I have a meeting with the editors of Bamboo Ridge Press." She pauses and stares at me. "Yes, another of my spirit-of-volunteerism nonprofits. Got a problem with my philanthropy?"

"No. I mean, fuck, Celeste, what's with the hostility? Get a grip . . ." I look at her, confused for a moment. I watch Heather take her breakfast and backpack into my bedroom. She crawls under the covers and snuggles with a sleeping Sonny Boy. She pats his head and he stirs, turning himself in to her warm body.

"I have been utterly philanthropic with Solomon," Celeste continues, a hair with my name on it obviously up her ass. "Haven't I secured services with the department of health *and* the school system for him? I personally interviewed therapists, doctors, teachers, and specialists. And with all my connections in this town, and it's all because of my extensive commitment to my many charities, I've pulled every proverbial string for Solomon's treatment plan."

"I'll take care of Heather, no problem," I tell her. "Today, tomorrow, every day. You don't have to feel so guilty. You're justifying—"

"You shut your smart mouth, Sonia. I'm a damn good mother."

I sigh deeply. Joseph and Grace pulse in my sister's guilty bones. A good mother, her physical and emotional absences with her own daughters, she's feeling it and knowing it.

"A damn good mother," she repeats. Celeste peers into the bedroom. "You listen to Mommy. Be nice to Solomon, you hear me, Heather?" she whispers. "Remember, he's you-know-what."

"Artistic," she says.

"Fuck you, Celeste." I roll my eyes at her.

"Better they know the truth," she tells me. Celeste follows me into the kitchen and pours herself a cup of coffee. "When's the old fart due in?" she asks. "I bet he found some miracle herbal cure for autism in Nepal that'll only give Solomon a bad case of diarrhea." She laughs uncomfortably at her own joke.

"Joseph came in last night at around three. Mark went to pick him up. Shh, they're asleep in the other room. And I am just about ready to believe anything anybody tells me about a cure."

"Whatever," Celeste says, dismissing me. "Typical you turning to every feel-good quick fix that comes your way. Always taking the easiest, most convenient way out, for yourself, that is. Got any Equal?"

"Nobody's totally cured autism with conventional treatments. Why not believe in the soft sciences? Did you hear what I said?"

"Yes, I heard you. A cure? Your cure? Joseph's cure?" She looks into the fridge and pours skim milk into her mug. "Did you hear me, Sonia? The soft sciences are full of nonsense. There's no cure other than early-intervention programs. And maybe a heavy psychopharmacologic regimen. That's what Solomon's psychiatrist, the best in town, mind you, alluded to when I ran into him at the Pacific Club. There's no cure."

"There is," I tell her.

"Is not. The end."

"The beginning . . ." I say.

"Oh, stop."

The door to my bedroom closes slowly.

I close my eyes. I remember the way Granny Alma taught me to pray as a little girl. "Never say, 'If You are God,' " she often said. "You pray, Sonia, Because You are God."

If You are God, You can lead me home.

No.

Because You are God, lead me home.

Because You are God, wake me at six-twenty tomorrow morning.

Child of God, I prayed with ease. I love Thee, Lord Jesus.

Child of God, I was inherently religious with innocent

belief. I had only one prayer. "*Because* You are God, take me home."

Nothing happened, days, months, years.

This happened, the formation of belief:

I am Alone in this world. No one can be trusted. Death lives in every breathless moment. I will not hurt. And Love. Love has only caused me hurt. They faded, my father, my mother, from my moment to moment, my breath to breath. And so faded my desire for God.

But You answered my prayer, because You are God.

It happens, years later.

We come home.

"Because You are God," I whisper.

"What?" Celeste says. "Now you made me burn my tongue. I'm not God. I hate when you get like this, Sonia, all cryptic like that father of yours."

"Heal my son."

"A healing? *If* He answers the prayers of the unrepentant," Celeste says, dipping a cream cracker into her mug. "He won't answer you, Sonia. You've fallen from grace. That's why Aunty Effie's been planting and replanting the Sonia Kurisu prayer tree for years now. And the rest of us have been fertilizing that damn tree. But I told them all myself, this time, we're not praying for a miracle."

"He came for all of us," I tell her. "And I will find a cure."

She laughs. "From denial to attempted suicide to outright delusion. You're a real work of art, Sonia. But like I said, this is typical you. You'll get tired of all this vigilante, champion, mother-of-the-affirmed crap. And then what? A return to the cop-out—alcohol, drugs, sex, your *art* in its varied but obviously amateurish forms. It's a pattern for you. Don't you see it? We do, and we're already preparing for the worst."

Sister/sadist.

"What the fuck are you talking about?"

"We know that one of us will eventually have to take him. Me, Granny Alma, or Grace."

"Do you pray for me?" I ask her. "Does God answer *your* prayers?"

She stares at me, hard, nods slowly, sucks her teeth, shaking her sarcastic head at me.

"Then you know," I tell her, my words choking in my throat, "that I am——"

"You are *what?*" she says, poking me in my chest, daring me to defy her Christianity.

"The Prodigal."

Celeste laughs, again. "Aren't we all," she says, rinsing her mug in the sink. "So should we kill the fatted calf?" She wipes her hands on a kitchen towel and gets ready to leave.

"I would. For Joseph. For Grace. For Sonny Boy. For you. You told me when Grace sent us to Honolulu that you and I are closer in blood than anyone else in this family."

"I *never* said that. I belong to the family of God," she says. "You listen carefully, Sonia. Granny told me a long time ago, if my own flesh-and-blood Father cannot take care of me, then let my heavenly Father take his place. That's why I'm not the bloody mess that you are." She places her finger under her eye to stop a tear from wrecking her makeup. "I am a child of God."

"And so am I."

Heather leads Sonny Boy by the hand out of the bedroom. She places bits of her breakfast in his mouth. She goes back into the bedroom and brings out a blanket that she puts on the kitchen floor. She empties her backpack of Barbie toys. She opens a margarine container and pours plastic Barbie shoes onto Sonny Boy's open palms. The falling of colors and textures makes a tinkling sound. He looks at her. She puts a bit of English muffin and cheese in his mouth. They put the shoes back in the container and pour them out again and again. They finish her breakfast. All without words.

Joseph gets up at noon. Sonny Boy watches a Disney tape. Heather draws beside him, their bodies touching. She hasn't spoken a word all day. Joseph kisses her on the head, and she acknowledges him with a small smile.

"The windows on your house look like eyes, Heather," he says. "And your door with the little doorknob looks like a mouth." She pauses for a brief moment. "When I was a little boy, I drew the very same house with the rooftop pointing to the sun. And the very same sun with yellow spikes."

"You want some coffee, Daddy?" I ask, getting up off the floor.

"And I like your green tree," he continues. "I used to think it looked like a mango tree, that tree that I drew over and over. But I always put apples on my trees." He is quiet for a long time. "Do you know this house?" Joseph asks me.

I nod.

"Do you?" he says, demanding my attention.

"I know this house," I tell him. "I drew it, too, over and over," I tell him, annoyed.

"You drew it for me on that card you sent to Kyushu," he says. "Or was it Celeste? You were so little. You drew a house you had only seen in picture books. Why, Sonia?"

I want to follow him, but as usual, I don't know where he's going.

"Oh, never mind," he says, irritated at me.

"I drew it," I tell him with a learned, fierce monotone. "And then I fucking sent it to you."

I never knew that he received those letters addressed in a child's scrawl:

Joseph Kurisu

JAPAN

Grace must've sent the letters. My mother addressed and sent my letters?

Like the letters I sent to Santa:

Santa Claus

NORTH POLE

Grace read my letters. And then she found the money for my presents.

Or the letters I send to Bob:

Bob

LAS VEGAS

Grace. God's.

"Your chimney's nice," Joseph says to Heather. He hands her a gray crayon and she draws a curlicue line of smoke. "No one had a chimney in our plantation camp," he whispers to me. "And the birds. I drew them with a wide black M just like that. Crows, I told myself, even if I had never seen the 'alala in these skies."

Mark hands Joseph a cup of hot coffee.

"It all makes sense, doesn't it, Sonia?" he asks me. I sigh loudly and shrug my shoulders.

"When I was at Aunty Teruko's in Ann Arbor, I saw this house," he says, pointing to Heather's drawing. "But we don't have houses like this here. Why did *I*, why did *you*, why does *she* draw this fucking house?"

Heather turns to look at my father. He looks at me. "You need to stop, Daddy," I tell him.

"This isn't our house," he says loudly, "but it's all we saw in their damn picture books. My house wasn't good enough. I never once drew the house I lived in because if I drew this house enough times, maybe it could all happen to me." My father rests his face in his hands.

"Oh, Daddy," I mutter.

I get up and walk toward the window. The rain, a filament of dusty mist, sprays through the jalousies. I swipe my finger over the dirty screen and close the mouth of glass.

"He *is* artistic," I hear Heather whispering to Joseph. I turn to face them. They are the first words she has spoken all day. We all watch as Sonny Boy takes the black crayon to Heather's house. With wide, bold circles, he covers the images, his jaw clenched, eyes focused. "Sonny Boy told me, 'This is not our house,' Grandpa," Heather whispers even more softly. My father cries into his hands.

"How did he tell you that?" I ask her.

"He told it to me," she says, unafraid and certain, "in here." She places her finger on her forehead.

"How?" I ask again.

"With words," she says. Sonny Boy stops, looks briefly at Heather, then puts the crayon down. She takes him by the hand and they sit in front of the aquarium, silent boy and silent girl.

Jacob drops by. He takes his cold-pack of Budweiser to the fridge. He hands one to Joseph, who sits on Mark's secondhand recliner. "Jacob Gomes," he says, his hand extended to my father.

"Frannie's boy?" Joseph asks. "You're a man?"

"Sometimes," Mark mutters. I nudge him hard.

"You want one?" he asks Mark and me. I nod. He passes his open can to me and gets up for another one.

Celeste calls on her cell phone, the static louder than her voice. I step out onto the porch and Jacob follows me. "Hey, Sonia, do me a favor," she says. "Go get Tiffany, right now, at the Art Academy. She doesn't like to be kept waiting. My meeting's running late and Mike's out in Waimānalo."

"Mark's taking Claire Yee grocery shopping in a little while. I won't have a car."

"Make him get Tiffie first, I mean it, Sonia. And I'll bring some Thai food for dinner, I promise."

"For all of us? Joseph, me, you, Tiffany, Heather, Sonny Boy, Mark," I tell her, "and Jacob?"

"What's he doing there?"

"He dropped over."

"Oh?"

"Oh, what?"

"Ask him to get Tiffany for me," she says, pausing. "He drives that crappy old Tercel without AC, doesn't he?"

"Yeah, so?"

"Tiffie's going to be so embarrassed to get in the car in front of all her Punahou friends. I know, park by Thomas Square behind the big banyan tree, and you run out to get her."

I place my hand over the receiver. "Can you take me to get Celeste's asshole princess at the Art Academy?" Jacob nods while taking a swig of his beer.

"Okay," I tell her.

"Thank you, thank you, thank you," she bubbles. "I've got dinner, don't worry. I'm so Japanesy in that way. Put me down to head the marketing plan, Wing Tek," she says to someone there with her. "Ta-ta, Sonia."

Jacob sits next to me on the steps. We watch Heather and Sonny Boy gathering smooth stones in the patch of yellow ginger. "So who's Claire Yee?" he asks.

"Some rich Chinese girl he met in grad school at UNLV. She just moved to Honolulu. She followed him here, I think."

"And you don't care?"

"Why should I?"

"You mean, you and Markie aren't—"

"No."

"Then why does he act so possessive?"

"Because he loves a fuck-up."

Jacob laughs. "But that's why he hates me." His eyes follow Sonny Boy in the yard. Heather leads him toward us, their hands full of yellow ginger. They throw them at our feet, Sonny Boy flapping madly at the falling of petals.

"You know what," Jacob says, a small smile at Sonny Boy, "you're not as fucked up as—" He puts his hand on my leg, a generous warmth in his stroke.

"Stay," I tell him, "for dinner."

He looks at me, and then at Heather and Sonny Boy picking up the flowers to throw them on the steps again. He nods, then goes inside to get another beer.

Celeste's late with dinner, all abluster with Styrofoam food containers spread over the kitchen counter. "Paper plates, paper plates," she says as she flings our cupboards open. "Tiffie, get over here and make a plate for yourself and your sister, now!"

Tiffany's cranky. Jacob had pulled up to the curb outside the Art Academy, bopped his horn, and yelled for her to get in the car. She pulls her headphones out of her ears. "Tiffie do this, Tiffie do that. Heather, make your own plate. Heather!" she yells.

"She's taking a bath with Sonny Boy," I tell her, leaning my body out of the bathroom door.

Tiffany stomps over. "Heather, Mommy said to make your plate right now." Heather doesn't answer. She spills water from an Evian bottle onto Sonny Boy's shoulders. "Heather, I'm talking to you!"

Sonny Boy looks at Tiffany's face and starts screaming. He hits the water, throws his toys, the shampoo, the soap. An autistic rage. He gets out of the tub and hurls himself onto the wet floor, slipping, then hitting his elbow hard on the linoleum. He screams louder, runs naked and wet to the living room, pauses to look at Mark, then runs to Jacob.

"C'mon, champ," he says, leading him toward the bathroom, "let's wipe you down and get some clothes on you."

Mark gets up. "I'll do it," he says, his hand on Jacob's shoulder.

"All yours," Jacob says, his hands raised in surrender.

"That's right," Mark mutters. Sonny Boy's still wailing, his hands covering his ears. "He's all mine."

I get Heather out of the tub. She's covered with bubbles but wipes herself down. Celeste comes rushing into the bathroom. "What's the matter with Solomon?" she asks Heather.

"Nothing," Heather answers. "Noise. Too much Tiffie noise."

Mark makes Thai coffee after dinner. It's quiet at last, Heather and Sonny Boy watching television in the bedroom, and Tiffany sulking with her CDs plugged into her head.

"I climbed a mountain," Joseph says. He leans back in Mark's secondhand recliner and takes a sip from his mug. He takes in the flavor and closes his eyes. He wears no shirt. There are red beauty marks, tiny keloids, dotting his chest. Connect the dots numerically. A picture. A map.

Jacob sits down next to me. He lights a cigarette, takes a couple of drags, and passes it to me.

"Rupees for the tuktuk, rupees for a decent walking stick, rupees for a Sherpa, rupees for a guide, a handkerchief, water, candles, matches, food, a toilet. What was the mountain about?" he asks.

"So what's it about, Joseph?" I ask. Celeste's cleaning up in the kitchen, bitching on and on to Mark.

"Consumerism?" Jacob asks.

"God," Joseph responds.

"God?" Celeste asks, standing behind Joseph. She laughs, mean. "All of those years in all of those filthy boulevards of the world, you were searching for God? You're full of crap, Joseph."

"And now you sound just like your mother."

"And that's supposed to hurt me? Dessert, anyone?" she snarls.

Joseph reaches his hand toward Sonny Boy when he wanders into the room. "C'mere, little guy," he coaxes. Sonny Boy dodges him and leaves for the kitchen. My father shrugs as though he's tried to reach out to his grandson but to no avail.

"We need to go toward *him*," I tell Joseph.

Joseph ignores me. "They told me God was there," he continues. "I stood in the middle of the square. Three wise men, orange-clad, approach me. They are yogis, I am sure. I give one fifty rupees—a blessing for my grandson; the next twenty—a blessing for my daughters and granddaughters; and the third ten—a blessing of small measure for me. They begin to argue over the money. A man in white tells me to disregard the street beggars. They were beggars, Sonia."

"Oh, please, Joseph," Celeste says, passing a plate of sweet custard pie to Jacob. "All your searching for false spirituality makes you such an easy target for all the con men of the world. What a foolish man."

"God," Joseph mutters.

"He's Aunty Effie's God, remember, Daddy?" I ask him. "You still looking for true freedom on all those mountaintops, maybe?"

"How do you remember all of the things I've said?" he asks, leaning forward now.

"Etched on the cells of my body," I tell him.

"And that's the problem with the both of you," Celeste says, sitting down at last. "It's biblical. You should read the Word every now and again. Both of you denied your eyes nothing they desired, refused your heart no pleasure. What futility it all was. What chasing after the wind. I've just quoted Ecclesiastes, mind you. And look at you now. Lost as ever. This whole conversation's making me nauseated."

"I'm here now."

"There's your prodigal, Sonia," Celeste laughs. "Go kill the fatted cow, but count me out. I have a heavenly Father. He's all I need. You," she says, pointing at Joseph, "are nothing to me."

"Celeste?" Mark says, calling to her from the kitchen. I hear them whispering, sibilant and angry. Jacob picks up Sonny Boy when he wanders past him, his tiny fingers lingering over Jacob's legs. They step out onto the porch. I listen to Jacob softly naming the stars, the moon. Joseph follows them out.

"What's going on?" I ask.

"Heather decided to stop speaking," Mark says.

"What?" I ask. "When did she tell you this?"

"Just now," he says.

"Maybe it's not such a bad thing," I say softly.

"What? Dammit, Sonia," Celeste yells. "It would be a bad thing if she were your child, now wouldn't it?"

"It's why they get along so well," Mark explains to Celeste. "She's not in his face bombarding him with audio confusion."

"So it's a good thing, right?" I ask. "I mean, we can explain to her that she can talk when she's with everyone else, right?"

"So that my daughter has decided to be an elective mute sits perfectly well with you, Sonia," Celeste yells even louder. "So long as your son's autism is served, the hell with my daughter, right? She'll be in therapy for years, dammit."

"There's something about Heather that helps Sonny Boy—" I start.

"Like there was something about you and all of those insane voices? Well, that helped no one," Celeste snipes. "She's going to talk if I have to pry the words right out of her mouth. Heather, you come here right now. Heather!" Celeste starts searching around the house for her daughter.

"Heather?" Mark follows, trying to calm Celeste, me yelling behind him for her to stop and think.

The music we hear amidst the din is soft at first. A girl and a man singing in hushed, small notes:

Amazing grace, how sweet the sound,
That saved a wretch like me.
I once was lost, but now am found,
Was blind, but now I see—

Celeste pulls open the door, a rush of wind in her face. Mark grabs her arm. She yanks herself away, but then she stops. No one on the porch turns to see her angry face. Sonny Boy sits with Heather on the stairs, Jacob beside them sipping a beer. Joseph moves slowly in the old rocking chair.

Heather hums. She gets up and searches the sky for the moon disappearing behind white clouds. Sonny Boy follows her. "Moon," she says, pointing.

He repeats her word, "Moon," and she nods, smiling at him.

"No noise," she says, turning toward her mother in the doorway.

Celeste looks at me. I remember that gaze, the way her eyes searched mine when we were little girls disembarking from a cold airplane in Honolulu. Her eyes in mine, and then, the way she took my hand in hers.

We're in this together. You and I are closer in blood than anyone else in this family.

It would be the only time she ever looked that way at me. The only time, until now. I take Celeste's hand in mine. We walk through the open door of Granny Alma's house, together. I lead her out onto the porch. She sits beside Jacob. I see her eyes follow her child's eyes that scan the skies above Kalihi Valley. Heather climbs onto Joseph's lap and rocks with him. And I hum like Bob says, amazed.

BECAUSE

THE PHONE RINGS at four-fourteen in the morning. "Hey, you awake?" the voice mumbles.

"No, dammit. Who's this?" I drop the phone on the side of the bed and fumble around for it in the darkness.

"Hello? Hello? Sonia, it's me."

"Jacob?"

"Sonia, come and get me." I hear a car passing on a wet street and distant music. "Man, they fucked me up bad."

I sit up in bed, the phone wedged between my ear and my neck as I pull on a pair of rumpled jeans. "What happened? Where are you?"

"Bring my gun."

"What gun?"

"Markie's gun."

"He doesn't have one." Glass breaks, a woman screams, tires screech on a wet street. "Where are you? I'm coming to get you. Jacob!" I listen to the long buzz of the phone line.

"Wizard of Oz," he murmurs at last.

The night is a fluorescent orange string of lights after the hostess bars close. I pull into the parking lot next to a faded gray BMW. Legs dangle out of the passenger door, a body sprawled over the front seat. A woman in a torn shirt staggers toward me in her four-inch heels.

"My name not Cindy," she sneers as she pushes on Jacob's legs, trying to get him into her car. "Ho-nee, get in. Ho-nee, I take care you." Jacob groans, his eyes rolling back and forth in a slow wave.

"Jacob, it's Sonia. Get up. Get in my car." Cindy shoves me away. I shove her back, and she stumbles into a pile of empty cardboard boxes.

"Sonia," he says as he tries to lift himself up, "you came." There's blood all over his face. His hands are red-purple swollen. I hoist his arm around my neck and drag him out of her car. Cindy lunges at me and the three of us fall onto the wet asphalt. "Go home, Anna. Go," he manages to tell her.

"Who this, Jake? Who this bitch? Tell her go home," she screams. "I gibee you money. They going kill you. I get money."

It starts to rain.

This can't be happening.

Another fucking drunken junkie.

It's almost five-thirty.

Fucking rolling the shit but doing all the shit, dead/man.

I have an early-morning class, classes all day.

Cold sweat, vomit, and blood.

I have to get Sonny Boy to school.

Cindy still has her green tassels on under her wet T-shirt.

I'm pulling a double shift at the Ten-Pin tonight.

I shove Jacob into the car. Cindy pounds on the hood. Jacob rolls up the window, and she hits it with her closed fist, her open palm, all the while screaming his name.

"Bitch," she yells at me as I pull away, "he no love you."

He loves me.

He loves me not.

A couple of weeks before, Jacob and I had shared a bottle of Bombay Sapphire on the porch. "If you saw me on the side of the street, Sonia, say at A'ala Park or say on River Street, would you take me home with you, bathe me, feed me, take care of me? Hypothetically speaking." We were past drunk, ready for another bottle.

"Yes, of course."

"You promise?" he asked, putting his arm around me, his smell on my skin, the warm weight of his leaning into me.

"Yes. Why?"

"Because," he whispered.

I love him.

I love him not.

It's almost six in the morning. I take him home. I bathe his filthy body, wash his matted hair, throw his dirty clothes in the washer, leave the warm shower running on his broken face, help him out of the tub, then wipe him down with a clean towel. He climbs naked into my bed. I cover him with the comforter.

Six-thirty in the morning. Sonny Boy's asleep in Mark's room. Mark gets up for work and brews a pot of coffee. He makes a home lunch for each of us, then he starts breakfast.

"Sonia," he calls to me, "don't forget to pick me up from school early today. Sonia?"

"Markie," I whisper.

He peers into my room. "What the fuck?" he says. "When did this happen?" Jacob, cold sweat and shivering, pulls himself into a fetal position. I wipe the damp cold from his brow, then his entire body goes hot. His teeth chatter, legs twitch, hands shake.

I'm sitting beside him, numb. "Should I take him to the emergency room?" I ask Mark.

"No," Jacob whispers, "please, no. Just let me stay for a few days, please, Markie. They're looking for me."

I look at Mark, speechless, wide-eyed, scared.

"Whatever," Mark says in pure disgust. His jaw tightens. "But if anything happens to Sonia or Sonny Boy, you fucking drug—" I put my hand on Mark's arm, and he yanks himself away from me.

Jacob, father of #2, father. Jacob, beautiful Jacob, the room is so dark this early morning. My breath is shallow, my eyes helpless, because I know:

I love you not, junkie.

I pick up Sonny Boy from school, Heather from voice lessons, Mark from work, and drive to the Ten-Pin. I feel drained, in need of three days of sleep. I call home on every break, hoping Jacob will pick up the phone. No answer.

"Finally," Granny Alma complains as we all trudge into the bar. "You're never on time for work, Sonia." Heather nudges Sonny Boy to sit on the inside of the orange booth as they wait for their hamburgers and saimin. He starts arranging the salt and pepper shakers, the shoyu bottle, the Tabasco, the ketchup, and the napkin dispenser into a set pattern.

"Soldiers," Heather whispers, "nice."

"Nice," he repeats.

"Can I live with you?" she asks when Granny Alma brings over a plate of fries and fruit punch.

"Don't be ridiculous," Granny grumbles. "You have a nice house."

"Not you," Heather says softly. "You," she says to me, "in your room full of stars."

"What stars? Oh, never mind," Mark says, dismissing her comment. "Hurry and finish your dinner, Heather." She puts a piece of burger in Sonny Boy's mouth. "Granny," Mark calls, "you almost ready to go home? I've got a shitload of paperwork to finish this weekend."

She nods, waving him off. "Sonia," she says to me as I open three bottles of Bud Light for the waitress, "you better call your mother after you get off tonight. She said she's been trying to reach you for a couple of weeks."

"Tell her I'm busy, Granny, you know that," I tell her. "I'm smack-dab in the middle of finals, shit. And I get off late tonight. Did Uncle Fu get the Christmas decorations out of storage yet? And when's the liquor distributor coming?"

"You damn hardhead. You call your mother, you hear me, Sonia?" Granny gets her handbag from under the bar.

"No."

"You better listen to me for once in your life, dammit."

"Why?"

Granny pauses. She clutches her handbag to her chest. She looks upset. "Grace says that she ran into your kuro-chan friend at the Open Market. There, you got it out of me."

"What?"

"Did he follow you here? Your mother's worried. No, I'm lying. I'm worried. Is he a stalker?"

"What? It can't be."

"You better get a restraining order."

"Bob?"

"Did you give him money in Las Vegas? Maybe he thinks you're an easy mark. They're all smooth talkers, those kuro-chans. I bet he was one of those welfare vagrants who got a one-way ticket to Hawai'i from the state of Nevada."

Bob.

My body floats. My head feels light, Granny's words buzzing on.

"You in love with the kuro-chan, Sonia?"

"Yes. Love."

"Oh, God help you."

"He has."

It's dark inside when I get home from my double shift at the Ten-Pin, late, one in the morning. I listen to them giggling from behind my bedroom door. Mark tiptoes out of his bedroom. "Claire's here," he says with his finger over his lips, then pointing to his bedroom. "Go on," he says, lifting his chin in the direction of my room, "look what he did."

I open the door. The walls, the ceiling are full of glowing stars, the fluorescent green illumination of constellations and universes.

"Sonny Boy can't get to sleep," Mark grumbles. "Overstim, I tell you, Sonia. I'm taking them all down tomorrow. Jacob's screwed up his sleep pattern that took us six months to regulate. Fuck. What an idiot."

"Claire's sleeping over's screwing up his sleep pattern."

"I doubt it. Whatever, Sonia," Mark says, running his hand through his hair. "He's a fucking alcoholic junkie, plain and simple. And you enable his lying, druggie ways."

"It's not so simple."

"It is. He's a loser. Run while you can, Sonia."

I walk into my room. "Heather, what are you doing here?" I ask as she peers at me from under the comforter.

"Sleeping under Jacob's stars."

"Come home, Sonia," Grace says when I call her the next morning, "you and Sonny Boy."

"Why?"

"They're coming to me for Sonny Boy, I just know it."

"Who?"

"They were waiting for him. It's what your friend told me. I saw him buying potted mints and herbs at the Open Market. Why didn't you return my calls?"

"What are you talking about? Who's coming to you for Sonny Boy?"

"Me, Sonia, they're coming to me, but it's not about me. It's about Sonny Boy. It must be Christmas. I told Effie I do, I do believe in miracles. They're going to hire him at the church as a groundskeeper. He needed a job."

"Who, Mommy, who?"

"Bob. He's here in Hilo. He wants you to come home. I want you to come home. You and Sonny Boy. I'll buy a nice tree, I promise."

"Why should I?"

"Because."

Should I speak aloud, Bob, would you hear me?

Hum, little girl.

Bob, is that you? Are you really in Hilo?

Come home.

I am home.

Deeper still, and deeper still.

Who's coming toward Grace?

The light-ones who walk among us.

Why her, of all the godforsaken people on this planet?

He heard her. He heard you.

God answered my prayers?

Because He Is.

This is crazy.

A mustard seed is all you need.

And nothing is impossible unto me. Will you wait for us, Bob? Don't leave.

Always near, always sitting on the shoulder of the Little Priest.

Why do you keep calling him that?

Embodiment of Eminence, my little champ. God within me. God behind me. God beside me. God beneath me. God above me.

Wait for me.

Amazing. Amazing grace.

"You're leaving when, Sonia?" Mark yells at me. "Tonight? You'll never get a flight out. It's Christmas Eve. My mother invited us over for Christmas dinner. She's been cooking all day. And Claire's coming with us. C'mon, Sonia, stop being so obsessive. You can leave in a few days."

Jacob steps away from us and turns on the light in the salt-water aquarium. He takes a drink of his beer and pulls on a clean T-shirt. I look at him and panic rises inside of me.

"I can't take Sonny Boy to Hilo by myself, Mark. It's too hard. He'll be running crazy at the airport," I tell him, my voice wavering. "You have to come with me, please."

"No," he says, "I'm not getting pulled into this nonsense. She talked to Bob in Hilo? And light-ones are coming toward her? Who the hell are they? Please, I don't think so. Your mother's nuts. And you know what, you're—"

"Fucked up?"

"Me too," Jacob adds without looking at me.

"Fucking-A," Mark mutters.

"I'll go with you," Jacob says. "I've got to get out of town for a few days and let all the shit blow over anyway."

"What did you do? You owe some drug dealer money? Is that why you've been hiding out here?" Mark asks point-blank. "Why not say you want to go home to see how Aunty Frannie's doing? You know, take care of your mother after her surgery and shit. And you want to be with her for Christmas, for chrissakes. I'd rather you lie."

"Markie, Markie, Markie," Jacob says, "what's with all the drama?"

"Fuck off and die," Mark says, snatching his car keys. "Same old shit, Sonia," he says, stopping at the door. "But this time, you have Sonny Boy. Use your head for once. And stop chasing after miracles and fuck-up loners, you bonehead, or you'll find yourself buying your own fucking shampoo again."

The Hilo rain falls on my mother's roof, rain the size of liquid pearls, sliding down the arms of the sweet night-blooming jasmine tree. It's the patter of rain on broad ti leaves, the funny song of a red cardinal, and the tinkling of wind chimes that bring Sonny Boy to the picture window of my mother's house. He presses his face to the glass, the same glass through which I watched my father leave.

"I have a secret, Grace," I tell my mother. She puts a bowl of hot rice covered with okara on the coffee table. She says nothing, blows on a spoonful and offers it to Sonny Boy.

"Du-rain, du-rain, du-rain," he says. Something Heather taught him while watching the mist cover Kalihi Valley. I look at him. I see myself, nights pressing against the window.

"I only know about leaving," I tell her. Grace says nothing. She continues to feed Sonny Boy. Such tenderness in her movements. "I know nothing about coming back." I speak in the monotone of resignation.

There is a knock at the door and more rain this morning, like the morning I saw lightning hit our front lawn, the shatter of white liquid momentarily stunning. Grace looks at me. I look at her. The door opens. It's Jacob. He enters the house in silence.

"I'm supposed to be here," he says at last, sitting down on the sofa next to Sonny Boy. He kisses his cheek. "Your friend told me. He was surfing at Honoli'i earlier this morning."

"What? Who? Bob? Black guy? Did he give you a phone number? Where is he?" I want to cry. Maybe Mark was right. This is all nonsense. It's another confusing Christmas morning. The mad rain that comes and goes. I put my face in my hands.

Hummmm.

And there is another knock on the door.

This is for Sonny Boy, this is for me, so I answer.

A petite woman in a blue linen dress stands there. She wears a turquoise necklace and bracelets. She's Japanese but with light eyes. This moment is liquid, this moment of our meeting, rain-wet skin, black shiny hair. A certain calm in her countenance.

"Faye," she says, holding out her tiny hand. "Faye Ouye. I'm a friend of a friend of Bob's." She removes her sandals. She steps through the threshold. Her eyes move quickly about the room, linger in the corners, scan the floors, and then the ceiling. She sits on the carpet and pats the empty space next to her for me.

Sonny Boy wriggles out of Jacob's arms and walks down the hallway. I hear the bedroom door shut.

"You're here for him, right?" I ask her. "And you're some kind of healer, right? Then why is he leaving? Shouldn't he be in the same room with you?"

"He understands better if he doesn't see our faces," Faye says. She crosses her legs and leans forward. "Words come out of our mouths at a confusing speed for him, we gesture, we use facial expressions—but they do not match what we are thinking in our minds. He has an incredible intuition. He's not in the room because he wants clarity."

Grace places her hands on my shoulders. My body tightens

to her touch. Jacob sits next to me. "Sit, please, Grace." Faye gestures to the floor. "I want you all to sit with your legs outstretched. He's going to come through one of us. I don't know who. Your son," she says to me, "can know the content of a person's heart within seconds of meeting. He cannot speak, so in order to survive, he has to know who might pose him harm. Those among us whose hearts are black for whatever reason, he needs to avoid. He's going to speak through one of us today."

I say nothing. This all seems so fucking bizarre. Maybe Celeste was right. My desperation brought me to this. Maybe Mark was right. I am fucked up. I want to leave. I want her to leave.

Where are her crystals? The shining lights? I hear no Voices. Where are her tarot cards, crucifixes, talismans, rosary beads, incense, and aura machine? What's with this healer?

"It's you," she says after a moment, looking at Grace. "He's going to come through you."

My mother takes a deep breath.

"Why her?" I ask, shaking my head in disapproval. "Tell him to come through me," I tell her, poking angrily at my chest. "I'm his mother. Why?"

"Because," Faye answers.

"No," I tell her, "it has to be me or this is over. It's not going to work."

Second chances, little girl. Lost, but now found.

"Bob?"

Hummmm.

Jacob rests his hand on my thigh.

"Your son's coming down the hallway, running his hand along the walls. Does he do this? Walk along the perimeter of the room?" Faye asks.

"All the time." Jacob nods.

"How does this happen?" Grace asks.

"He will enter through your feet. You will speak for him through my own biofeedback method."

My mother's body shivers slightly.

"Hold out your arm for me, Grace," Faye asks. She lightly touches my mother's forearm.

"You say you like the stars?"

The stars in my room. Yes.

"Whose stars?"

Jacob's. And God's.

"You say you want the water?"

The ocean. Yes.

"How often?"

Three, four times a week. And blue. Cover me with blue.

"You say you are in a box?"

I want to come out.

"Then come."

I cannot.

"Yes, you can."

Trapped inside.

"You want words. What do you want to say?"

I love you, Mommy. Help me out of this box.

Faye stops. She leans her body toward the dark hallway. "Somebody's coming," she says, her voice high, "out of a box, and it's not Sonny Boy."

"What?" I ask. "Who's coming?" I feel my heart in my mouth.

"What's going on?" Jacob says, getting up. "Who's coming?"

"Sit," Grace tells him.

"Such a tall, handsome man in a small, small box. He's been trapped too, for such a long time. What an attractive man, but buck naked," Faye giggles. "Yours?" she asks me. "He says he's yours. He will help the Little Priest."

"Mine?" I whisper, crumbling to the sound of his approaching footsteps. "My Number One." He whose body traveled toward light in the corner of a cold hospital room.

The door to Sonny Boy's bedroom opens.

"Your Number One is bowing to the Little Priest. He is on his knees. The Little Priest is asking him to rise. They're holding hands," Faye announces. "Your number-one son has shattered the boxes."

Sonny Boy walks toward the living room. He stops and stands outside our circle of bodies. He has aged in demeanor in this strange fusion of selves, this union of a prince and a priest. He looks at Grace, who cries as she names herself. "Grandma," she says, pointing softly at her heart.

He looks at me, never known by name to him who leads me by the hand to meet his needs, who gestures to me, who cries inconsolably, who longs for words. I feel myself falling, slain in the utter power and significance of words that parallel the image: "I love you, Solomon," I tell him.

He looks at Jacob, Jacob who kneels before him, his arms held out, Sonny Boy moving toward him, inside the circle now. "Da," Sonny Boy whispers into the curve of Jacob's neck.

I look at Faye, and she nods. Jacob looks for me, but I cannot meet his eyes. "Is this why I'm here?" he asks Faye.

"Give him your blue," she says.

"He's a fucking junkie," I whisper.

Faye shoots her eyes at me. "Didn't Bob tell you, Sonia? The Little Priest came for *all* of you."

"I have to heal *him*, or I'll be in for more punishment for all the babies and bullshit I—"

"Sonia," Grace says, stopping me. She takes Sonny Boy in her arms and walks toward the picture window.

"You have it backwards, Sonia," Faye says. "You don't have to heal him. He is here to heal you. You died, didn't you?" she asks me. I say nothing. "And you, Grace, you have died too?" My mother nods. "Rise from the ash, all of you."

I can't take it all in. I get up and stand next to Grace at the window. The smell of night-blooming jasmine holds me. "Your father," Grace says to Sonny Boy, who turns his gaze to Jacob. "And *your* father," Grace says to me, the rain outside a white sheet, a curtain for a child's puppet show, lifting before me. My father with his duffel bag walks out of the rain and toward the front door.

◆ 16 ◆

Expanse

GIVE ME BLUE, he asks me;
    the expanse of the mountaintops, he asks me;
    the expanse of sky, he asks me;
    the expanse of ocean, he asks me.
    The universe is blue.

The expanse of mountaintops. My father climbs to the summit of the venerable Fuji-san at last.

What did you see, Father? *Seek?*

"A journey before me, a journey behind me," he tells me. "Switchbacks and mountain paths, pollutants distorting the summit, heavily forested terrain below the Fifth Station, where I begin my passage. There, I buy a tsue for eight hundred yen and take the path covered with gravel and sand to the Sixth Station."

The mountain, Father, is a patriarch. *Seek/and?*

"The higher I walk, the higher the price for soda, beer, tea, water, and food. They brand my tsue at the Seventh Station for a hundred yen. The longer I walk, the longer I wonder: Has every step I have taken had its cost?"

The mountain, Father, is a matriarch. *Seek/and/you?*

"Death, this is death, the air so thin it burns. I pray for a rebirth, a rise from my own ash, the burning of my lungs. I stay the night in the Eighth Station. For four thousand yen, I find a place to lie down, a futon, a pillow, and two meals. At three in the morning, the oka-san wakes me for a miso breakfast, then sends me out the door."

A holy mountain, Father? *Seek/and/you/shall?*

"I push my body forward to the Ninth Station, leaning heavily on my tsue. I reach for rocks to hold on to, I pull myself along the chains and ropes that flank the path. I crawl through the gate with two guardian lions and enter the top of the world, the summit of Fuji-san."

What did you see, Father? *Find?*

"Concessions, sweet Sonia. Capitalists. Charlatans. Soda, three hundred yen. Beer, six hundred yen. A hot brand for my tsue, two hundred yen. Toilet, fifty yen. I am delirious and weary, a spent man drinking lukewarm tea on the side of a filthy john. There are no more mountains to climb. I must return home."

Home, Father? Where is home? *Seek/and/you/shall/find.*

"I have found it, sweet Sonia, inside of me."

Come, Father, come home. We are both the Prodigal.

Joseph sits in the living room. He hasn't spoken to us for days since his return. Sonny Boy runs his hand up and down along the sofa where my father rests. He gathers his Winnie-the-Pooh toys into a strand of morning sunlight.

Joseph gets up slowly. He attempts eye contact, but Sonny Boy averts his gaze.

"You of the empty intellect," Joseph whispers, holding a stuffed owl in his hands. "How you know nothing but words and trivial philosophy. What good is that? Only more confusion, I think. But what shall we do to help Solomon, old friend?" He holds Owl to his ear as if expecting an answer. Sonny Boy watches.

"And you," Joseph whispers to Rabbit, "have such a crafty mind. Cunning, but alas, without wisdom or heart. You say we should devise a plan to help our little Solomon?" And with his finger, Rabbit's head nods. Sonny Boy moves closer and snatches at Piglet. "A plan, a plan," Joseph muses.

"Eccentric as ever," Grace mumbles. "What did they feed you in Kobe?" She hoists herself up, the tight squint of her eyes in the stinging sunlight. "Did the altitude affect your mind? Oh, I know, somebody handed you a used copy of *The Tao of Pooh.*" My mother laughs at him.

Joseph touches Eeyore. "Gloom," he says, touching the donkey's sad face. "Moan, why don't you." Sonny Boy peers at his exaggerated scowl. "Lamentation." He feigns crying. "Poor me. How will you help our Solomon with your constant complaining?"

I sit with Sonny Boy and my father on the living room floor. Joseph holds Tigger in his hands. "You, dear friend, think you can do just about anything you wish. You think life has no boundaries." A small tear forms in my father's eye. "Sorry, my friend, it does."

Sonny Boy slowly hands Piglet to Joseph without meeting his gaze. It is as though he understands the words my father whispers this early morning. "And you, our doubting and stammering friend, hesitating and fumbling through life, never trusting your own intuition—" Joseph looks at me. "How will you ever be of help to our Solomon?"

"Daddy," I sigh, "I want Sonny Boy's condition to be about you as much as you do, but it's all about words again, your words, and thought—what good has thought ever been to us? It only makes you and me run when we shouldn't. We think too much."

"Or too little," Grace adds. "But it's his pronouns that really bother me," Grace says. "All those *we*s, as though we've ever been *we*."

"It's you, O bear of little brain," he says, ignoring us. He takes Pooh from the middle of the circle. "Can you teach us how to help our Solomon with your intuitive spirit? How did you ever learn such be-so?"

"Be-so," Sonny Boy repeats.

Joseph takes Sonny Boy's face in his hands and kisses his forehead. I want to believe my father. I have always wanted to believe my father. "We all could use a little be-just-so," I tell him at last. I look at Grace, who is looking at my father, who is looking at my son, who is looking at me.

Be-so, because it is at this moment I realize that outside, the sky is blue.

The expanse of sky, it is evening when the fragrance of the night-blooming jasmine moves into the space of the bedroom where I sleep. The real and the dream merge. I walk down passageways filled with honeysuckle and puakenikeni. The arms of night-blooming jasmine no longer hold back a little girl wandering too far behind the shadow of a gone father.

"The expanse of sky," rasps a voice from a bottle.

Thin air, I remember, my Jar. I haven't heard your voice in such a long time. I remember. Rarefied air like the Sierra Nevadas.

"Give me blue," says a voice from a bottle.

My Jar, I know it is dark and wet, the place where you find yourself trapped in a bottle.

"Flight," says a voice from a bottle.

Tsuru of the thousand and one years, I will take four yards of blue silk cloth made from the feathers of your bloody breast, blue silk left on the porch of my granny's house in a box marked:

Sonia Kurisu

Granny Alma's house

I will wrap your ashes in it on the day your lungs breathe in your father and your mother in the kingdom of mountains high above the cloud line.

"On my flight of finding?" asks a voice from a bottle.

High on the Kohala Mountains, I will release white feathers in an updraft.

High on Hualālai, I will release granulated glass in a zephyr.

High on Mauna Loa, I will release a thousand and one, golden folded in papery flight.

Then on Mauna Kea, I will release ashen you, breathing blue.

"Promise me ash," says a voice from a bottle.

Then will you be mine?

No answer. The real and the dream unhinge. I am on my bed in the room filled with the smell of night-blooming jasmine, Sonny Boy's warm body pressing against mine. I open my eyes.

"I will be his," answers a voice from a bottle.

I get my father's shovel from the garage. Sonny Boy watches me from the picture window as I thrust the spade into the soil surrounding the night-blooming jasmine tree.

"Sonia!" I hear Joseph calling from the front door. "What now, for chrissakes. You're going to kill the damn tree. Watch out for the roots."

"Let her go," Grace tells him as they stand with Sonny Boy.

Deeper and deeper still, I dig into the ground. I don't remember where I buried the bottle. I think it gone, a dream, or broken glass disintegrated underground so long. I get on my knees and dig with my bare hands. The moss around me is like a carpet of sweet spores, the smell of Hilo soil rich and elegant, cool to the touch. I feel frantic, my search seems futile on this, another morning of blue sky.

And then, my hands touch the cold of glass. I unearth the bottle wedged deep in the wet claylike sediment that sucks at its sides as I pull it into the sunlight.

I wipe the bottle clean with blue silk cloth and look inside at his black eyes, fisted hands, his body a fetal pink curl, the water thick and murky. I bring the bottle inside.

"You don't have to look at me, Daddy," I tell him. He turns to look at the bottle. "Your every thought, your every word, years, Daddy—they meant something to me, because I knew I was your child. You were me and I was you. So alike, they always said, I was just like you. To hurt me, I think. Their words never hurt me." I feel the pulsing of my heart. "But you did, whenever it mattered most. Daddy, you never saw me, did you?"

"This time I will," he says, lifting his gaze.

"Then stare truth in the face, Daddy. And this time, there's nowhere to run. My first child, Number One I call him, was a boy, a prince in a box. My second child, #2, was also a boy, a turtle boy. And here is my third, another boy, the one I call Jar." I press the bottle to my face. "A crane I drowned and buried."

"Elegant, noble tsuru," Grace whispers.

"You're all fucking crazy," Joseph begins.

"And kame," Grace continues, "the turtle never giving up the struggle. And the Prince that Faye said came on his knees to Solomon—"

"Does this make sense to you, Gracie? Tell me," Joseph pleads.

"It has to," she says, "everything we've done, you and I, has brought us to this. Sonia brought us here. No," she says gazing softly at Sonny Boy, "Solomon has. It has to all make sense," she repeats softly.

Sonny Boy sits on my lap. He looks at the bottle. "He is my fourth," I tell Joseph, "the Little Priest. He chose us—" I feel myself breaking. Breathe. "To teach us. We need to be taught, Daddy, don't you see? We tried, we tried, but we've all been such fucking failures. Thank God they're coming, more and more of them."

"I believe you, Sonia," Grace says.

Joseph sits on the sofa, his face in his hands. "We're all fucking losing it," he says. "All of us, this fucking insanity that keeps going round and round this goddamned house. I can't take it. Never could."

"Then it's my fault," Grace says.

Joseph takes the bottle from Sonny Boy. He holds it up to the light, examines it in the round. My father shakes his head. And then he looks at me. And then he looks at her. "No, Gracie, it's me," he says at last. "It was me. Three babies? Oh, Sonia, what have you done?" He turns his horrified eyes to me. "What have I done?"

"True freedom is not given but seized," I tell him.

"Why do you remember every fucking stupid cliché I've said to you?"

"Because, Daddy, you were right. True freedom is holding on and seizing—"

"Seizing what?"

"Love—no matter the cost or ferocity of that love."

Joseph clutches the bottle to his chest. He reaches for Sonny Boy, who puts his arms around my father's neck. Joseph rocks slowly back and forth. "I am so sorry," he says again and again. And then he asks, "What do we do now, Solomon?"

"We?" I ask him.

"You heard me. I said we," he repeats softly.

"Rise," I tell him, "all of us from the ash."

The expanse of ocean, the waters of Punaluʻu deepen into indigo where a turtle boy, #2, greets me in dream. Brackish fresh water meets the ocean seawater, the two merging the real and the unreal. The day-moon curtsies in the sky.

His arms unfold into dorsals, feet, tail fin, tiny head, shiny amber shell. A whistling spins from his mouth.

"This shore, our return," says a voice from water, #2.

Come. Son of Jacob. Son of Sonia. Grandson of Joseph and Grace. Brother of Solomon. Come back to this shore.

"Give him blue," says a voice from water.

The expanse of mountaintops, the expanse of sky, the expanse of ocean.

"The universe is blue," says a voice from water.

What will we see?

"A journey before you," says a voice from water. *"A journey behind you."*

The ocean, #2, is a father.

"A changing current," says a voice from water.

"I am his father," says a voice sharp as a sliver of moon.

Jacob?

"Gone with the rising tide, soon, Sonia, soon," says the voice of the sliver of moon.

Stay with me, Jacob. Don't go. Stay with us. I can change you. I can fix you. I can love away your addiction.

"I cannot love you, Sonia. I cannot love Solomon. He is second, you are third," says the voice of the sliver of moon.

"Then I am his father," says a Voice from an expanse.

God?

The real and the dream unhinge.

Jacob hadn't called me for days since meeting Faye.

"It's the all-of-a-sudden-he's-a-father thing," Grace tells me over coffee one morning. "Probably scared the crap out of him. He's off somewhere denying it right now, I bet you. So don't expect him to be any part of Sonny Boy's life. Just let him go, Sonia. I hate to say it, but he's a loser. And he's weak."

"It's not about weakness. He's afraid," Joseph says. "Fear, it's all about fear."

"And you should know," Grace says.

"I should and I do," he says.

The phone rings.

"Let it go," Grace says. "Let the machine pick it up."

"Answer it," Joseph says. "It's more than I did. I never called you."

The phone rings two more times. I pick it up without a hello. The line is silent.

"Sonia?" He doesn't wait for my response. "It's Jacob. I'm taking you and Sonny Boy to Punaluʻu," he says, his voice distant but sure. "To see the turtles."

"What turtles?"

"They're all there, Sonia."

"Who's all there? What are you talking about?" I feel the panic of another lie. I never told him about turtles or #2. "You been smoking?"

"That's none of your fucking business. Yeah, maybe a bit more than recreationally. But okay, yes, all day, every day, all night, every night. Can't think of nothing but—but here I am on the phone with you. You're coming with me. Both of you."

"Oh, Jacob, you break my fucking heart—"

"Don't you fucking 'Oh, Jacob' me. We're taking him to the water. I'll be there in a few minutes."

When Jacob arrives for us, Joseph volunteers to drive us to Punaluʻu in one of the Jack's Tours stretch limos. Jacob sits up front with him. He says nothing, his eyes flitting back and forth over the passing landscape. His hand shakes when he smokes his cigarette. Sonny Boy falls asleep in the cavernous back.

"You haven't dismissed conventional treatments, have you, Sonia?" Joseph asks somewhere near Volcano.

"Celeste and Mark make sure he gets all the services he's entitled to—she's a fucking ballbusting special-needs advocate."

Joseph laughs, nervously. "Celeste," he muses, "can probably move a mountain like Fuji-san. I mean, this Faye lady sounds good enough, but—"

"Mind, body, and spirit," Jacob whispers, "holistic."

"But Celeste and Mark," I tell Joseph, "they don't get this, what I'm doing now, and it's just as important to Sonny Boy, to all of us . . ."

I stare at the back of Jacob's head. In the days of his silence, I wanted to believe he was soul-searching. I picked up the phone many times, called him, but always hung up. I drove past his mother's house, stopping, then driving on. I knew I had to give him time and space. Then he would choose me and Sonny Boy.

Wrong.

Second in his life is Sonny Boy. Third in his life, me. Junk is First. Junk sits on his shoulder. Junk is the devil. Junk is forever. I expect nothing from him.

So much, so much heart. So much, so much beauty. So much, so much intelligence. This junkie, this good man. I want to expect everything from him.

"I know all about leaving," I tell him. He doesn't turn to look at me.

"I'm here, godfuckingdammit." He hits his fist against the window.

"Sweet ice," I tell him.

Jacob turns to glare at me. "It's cold, this shit," he says. "Like a woman. What a dreary life. I need the water as much as him," he says, looking at Sonny Boy.

"It's you," I say.

"It's you," he says, "all your secrets. I can't, I won't be a part of your lies. And I'm not going back to Honolulu."

"What?"

"My last hurrah, this little swim with the champ," he says. "My doctorate adviser arranged an internship for me up on Mauna Kea."

"How long?"

"A year."

And now I'm sure. "I expect nothing from you," I tell him.

"Liar," he whispers.

The drive from Hilo to Ka'u is long, deeper and deeper still into a geography of stark revelation. We travel down the winding road from mountain to seashore, a black sand beach, weathered coconut trees, and a row of lei stands where Joseph parks the limo. He gets out and sits on a fallen log near the tidal pools.

Sonny Boy lifts his groggy eyes and sees the waves bursting on the shoreline, the smell of saltwater mist, the southerly Ka'u wind in his tousled hair. Jacob carries him to the water. I sit with my father.

"Can he swim?" Joseph asks me.

"Yes," I tell him. "Jacob's been taking him to gather fish near the Waikīkī Aquarium."

"He's really leaving," Joseph says. "And he may never come back."

"Can you tell?" I ask, resting my head on his shoulder.

"Yes," my father says, putting his arm around me.

Jacob and Sonny Boy move farther and farther away from the shore. I stand at the water's edge, the brackish cold swirling around my feet. Sonny Boy laughs, his swim trunks washing up on the beach.

The turtles remain in the breaking waves, their heads lifting up out of the black water, teary eyes blinking. Jacob and Sonny Boy tread water near the far reef.

"Mommy!" Sonny Boy cries out to me. I move into the water that surrounds me with its warm and its cold. The turtles turn their eyes toward me. I submerge my body in the waters of Punaluʻu. And when I rise, I look back to the shore.

My father stands at the water's edge, pointing me toward my son. "There, over there," he calls to me. Father ocean, a changing current.

"Here, Sonia," Jacob waves to me. I begin swimming toward them. The turtles, such smooth grace in the water. A small hawksbill swims in front of me. He seems to fly underwater like a bird in liquid current. I close my eyes to the sting of salt, the water, my tears, and follow him by sound and breath.

The hawksbill sinks beneath the surface of the water. Sonny Boy swims to me. He's tired, the current changing, the tide rising. He locks his arms around my neck and I go under, taking in water. I tread faster.

"We better go in," Jacob says, taking a few strong strokes, then holding out his hand to Sonny Boy.

"The hawksbill, Jacob, where did it go?" I ask him as I scan the water beneath me.

"The small one? He's gone. Went under. C'mon, Sonny Boy," he says. "Your mother can't bear your weight."

Sonny Boy lets go of me and swims away from us. He swims naked behind the small hawksbill, who throws his chirping head at him, the splash of sea spray. Jacob and I catch up to Sonny Boy. Then, the hawksbill lifts his head above the water, the four of us treading water in a small circle. The turtle looks at Sonny Boy and then at Jacob. Sonny Boy nods.

The hawksbill moans before descending one last time. Sonny Boy with Jacob and me behind him moves into the shallow waters. Joseph meets Sonny Boy on the sand and wraps a towel around him. We stand at the water's edge waiting for the small turtle to come up for air; it seems forever. Sonny Boy turns away from the water and faces Mauna Loa.

"Where is he?" Jacob says.

Sonny Boy sits on the fallen log, his back to the water. He watches the rippling of his fingers, then the rippling of coconut fronds in a light trade wind. I sit with him, my back to the ocean.

"Where did the fucking turtle go? He was there, right there in the water with me. Looking right at me like he knew me. Where is he, Sonia?" Jacob asks. "Man, I'm losing my fucking mind. Where's the fucking turtle, Sonia?"

I turn to him. "Inside," I tell him.

"Inside the water? A cave? Where?"

"Inside both of you."

"No, Sonia," Jacob says, falling to his knees. "Stop fucking with me, please."

"He is yours."

"Stop fucking with my head. Stop it."

The waters of Punalu'u, a deep indigo; the day-moon curtsies in the expanse of sky. Sonny Boy gets up from the fallen log, walks in the black sand, and leads us all back.

Home

"MARKIE, IT'S SONIA." There is a long silence on the other end of the line.

"When the fuck are you coming home?" he says at last. "The school's been calling about Sonny Boy's absences. Has Celeste called you? She's fucking fit to be tied, Sonia. You better get your ass home."

"I am," I tell him, "home."

"I knew you'd say that. You're so fucking predictable. And Jacob?" he asks. "Where's he in all of this? So what, you and my asshole cousin finally found a fucking love connection? You piss me off."

"Sonny Boy and I have just one more thing to do and we'll be back in Honolulu, I promise."

"You have to take him to see another healer, right? His chakras are clogged, right? And you need a crystal cleansing, right? This holistic, New Age bullshit you're chasing in Hilo, of all backwater, provincial places, just makes me sick. You should talk to Celeste. She's got a few words about paganism for you. And here we busted our asses to secure him a shitload of *real* treatments, and now you're about to fuck that up too."

"Mark, I need you here. Soon . . ." I shift my gaze to Sonny

Boy, who has created an altar of sorts with all of the trinkets Joseph has brought home over the years. A carved Burmese elephant, an Indonesian tiger's tooth, Pompeii ash-fired owl, Tibetan beads, kokeshi dolls, sandalwood carvings, incense urns, an olive-wood cross, and Jar in his bottle surrounded by my father's talismanic souvenirs. "Markie?"

"There's no reason for me to be in Hilo. There's every reason for you to bring Solomon home."

"It's Jar, Markie. What you and I did to him. He's followed me here. We have to listen to him. We need to take care of—"

"I've made my peace. I have begged for God's forgiveness every day of my fucking life. So knock off this *we* business, dammit."

"Please, Mark. Please come."

"No."

No.

A word I just cannot swallow into the shallow hollow of me. Mark, pillar friend, come and lay hands on us, believe the way we did with the innocence of our childhood. Remember the way we prayed. Remember the way we lost our way. Remember the way we found each other time and time again. This burning is for you. See the tsuru lift like sweet ash over this island. My promise kept. Your guilt, a goodbye. My sin, your sin, absolved.

"Sonia? It's Celeste. Mark and I talked and it's imperative that you—"

"Come home, Celeste, to Hilo. I know you think what I'm doing for Sonny Boy is all a crock of shit, but I need you for once in your life to trust what I'm doing."

"You stop right there," she says. "Trust you? You've got to be kidding."

"I'm asking you to come home for me, for Sonny Boy, for Grace, for Joseph, and for you."

"Grace and Joseph? You? Me? Oh, please, Sonia."

"For you," I tell her, "the spaciousness of God's grace. It's on that mountain, I know it."

"What mountain? I swear, Sonia. And speaking of mountain, Aunty Frieda told me that Aunty Frannie told her that Jacob's sequestered himself away on Mauna Kea for the next year. You know that Aunty Frieda, Mark, Claire, and I went to clean up Jacob's apartment? It was a filthy mess. He was evicted, you know. There was all this drug paraphernalia. What's going on?"

"You need to come home. My baby, my babies, Jacob's, they're all here, waiting for all of us to come clean. All of us—"

"All of us? You have got to be kidding. You've gotten yourself, once again I might add, caught up in some kind of mysticism hoodoo when all you had to do was turn to God."

"God loves me, Celeste. God loves the Little Priest."

"The little who? You're Buddhist now? Oh, never mind. You listen to me, Sonia, and you listen good. God loves *me*. And God has forgiven me for killing . . . for my part in your . . . abortion. Mark warned me that you were pointing fingers. All I did was tell Granny. She told Dr. Wee. You made your choice. Did I hear you say that Solomon was Jacob's baby? You need some serious help. Both of you."

"I need your help," I tell her. "Come home."

"No."

No.

She of the supreme righteousness, she of the absolute judgment, listen for once. I have *always* spoken to God, Celeste, and He has *always* spoken to me. I have walked with the angels among us. I know the miracle of reaching out my hand to touch His robe. Don't you see? When I ask you to come home, I don't mean our earthly home, an island, a bay town, a small house full of a mother's misery and a father's absences. I ask you to come home, take off your shoes, sing your hymns of forgiveness. Home is heavenly, don't you know? We are only strangers here catching glimpses of light. To come home brings you closer to the home you and I can never truly visualize. The home beyond our simplistic imagination.

"Aunty Frannie, is Jacob there?" I ask.

"He packed his things and left for Hale Pōhaku this morning."

"Did he say anything before he left? About me or Sonny Boy—"

"No. Just something about beating the Devil. He has to run and hide from the Devil on that mountain. What in God's holy name does he mean?"

"It's cold, Aunty Frannie, what he's gotten himself into."

"And he said the Devil's sitting on his shoulder every day. It's all he can think about. It's all he wants. Sonia, you better start talking."

"You *know*, Aunty Frannie. You've known all along from the time we were kids. But you and Aunty Effie chose not to see all the shit he was getting himself into. He was so clever."

"Are you calling my son the Devil? How dare you? No, you're wrong."

"They're all clever and charming, manipulators, liars, and thieves. He's saving you from himself. He's a fucking drug addict."

"You shut your mouth. They all said you were a liar from the get-go," she sobs. "They said worse about you, so don't you dare cast stones. My son is not, you liar—oh, I don't know what he is, maybe you're right."

"Did he say if he'll be coming down from the mountain?"

"No."

"Did he leave a phone number?"

"No."

"Do you think you can save him?" I ask her. "Do you think I can save him?" I ask again.

Aunty Frannie cries some more. "No," she says at last.

No.

Not again, promise yourself. Not another junkie. Never be second to drugs again. Never try to save another man. Never try to fix another man. Never say you'll be just friends. Never believe in the hope of change. Never pass him a twenty, a fifty, a hundred. The mountain is cold. His addiction, colder than a woman. Jacob, exhale the mountain's visible vapor. Whistle and sigh. Moan and howl out the vowels of your dreary life. Look to the sliver of moon.

I ask Grace to wait for the sliver of moon.

"A week then," she says, looking at her tide calendar. "We'll do it on Wednesday."

I look at the altar Sonny Boy obsessively arranges and re-arranges.

"You're waiting for the sliver of moon?" Joseph asks. "To do what?"

"To turn him to ash," I tell him. Sonny Boy lifts the bottle. "And everything Sonny Boy has placed on his altar, I want to burn it all."

"Are you crazy?" Joseph asks. "You know how long it took me to get all those things?"

"Things," Sonny Boy repeats.

"A prince, a turtle, and a crane," Joseph says. "I'm eccentric enough to be with you on this, Sonia, if you think it's going to make, to cure, to help Solomon. I'd do anything to make him right—" My father stumbles.

"He is already right."

"But not my things. They represent years. All of my journeys—"

"Things," Sonny Boy says again.

"No," Joseph says.

No.

Grace, you become my mother when I become a mother. The babies you discarded, the babies I've discarded come back through the one we've kept. They all tell us, We are One child. And they are. One in blood. Blood, Joseph. The trauma of your distancing spirals down in our bones, two generations now. Come with me, climb this final mountain and throw the trinkets of your journeys to foreign mountains into the fire of our blood.

"I don't think Mark and Celeste are coming, Sonia," Grace says to me late one evening. "They won't make it for the sliver of moon."

"Yes, they will."

Hear the word.
Yes.

"Sonia? It's me, Celeste." She pauses and sighs.

"When are you coming? You need to be here in a couple of days."

"It's Heather, Sonia. She won't stop crying. She's been wetting her bed. I change the bedding, and she does it again in a couple of hours. And she's wetting herself in school. We haven't been sleeping at night. Mike's about to kill her."

I listen to Heather wailing in the background. "What's she saying?"

"She's unintelligible. This gobbledegook. 'Yooni, yooni, yooni,' over and over, like some kind of mantra. Mark and Granny have been over to try to help, but she just screams louder. She's not really close to them. I don't know what to do. Will you talk to her?"

"Will you come home?"

And after a long pause, she says, "Yes, dammit."

"Then, yes, I'll talk to her."

"Come here, Heather, Aunty Sonia wants to talk to you." I listen to Heather's staccato gasping, her shivering breath.

"Hey, baby girl, we miss you."

"Yooni, yooni, yooni. Dimmy, dimmy, dimmy." She's screaming, high-pitched vowel sounds.

"Heather, listen to Aunty Sonia. Your mommy's coming to Hilo to help me. Will you come with her to help Solomon?"

"Sol?" The crying stops for a moment.

"I'll see you tomorrow."

"Solomon!" she screams. Sonny Boy turns his head and walks over to me. "Solomon!"

"The Little Priest," I whisper, "is waiting for you."

"Priest," she repeats over and over.

Celeste takes the phone from her. "What's she saying now? What is it with her and your boy, Sonia?"

"Blood," I tell her.

"I'll be there tomorrow," Celeste says, resigned.

"What's Heather doing? I don't hear her."

"She's packing."

Heather walks through the door of the house. She walks toward Sonny Boy's altar, circles it, then sits down. She places on the bottle a picture of Sonny Boy, its edges jagged as though cut by a child's dull scissors. He peers at her from the kitchen. She does not meet his gaze. She waits for him to approach her for what must seem hours to a little girl. He steps tentatively toward her from behind, places both hands on her hair, breathes in the sweet scent, then kisses the crown of her head.

"Hey, Sonia, it's me, Mark, just listen. I was at Magic Island with Claire. You know we've been jogging every day. I mean, I was waiting for her near the rest room, you know, where you got rid of, where I drove you that night when you lost, you got rid of, I said that. The second baby, Sonia, do you know what I'm talking about?" Mark starts to cry.

"Yes," I tell him, "I know."

"And then, I looked toward one of the yellow shower trees. I was looking for Claire. And there was Bob, Sonia. I swear it, he's here in Honolulu. So he motions for me to come over. Something's pulling me toward him. Some light coming from—"

"The center of his chest," I finish.

"Yes," Mark gasps. "He holds out his arms to greet me. But get this, Sonia, when he touches me, I feel my knees buckle and my legs melting into the ground."

"When will you be home?"

"Bob says to me, he says, 'The laying of hands, champ needs you, go home in truth, buddy. The truth will set you free.' Claire calls my name, I turn, and when I look back, Bob's gone."

"Come soon."

"I lied, Sonia."

"I know."

"I was with you all three times—you . . . me . . . we . . . those babies. I never prayed for forgiveness, because I thought the two of us and what we did—we went beyond any kind of grace."

"Second chances, Bob once told me," I tell Mark. "It's all about second chances."

"I'll be there tonight."

Mark brings a gift for Sonny Boy. It is a drawstring bag of blue magnetic letters. Heather places each letter on the refrigerator. Sonny Boy tilts his head and flaps his hands as each blue piece snaps onto the cold metal. She doesn't spell her name or his name. "Yooni, yooni, yooni," she says.

"Oh, sweet Lord Jesus, here we go again," Celeste panics.

Sonny Boy laughs. He takes the letter *L* and places it to the far right, and then he composes a word starting at the end of the word, right to left:

U—N—I—V—E—R—S—A—L

"Yooni, yooni, yooni!" Heather claps. "Dimmy, dimmy, dimmy!"

Sonny Boy scans the remaining letters. His small hands start with the letter *L*:

D—I—M—E—N—S—I—O—N—A—L

"Yes," I tell my son. "Yes, you are."

Night, the sliver of moon in the early-evening sky, is a blue-gray canvas. I open the bottle as Mark puts his hand on my shoulder.

"Where can I go from your Spirit?" Celeste whispers. "Where can I flee from your presence?"

I light the liquid. A diaphanous blue flame circles the surface of the liquid, fire consuming water.

"If I go up to the heavens," Grace says, "you are there."

Jar's body stirs in the slow burning blue above him. Sonny

Boy sees his movement within the bottle and begins flapping his arms in excitement.

"If I make my bed in the depths," Mark says, "you are there."

Joseph stares blankly at the flames, the trinkets laid before him on a goza. Heather takes the photograph of Sonny Boy and places it on the fire, nearly extinguishing it. She cups her hands around the bottle and blows softly.

"Why are you burning his picture?" Joseph cries. He tries to lift it, the edges black, crackling. A night trade wind lifts the papery black ash from his fingers.

"He is dimmy, Grandpa," Heather tells him.

"This is so full of it," my father says as he gathers his trinkets. He turns to go inside. Jar's body begins circling in the remaining liquid, his eyes, black seeds, opening. "I'm out of here. I can't——" He looks back at Jar, his fists opening, his pod-tail moving back and forth. Joseph backs up, three frightened steps away from us.

"If I rise on the wings of dawn——"

I turn to the Voice.

Bob.

"If I settle on the far side of the sea," he says to my father, gently placing both hands on his shoulders, "even there your hand will guide me, your right hand will hold me fast." The trinkets fall to Joseph's feet. "Go on, Joe," he says to my father, "enkindle them before the fire goes out."

Sonny Boy moves on the outside of the circle of bodies. It is dark now but for the light of the fire. Bob kneels to him and wraps him in his huge arms.

We watch the flames transform color with each trinket my father places in the expanding fire. No one speaks. No one cries.

Jar's body writhes; the blue flame enters his tail that coils tightly into his body that stiffens, then spasms. He is red. He is maroon. He is black. The bottle bursts.

Joseph looks at me. "I stayed," he says, almost surprised, "for you."

"You and I always to the very end of the age," I tell him.

The smell of formaldehyde is gone. What remains is the smell of sandalwood, olive, gingko, ash, and night-blooming jasmine.

Mark leads Celeste, Grace, and Heather into the house. Bob carries Sonny Boy until Joseph holds out his arms to my son. And for the first time, my son reaches out his arms to him. He turns to take him inside, Bob behind him.

"Hey, Sonia," Bob says, "throw your words in the fire. Quick."

The embers fade and crackle.

"But I am the keeper of words," I tell him.

"Forgive," he says, "they all have but you."

I feel my tears rising, choking me.

"No."

"Yes," he says.

I turn back toward the dying flames. "Sister/sadist," I begin.

"Sister with the psalmist's words," Bob finishes.

"Mother, burn/in/hell," I say to the fire.

"Burn because we rise from the ash," Bob finishes.

"Father," I say. I want to believe I can give these words to fire. "Seek/and/you/shall/find."

"And now he has found," Bob says.

I gather the bits of glass and ash in a small porcelain rice bowl, cover it, and turn to go inside. Bob is humming. And so am I.

Epilogue

NINE THOUSAND FEET ABOVE SEA LEVEL, we are above the cloud line, a bed of cotton covering the brush grass and lava fields of the rising lowlands. The diamantine sun etches itself on my face. A cold wind slices through me in gusts. I secure a cap on Sonny Boy's head. I pull his jacket's hood over his head and draw it tight around his face.

I look at my mother, Celeste, Heather, and Mark one last time. "Wait for us at Hale Pōhaku," I tell them.

Joseph peers up at the blinding sky, the sharp rise of Mauna Kea's stark slope, and motions for me to follow him. "Our mountain, champ," he says to Sonny Boy. "One last mountain," Joseph says to me. We will trek to the summit. Sonny Boy starts ahead of us on the trail.

Ten thousand feet above sea level, my ears start to hum, like the ringing of chimes in my head. My breath is short, my step measured. I hear no external sound. The landscape is volcanic and lunar, the sky, a canvas of pure blue.

Sonny Boy slows down. Joseph pulls another pair of athletic socks over his tiny hands and they walk on together. The polemic union of heat and cold nauseates me; the tangible silence pierces my eardrums like the injection of slow needles full of heavy serum.

Eleven thousand feet above sea level, I stumble and fall onto the lava rocks. Sonny Boy stops, gasping for air, and then sits on the side of the road. There's blood all over my hands and face, cut by the sharp a'a. Joseph pulls a T-shirt from his pack and wraps my injuries. My nose and throat burn. The altitude pulls my scalp tight around my skull.

I manage to get up and pour water into Sonny Boy's mouth. He's crying. He won't stand to go on. A wind kicks up, whipping dust and gravel in a crackling whirlwind around us. Joseph picks up my son and carries him on his back.

Twelve thousand feet above sea level, Joseph finds two māmane-wood walking sticks. I lean heavily on mine with each labored step. My head seethes with solar heat, my nose mucus-filled. I am panting in dizzying, heaving breaths. I vomit a bubbly, bloody phlegm on the lava. Sonny Boy collapses beside me, his eyes rolling in their sockets. He covers his ears with both hands and presses hard. His lips turn blue.

I hear the distant whining of a Jeep, pulling itself up the mountainous terrain. I see the rumbling of a trail of dust left in its wake. Joseph crawls to the side of the road. White-burning with altitude heat, I watch the undulation of light waves when I look up toward the summit. My mind slurs in confusion. The Jeep approaches and stops. The door opens.

"Get in," says a voice, enshrouded in the dark cab. I tighten my eyes for a better look, but seeing nothing, I turn to lift Sonny Boy in my arms. Jacob gets out and steadies me. He takes Sonny Boy into his arms. Sonny Boy opens his eyes to him.

"Solomon," Jacob whispers as he pulls him close. Jacob

looks at me. He's saying something. I watch his lips move with tired eyes, try to listen with deaf ears. His words whirl about me, spinning in and out of my head. "The stars, Sonia," he's saying, "two kinds—"

"What two stars?" I manage to repeat.

"Steady light and variable light," he says, wrapping Sonny Boy in a cocoon of blankets. "Such variable light," he says to me, his eyes in mine. "I can't hold on to it. Steady your light, Sonia."

"Find yours, dammit," I tell him as I stumble into the Jeep, Joseph behind me.

"Keep the light on for me," he says to Sonny Boy, kissing his forehead, then laying his body down in the back of the Jeep.

Thirteen thousand seven hundred ninety-six feet above sea level, the summit of Mauna Kea, Jacob wraps me in a parka. He carries Sonny Boy into the Keck Observatory. Joseph hacks and coughs as he moves behind us as if in slow motion. Jacob leads us into a small room, warm and musty, the heavy door closing.

Jacob puts Sonny Boy on an army cot. He sleeps fitfully on a dirty pillow. Jacob removes the bloody cloth from my hands and cleans the bits of lava rock from each cut, dressing each wound. He pours green tea in coffee-stained mugs for Joseph and me. In minutes, I pull myself close to my son and close my eyes.

We sleep for what seems hours. But Sonny Boy wakes. He is hungry. Jacob prepares a bowl of rice and hot miso soup from a crusty Crock-Pot. Sonny Boy eats, then takes my limp hand in his. He pulls at me without words.

"Wake up, Mommy," Joseph says for him. Sonny Boy tugs

more insistently on my arm. I open my eyes and see my father sitting in an old chair.

"What time is it?" I ask.

"It's five twenty-five," Joseph answers.

"What color is the sky?" I ask.

"Still blue," he answers, "but the sun's going down fast."

I pull myself up, my head spinning. I open my pack and take out the porcelain bowl, wrapping it in the blue silk cloth. Joseph helps me into another jacket, and Jacob puts his warm gloves on my hands.

"You stay here," I tell Sonny Boy. Jacob moves the cot near the window and sits with him. Joseph walks me to the door. When it pulls open, I see that the sun has gone, but the sky remains indigo.

Joseph puts his hands on my shoulders. "Believe in the sun. Believe in love. Believe in God," my father tells me. He looks back at Sonny Boy. "He's restored it in me. Can you believe that, Sonia?" my father asks.

"One mountain. One child," I tell him.

I move through a pressing cold wind toward a small grove of māmane trees.

I hold the bowl in the palms of my hands.

I watch the gray ash and granulated glass circle the surface of the bowl. Round and round it spins until a cloud of ash levitates and hovers in a whirlpool above me.

"Here is your father," I cry into the glacial wind. The blue cloth lifts and pulls itself into the expanse of sky. I watch it rise, a carnival balloon, a kite's blue tail, until it is gone. Particles of gold paper fall around me like snow, snow falling, falling like a thousand and one white feathers. I lift my hands to catch each one.

"Father," says the voice of a prince.

"Father," says the voice of a turtle.

"Father!" a voice beckons from above me. I lift my eyes to the flight of a magnificent tsuru circling the summit in a current of rarefied air.

Behind me, Joseph stands shivering in a small square of golden light. He reaches his hand to me. "Daddy," I whisper.

Jacob carries Solomon into the square of light. He reaches his small arms to me in the piercing wind.

"Here is *your* father," I tell him. I place his cold hands on Jacob's face.

"Da," Sonny Boy whispers.

Jacob lowers his weary eyes.

"Bird," Sonny Boy calls, pointing to the white crane in the distant sky.

Jacob slowly lifts his eyes. We watch until the speck of white is drawn into the passage of indigo to black.

We stand for a moment longer on the summit of Mauna Kea in a dome of luminous stars, quieted by the spaciousness of found grace.

My thanks to the angels who walk among us:

JohnJohn T.S.Y., for the beautiful that is you, for the lessons you teach us by being universal and dimensional.

Robert Teixeira, computer mentor extraordinaire, who believed a techno-peasant could double-space; Doreen Teixeira, Corie and Travis, whose home and hearts have always welcomed us all.

Melvin Everett Spencer III, a northern wing with your name, an eastern wing with mine; Nancy H. Hoshida, best pal of mine; Shari T. Nakamura, dear friend of the Portagee old lady; Claire Shimizu, friend, you are the bravery of digging and dredging; and Don L. Sumada, oldest friend of mine—the amazing I found in all of you: a deep sense of like in this lifetime.

My father, Harry T. Yamanaka, whose many life passages inspired this book, and my mother, Jean N. Yamanaka, whose feisty life inspires me. Mona, Shane, and Sammie Rei Saiki, for the extra room and a typewriter; Kathy, Jeff, and Charlie Tatsuhara my best nephew in the world; Carla B.Y., home is wherever and whenever we are together.

Aunty Charlene, Uncle Sonny, Ian, and Ira Nobriga, and Christopher Ano for loving JohnJohn so very much. John Inferrera, who profoundly loves a boy who in turn profoundly loves you.

Susan Bergholz, I love you plain and simple, my beloved sista, my trusted friend; Bert Snyder, my mother loves you, good man (me, too); Ito Romo, the ranch awaits you; La Sandra Cisneros, always a muse.

John Glusman, for seeing into the words, belief in the words.

Josie Woll, for kicking ass when, for holding me when, for counseling me when, for being always you whenever I call.

Aunty Sue Stigar, for being a part of our family, steady, strong, spirit-filled, and loving. Uncle Lester, the roasted chicken and dinosaur pool on a Sunday night, our thanks.

Nohea Kanaka'ole, you are our saint, incredible heart; LuAnn Oca-lada, Mrs. T., Mrs. Charlotte White, Miss Heidi, Mrs. Inter, Sherri Poll, Miss Laura, Miss Joy; Aunty Bridget Kanaka'ole support and truth; Aunty Katherine; and Denise Webb, nobody like you, beautiful teacher, who dreams of my son.

Miss Marisa, Miss Kim, Rhonda Scott, Aunty Roxanne, Sandi Ishi-kawa, Melanie Migrar, Amanda Martina, Lianne Koki, Dr. Sada Oku-mura, Dr. Kimo Chan, Dr. Maggie Koven, Dr. Patti Dukes, and Mr. Mark, who see and believe in the greatest of possibilities.

Aunty Kui, for your tita spirit that is honest and magical.

Nora Okja Keller, Marie Hara, Wing Tek Lum, Eric Chock, Darrell H. Y. Lum, Joy Kobayashi-Cintron, and the extended family of Bamboo Ridge Press: you give me a place to be, a place to return, a place to know lasting friendship.

Cora Yee, who creates in a parallel universe and weds my work in this one, my life so full of your good energy.

Michael Harada and Yuki Shiroma, treasured paintings on my doorstep now framed on my walls, my thanks. Noe Tanigawa, artist and sista, I thank you.

You who come back at just the right time, still kind and warm with soft voice, such good company over a six-pack and maybe a bottle of merlot, the history of broken crayons, brothers, sisters, ours still, ours always. My thanks for the hedonism and the occasional deep thought.

Donna Choo, the good-fun half (though I adore David) and Simone; Kenn Sakamoto, always a moment for aromatherapy, and Dayle Fujii;

Lynden Shigezawa, inspiration; Mark Romoser, my buddy, my touchstone; Sherri Ida for courage; Suzette Shigemasa for history; Glenn Nakaya for depth; Cary Tanaka for grounding; Michael Y. P. Chock for financial truth; Geri and Lindy; Pono my man—frenz, all dear frenz.

Eh, Gerald, at least I know WordPad. Thank you for fixing the dinosaur.

Friday Night Writing Club, Jordan M. Harrison exquisite like-mind, Marisa Sue Pang, Rex and Bert Matsuo, Rachel and Julie Yamashita, Kristen/Kim/Kurt Komatsubara, Elele Pavlosky, Matt Won, Makoa Doo, Traci Kutaka, and Steven Kunishma: believe me, it's butter! Write the scenes, baby.

Aunty Jan, Aunty Bing, Ross and Dustin Narikiyo, my blood forever.

My grandma, Yoshiko Narikiyo, the glorious God you love, who loves me too just as I am. You are my light. He is my God, a light for us all.